PROTECTING REMI

SEAL OF PROTECTION: ALLIANCE
BOOK 1

SUSAN STOKER

Edited by Kelli Collins

Cover Design by AURA Design Group

Cover Photographer: Emma Jane Photos

Cover Model: Sterling Snedigar

Manufactured in the United States

CHAPTER ONE

"You're going without me?"

Remi Stephenson refrained from rolling her eyes. Barely. "Miles, we broke up. Of course I'm going without you."

"But we planned this trip to Hawaii together," her ex-boyfriend whined.

Remi wondered if he'd always been this annoying and she'd just refused to see it. She mentally shook her head. Of *course* he'd always been like this. Hadn't her best friend, Marley, tried to tell her time and time again that Miles was a jerk?

She'd broken up with Miles just over a week ago, after he'd stood her up for what seemed like the hundredth time, and this time he'd messed up so badly, she couldn't overlook or excuse his asshole-ness. He'd accidentally sent her a text that was meant for the woman he'd been sleeping with behind her back.

Miles: Remi doesn't suspect anything. I told her I was coming down with the flu. So we've got at least the next few days to be together before I need to see her again. Can't wait to be with you, baby. Wear that red dress I like so much and I'll see you in thirty minutes or so.

Remi supposed she should be more upset or angry that her boyfriend had been cheating on her, but honestly, she was simply relieved. He wasn't a very nice man, even though she'd made excuses for him time and time again. Now *she* was done being nice.

"Did you hear me?" Miles bitched once more. "We planned this trip together. Everything from the hotel to the things we wanted to do."

"Wrong," Remi told him with a frown. "*I* planned this trip. By myself. The only thing you cared about was which hotel we were staying in and making sure I made reservations at the most expensive restaurants in the city."

"That's not true."

Remi was done. "Why are you even here, Miles?" she asked. When someone knocked on her door earlier, she'd expected it to be Marley. Her friend was coming over so they could hang out. They'd planned on watching a movie and chilling on her couch, something they hadn't done in a long while. Marley had a busy life with her husband and two kids, and Remi had put all her energy into trying to make the relationship with Miles work, something she was definitely regretting.

But instead of seeing her friend, she found Miles standing at her door...and now she was done listening to him whine.

"I'm here because I know I messed up. I want to be with *you*."

Remi *did* roll her eyes then. She was thirty-five. Way too old to buy his crap. "No, you don't. Maybe you did when we first started dating a year and a half ago. But now you want to be with the stripper you were cheating on me with. Oh—and you want my money. You want to do what you want, when you want, and screw anyone's feelings you stomp on along the way."

Miles stood taller. Remi hadn't invited him to sit. Hadn't really invited him inside her condo, he'd just pushed past her when she'd opened the door.

"You're such a bitch," he told her in a harsh tone.

Remi couldn't help it. She laughed.

Miles took a step toward her. "You think this is funny? And if you're not taking me, I want half the damn money for this trip!" he demanded.

That made her smile die. "No. This is definitely not *funny*. You have some nerve coming over here to bitch about me going to Hawaii without you. Miles, *you* cheated on *me*. With a damn stripper. It's so cliché it's ridiculous. I'm going to Hawaii without you. I'm going to go snorkeling, to the zoo, hike to the top of Diamond Head, eat hula pie at Duke's, watch the surfers on Waikiki, go to the North Shore and eat dinner from a food truck, get lost in the pineapple maze at the Dole Plantation, and flirt with hot strangers at the hotel bar every night while I sip on some fruity alcoholic drink."

That last bit was a stretch, as Remi wasn't the flirting type. She was an introvert and wouldn't even know what to say to an attractive stranger. But she was on a roll, so she pushed that thought aside. "And why *shouldn't* I go on this trip? I paid for it! The airline tickets, the hotel, the excursions, all of it—you paid nothing, so you *get* nothing. I'm going enjoy myself for once, without having to worry about trying to please you."

"You've *never* worried about that," he barked, his face red with anger.

Remi didn't understand where his ire was coming from. The Miles she knew was fairly laid-back. But then again, she'd always done everything he'd ever wanted, so why *shouldn't* he have been that way?

"You're a bitch," Miles repeated. "An ugly, fat bitch! All you want to do is sit around the house and draw your stupid cartoon. You were *lucky* to have me as a boyfriend. I did you a favor."

"A favor?" Remi asked incredulously.

"Yes. You're a fucking nerd. Pathetic. You have no friends except for that bitch, Marley, and you suck in bed. You have no life whatsoever. I was trying to help you change for the better, but instead of wanting to go out to have some fun, or learning how to suck cock like a *real* woman, all you ever want to do is stay here. You're *boring*, Remi. You're going to end up like one of those disgusting cat women...old, obese, smelly because your house is overrun with twenty cats, and content to sit on your couch and read or draw those fucked-up cartoons of yours."

First of all, Remi thought what he'd described sounded pretty good. Reading and drawing while surrounded by cats? Sign her up.

But second of all...what an *asshole*.

"Get out," she told Miles, pointing at the door.

"I'm not done," he told her pompously.

"Yes, you are," she countered.

"What are you gonna do? You gonna *make* me leave?" he asked with a mean scowl, crossing his arms over his chest.

For the first time, Remi felt a small niggling of unease. She'd never been afraid of Miles. But right now, he was kind of scaring her.

"That's what I thought. You can't do shit."

Remi stared at her ex for a beat, before turning her back on him and heading for the short hallway that led to her small one-car garage.

"Where are you going? I'm not done talking to you," Miles called out. "Wait—stop! *Don't*, Remi."

Too late. Remi had already pressed the panic button on the security system.

"Fuck! Why'd you do that?" Miles asked, back to whining once more.

"I told you to leave. Did you think I was going to be

one of those too-stupid-to-live women in the movies you love to watch, who stand around doing nothing while their ex-boyfriends put their hands on them? No way. Leave, Miles. I don't ever want to see you again. I don't want to talk to you again. I don't give a shit if you get some sort of sexually transmitted disease and your dick falls off."

"Nice, Remi."

"I *am* being nice," she countered.

They stood staring at each other for a moment before Remi's phone started ringing in the other room.

"That's the security company wanting to know if everything's all right," she told him. "And when I don't answer, they'll tell the cops to step on it and they're going to be here in minutes. *Get out*."

Remi held her breath. The truth was, her heart was beating a mile a minute and her hands felt clammy. She didn't like confrontations, but she wasn't about to back down from Miles.

"Fuck you!" Miles spat. "Fine, go to Hawaii alone. I hope it sucks. I hope your room has bedbugs, the food is terrible, and you get left in the middle of the fucking ocean while you're on that stupid snorkeling trip you insisted on booking even though you know I get seasick."

Remi didn't reply. She simply stood at the security panel and stared at the man she'd thought was so mild mannered...and too enamored of her family's money to dare speak to her the way he was right now.

He took a step toward her—to do what, she had no idea—but stopped when the sound of sirens was finally audible. His fists were clenched tight and he stared at her for another beat.

"What the hell is going on?"

Every muscle in Remi's body relaxed.

Marley. Her best friend was kick-ass. She was everything Remi wasn't. And her showing up right when she needed her seemed like a freaking miracle.

"Miles was just leaving. Right?" Remi told her ex.

"Bitch," Miles muttered yet again—the insult was getting old—before turning and heading for the front door. His shoulder brushed against Marley's as he passed, knocking her back a step. But her best friend didn't shrink away from him, just stood taller, her feet braced as she glared at Miles, who wrenched open the front door and slammed it behind him.

Remi sagged against the wall. She couldn't believe that had just happened. Then the ringing of her phone registered and she hurried into her living area to grab it. She answered and breathlessly told the woman from the security company her code word and explained what happened. It was too late to call the police and have them stand down, which was all right with Remi. She'd make sure the officers who responded made a note of what happened with her ex, just in case.

* * *

An hour later, Remi was finally on her couch with a glass of wine in her hand, her best friend sitting right next to her, hovering in concern.

"I can't believe he had the nerve to say all that shit," Marley said with a frown.

Remi had told the cops everything, and of course, Marley had heard it all at the same time. The police had taken notes, told her to make sure her doors were locked and the security system on, and had left.

"I know, right? I mean, like Miles really thought telling me I was going to become a cat lady was an insult," Remi said, attempting to lighten the mood.

Marley shook her head. "He's dead to us," she declared dramatically. "His name is never to cross our lips again. From here on out, his name is Douchecanoe."

Remi laughed. More accurately, she snort-laughed. Marley was obviously influenced by her twelve-year-old daughter, who was currently in the running for the Drama-Queen-of-the-World crown.

Marley's lips twitched as she fought a smile. "I mean it," she told Remi.

"And I heard you. Henceforth, Douchecanoe is forgotten."

"Good." Marley reached for her hand. "Are you sure you're okay? That whole scene sounded like it was intense."

"It didn't start that way. Douchecanoe was here to beg me to come back to him. Or honestly, beg me to take him to Hawaii. And I think he thought it would be easy. He never really liked me, Marl, it was about my money. It's *always* about that."

"There's someone out there for you. A guy who'll see

you for who you are. An amazing, talented, beautiful, sensual woman."

Remi sighed. She loved her friend for being supportive, but she knew what she was and what she wasn't. Douchecanoe wasn't exactly wrong. She *was* a nerd. She had too many pounds on her frame and was definitely much more content to hang out in her condo, drawing her latest cartoon, than going out and being seen. But the thing was...she was all right with that. She didn't wish she was taller, thinner, prettier, or more social. She liked her life. She just wished she had someone to share it with.

"I know," she said belatedly.

Her best friend, knowing her as well as anyone ever had, didn't challenge Remi on her less-than-exuberant-response. Instead, she changed the subject. "So...you're really going to Hawaii by yourself?"

Remi sat up straighter and nodded. "I am. I was still waffling on going before tonight, but now I'm definitely going."

"Good for you. I wish I could go with you," Marley said a little sadly.

"I know. But you have too much going on here. We'll get our girls' trip some other time."

"I'm holding you to that. I'm so proud of you, Remi. Just promise me you won't sit in your hotel room the whole time. That you'll actually go out and do all those things you've booked."

"I will. I mean, I'm sure there will be some sitting in my room. I did pay for that kick-ass corner room with the ocean view, after all. Have to get my money's worth out of it. But I want to explore. I want to see the North Shore, and get a Dole Whip, and taste this hula pie everyone always talks about. And I want to go snorkeling. I've heard the turtles are everywhere in Hawaii. I want to see one in the wild."

"You better take a ton of pictures," Marley warned.

"You know it."

"And send them to me," her best friend went on. "I'm gonna need proof of life every day from you or I'll be calling the cops to storm into your room to make sure you're all right."

Remi snort-laughed again. Lord, she was such a dork. She wished she had a cute laugh, but thankfully Marley didn't care that she had such a weird laugh. "You *would*, too, wouldn't you?"

"Of course. I love you, Remi. Who else has always been there for me?"

Surprisingly, tears came to her eyes. The truth was, Marley had always been there for *Remi*, not the other way around. From the outside looking in, Remi had it all. Her parents were loaded, she lived in a nice condo, had a closetful of designer clothes...but outside of Marley, she had no other friends. She'd been lonely for as long as she could remember.

She'd always been eccentric, even as a child. She loved to draw and doodle, did so anytime she could, preferring to do that over playing outside with her classmates. The other kids didn't understand her, and since she was different from them, they found she was an easy target for making fun of.

Marley had smashed through all her shields and basically informed her in the third grade that they were going to be best friends, and that was that.

"Don't cry!" Marley insisted. "If you start, you'll make me lose it, and you know I'm not a pretty crier!"

That was true. Marley might be beautiful and petite, with gorgeous, thick red hair and green eyes that looked like the water in the Caribbean, but when she cried, her face got red and blotchy, her eyes bloodshot, and she looked like a hot mess.

"Right, so what movie are we watching?" Remi asked as she wiped the tears from her eyes.

"*Legally Blonde*, definitely! I love watching what's-his-name get what's coming to him!" Marley exclaimed.

Remi smiled. She wasn't surprised that was the movie her friend chose. Truth be told, it was one of Remi's favorites too. And she needed to watch something where the ex-boyfriend lost in the end.

Picking up the remote, she clicked on the streaming app that had the movie and brought it up.

Marley leaned into Remi as the movie started and said softly, "It's Douchecanoe's loss. He might not know it now, but he fucked up and lost the best thing that's ever happened to him. You're gonna find the right person for you, Remi. I know it."

Remi nodded, but she wasn't so sure. She felt the clock ticking away. She wasn't getting any younger, and so far, she hadn't found a man who could look past her family's money and her introverted exterior to the woman underneath. She was more than ready to love someone, but she simply hadn't found a man who liked her exactly as she was.

Forcing the depressing thoughts from her mind, she took a sip of wine and settled in to watch Elle Woods kick some lawyer butt.

CHAPTER TWO

"Are you seriously going to Hawaii on your own?" Safe asked.

Vincent "Kevlar" Hill smiled. "Hell yeah, I am."

Smiley held up a hand and waited for Kevlar to give him a high-five.

"Good for you," Preacher said.

"Ballsy," MacGyver added.

"It'll be easier to get some without the ol' ball and chain at your side," Howler said with a smirk.

Flash smacked him on the back of his head. "Rude, man!" he exclaimed.

Kevlar didn't get upset by his friends' razzing. These were men he'd die for, and who would die for him in return. As Navy SEALs, they'd been through hell and back together and come out mostly unscathed on the other side.

They were currently sitting in Aces Bar and Grill, a bar

near the Naval base where they were stationed. In the past, the bar had been *the* place for men and women who were looking for a no-strings sexual interlude. But ever since changing ownership several years ago, with Jessyka Sawyer taking over, it had morphed into a laid-back hangout spot for Naval men and women and not so much a pick-up joint.

Which suited Kevlar just fine. At thirty-five, he'd gone through a phase of enjoying meaningless sex with hot women who just wanted to sleep with a Navy SEAL, but that kind of lifestyle had quickly lost its luster. Maybe it was all the missions he'd been on where he'd been inches from death, highlighting what was really important in life. Maybe it was seeing the repercussions of those kinds of liaisons through other SEALs he knew—everything from unexpected pregnancies to sexually transmitted diseases.

But more likely, it was seeing the relationships his mentors had with their wives and children.

His friend Wolf Steel—and all of the man's former teammates—had stayed in the Riverton area after retiring from the Navy to help with training and mentoring SEALs as they rotated in and out of the base. From the first time Kevlar had met the man, he'd felt a connection with him and his team. They were legendary in SEAL circles; everyone knew their stats, how many missions they'd been on and the things they'd done.

But for Kevlar, what was most impressive was the closeness they had with their families and with each other. The men were teammates on the battlefield, but also in life. It was something that was extremely rare. Kevlar knew it, as did Wolf and the others. Anyone who messed with any of their wives or children found themselves face-to-face with seven pissed-off former Navy SEALs who wouldn't hesitate to do whatever it took to mitigate any threat to their families.

Looking around the table at Aces Bar and Grill, Kevlar felt the same bond with the men on his team. He was team leader, a position he didn't take lightly. He felt responsible for each and every one of the guys. Both when they were on missions and when they were at home. He'd always had what some would call an inflated sense of responsibility toward others.

Only one of his teammates had been in his BUD/S class. Brandon "Howler" Starrett was younger than him, as Kevlar had decided to go into the Navy only after failing out of college, then floundering for a few years, trying to figure out what he wanted to do. Howler had known since he was a kid that he wanted to be a SEAL. They'd kept each other going during Hell Week and beyond. Whenever they'd wanted to ring the bell, to just quit, they'd convinced each other to stick it out one more day.

And here they were. Serving on the same SEAL team together. Kevlar was proud of both himself and Howler for how far they'd come. It was an honor to be on the same team as his friend.

But the other men were just as important to Kevlar. Bo "Safe" Cyders, Jude "Smiley" Stark, Shawn "Preacher" Franklin, Ricardo "MacGyver" Douglas, and Wade "Flash" Gordon were more than mere teammates. They were family. And being family, that meant they rubbed each other the wrong way sometimes. It meant they picked on each other and never let a chance go by to pry into each other's business.

Meeting up for drinks at Aces, he'd just told them about his decision not to cancel his trip to Hawaii, which he'd planned with his ex. They all knew about his break-up with his girlfriend of the last year, Bertie. They'd been supportive of his decision, but that wasn't a surprise, since Kevlar was well aware none of his teammates really liked his ex. The relief he'd felt when she'd been the one to make the break made him realize just how wrong their relationship had been. He'd been holding on for reasons even he wasn't really sure about. He should've had the balls to be the one to break up with her, but however it came about, it was a relief.

"I decided since I paid for the entire vacation, and the plane ticket is nonrefundable, I might as well go," Kevlar told his friends.

"I think that's awesome," Flash told him.

"Me too. But what does Bertie think about it?" Preacher asked.

Kevlar gave him a look. "She's not a fan."

The other men all chuckled.

"You mean she pitched a royal fit," MacGyver corrected.

"Pretty much," Kevlar agreed.

"She was the one to break up with *you*, though," Safe said. "So what does she have to bitch about?"

"I guess she thought I was going to be a gentleman or something and let her go with one of her girlfriends," Kevlar said with a shrug.

"As if," Smiley said under his breath.

"I mean, you could've let her," Howler said nonchalantly as he took a swig of his beer. "We could've gone on that mission to Syria if you weren't leaving."

Kevlar wasn't going to feel guilty about that. He'd been approved well in advance to take a week's leave, so another SEAL team was being sent overseas on that mission. He was aware that Howler had really wanted to go, but he refused to feel bad about taking some downtime. It had been ages since he'd taken any kind of break. Hell, since *any* of them had taken leave. Their work/life balance was out of whack—a fact brought home to him even more after Bertie broke up with him because he was always gone.

It wasn't a surprise. Kevlar had known of Bertie's unhappiness with how often he was away and how little of his time she got. But she knew what she'd signed up for when she started dating a SEAL. And it hadn't taken her long to move on, anyway. From what he'd heard through the gossip grapevine, she was already dating someone else. The accountant who did her taxes. He wouldn't be surprised if she'd been cheating on him before they'd officially broken up.

He wasn't upset over the idea. To say they'd grown apart was an understatement. The last four months had been anything but healthy. They fought all the time, and it hadn't taken her long to show a part of her personality she'd kept hidden during the honeymoon phase of their relationship. Bertie *hated* it when she didn't get her way. And not being able to go to Hawaii on the trip she'd planned—without *any* input from him, even though he'd been willing and eager to sit down and discuss what they should do while there—had royally pissed her off.

"Lay off the Syrian mission already, Howler," Safe said. "Enjoy the break. Lord knows we deserve it."

"Whatever, man," Howler said.

"I know you're not going to follow the itinerary Bertie set though, right?" MacGyver asked. "Last you mentioned, it involved lots of shopping and bus tours."

Kevlar winced. "Yeah, no. Not my idea of a good time. Canceled nearly all of that crap. I'm mostly going to wing it. I'll take the rental car and cruise around the island. Find some good hole-in-the-wall restaurants, go on some hikes, shit like that. But I'm definitely keeping that private scuba trip on the agenda. It was the only thing I was really looking forward to."

"Right, because it's the only input you had on the entire trip," Preacher said with a scowl.

Kevlar nodded. It was true the dive was his only contribution to the planning. But he hadn't told his friends about yet another fight it caused between him and Bertie. She didn't want to book the semi-private tour. Said it would be boring, and she didn't know how to scuba. He'd argued that she could snorkel while he went diving, but she still wasn't happy. She'd stormed out of his apartment and hadn't spoken to him for two days when he wouldn't back down, insisting on doing just one thing *he* wanted to do while they were on vacation.

She'd finally given in and booked the outing, but Kevlar had the impression when it came time to get on the boat, she probably would've found something else to do, or claimed she was sick that day or something. Which didn't bother him as much as it should have. It was just one more indication that their relationship didn't work.

But he knew why he didn't end it first—he was just as stubborn when it came to trying to keep a relationship going as he was with mission planning. Because the truth was, Kevlar wanted what Wolf and his other mentors had. A woman who loved him with every fiber of her being, and who he loved the same way. Some people would scoff and think he was being unrealistic. That as a Navy SEAL, he should know better than to crave a normal relationship. But he did.

"You still staying at that fancy-ass hotel she picked out?" Smiley asked.

Kevlar shook his head. "Naw. Downgraded. Don't care much about where I stay as long as the sheets are clean. I'd rather spend my money on other things."

Safe leaned forward, his elbows on the table and his brow furrowed. "She gonna continue to give you a hard time about this?"

That was what Kevlar liked about his friends. They could be annoying assholes, all up in his business, but when push came to shove, they cared.

His first inclination was to shake his head. To blow off Safe's concerns, but he couldn't. "Maybe."

"What does that mean?" Howler asked. "Do we need to head to her place and make sure she knows to leave you the fuck alone?"

Kevlar looked at his friend, surprised to find he was serious. "No. First, I'd never threaten a woman, no matter how much of a bitch she was. And second, I can handle Bertie."

"What's she done so far?" Flash asked.

"Mostly just been annoying," Kevlar admitted.

"Which means what?" Preacher asked. "Come on, man, if we're gonna have your back, we need intel."

"It just means she's going to spend every minute before I actually board that plane to Hawaii trying to convince me to let *her* go instead. She doesn't care that I paid for it; she thinks that since she planned everything, she should be the one to go."

"Stay strong, dude," Smiley told him.

"Planning on it."

"Good."

"So...what are you guys going to do on our week off?" Kevlar asked.

He wasn't really surprised when no one had any concrete plans. MacGyver was going to visit his family up in Los Angeles over the weekend, but no one else had anything planned.

"I'll probably hang out at The Golden Oyster," Howler said.

"That bar's a dive," Flash said as he wrinkled his nose in disgust.

"Yeah, but they've got plenty of women looking to bag a SEAL."

It was times like this when Kevlar felt as if he was decades older than his friend, instead of only seven years.

"You aren't sick of that shit yet?" Preacher asked.

"Says the man with the nickname 'Preacher'," Howler teased.

"Seriously, that place is gross," Smiley said.

But Howler merely shrugged. "If we can't go kick some ass in Syria, might as well have some fun while we're forced to take leave."

Kevlar hated that his friend felt that way.

"Well, I, for one, am happy to sit on my ass," Flash told them.

"Same," Safe agreed.

"Me too," Smiley said with a nod.

"Fuddy-duddies. You guys act like you're seventy instead of in the prime of your lives," Howler complained.

"I'm just sick of the meat market," Safe said. "I'm not going to find the love of my life in a bar."

"You don't know that. Plenty of people have found their significant others in a bar," Howler countered. "Hell, even Jess, the chick who owns this place, found *her* man here."

"That's different," Safe argued.

"Is it?" Howler asked.

Kevlar couldn't really argue with his friend. They all

knew the story of how Jessyka was a waitress in this very bar when she'd befriended Benny and his friends, and the rest was history.

The bell over the front door tinkled and, as one, the seven men at the table turned their heads to see who'd just entered. It was built into their DNA. To be cautious, to know everything about their surroundings, just in case.

"*He's* here again," Howler said to no one in particular.

"He" was Blink Davis. A fellow SEAL who was on another team. Word on base said he was on convalescent leave—not by his own choice—after an especially gnarly mission had gone sideways. Three of his teammates had been killed, two others were still in the hospital with career-ending injuries. Blink had been the only one to come out of the clusterfuck of a mission unscathed physically.

Mentally, it was another story. Whatever happened on that mission had fucked with Blink's head, and his commander decided he wasn't yet fit to go back on active duty. Had forced him to take a mental health leave to get his head back in the game.

From what Kevlar could tell, Blink spent most of that leave time at Aces. He sat at the bar for hours on end, not talking to anyone, nursing a beer and staring straight ahead.

"Pathetic," Howler muttered.

Kevlar shot him a glare. "Not cool," he growled.

"He's done, man. No way will he ever be able to get

back on the teams. You can't tell me that you'd want him on a team *you* were leading. Not with his mental state."

"You don't know *what* his mental state is," Smiley countered. "You don't know anything about him."

"I know what I've heard. That when the shit hit the fan, he ran *away* from the bullets instead of toward them."

"Who'd you hear that from?" Kevlar asked in a low voice. "Because that's not what I heard at all. And I got *my* intel from his commander, not some little-girl gossip group in the bathrooms."

"Whatever," Howler said. He chugged the rest of his beer and slammed the glass on the table. Then he pushed back his chair and stood. "I'm going to The Golden Oyster. Anyone want to stop sitting around like an old man and come with me?"

When no one spoke, Howler rolled his eyes and headed for the door.

"I'm not paying for his beer," Smiley said after a moment.

"Not it!" Flash agreed.

"I've got it," Kevlar told his friends.

"He's such an asshole sometimes," Safe said with a shake of his head.

Kevlar didn't disagree. But then again, they all had their asshole moments, and he didn't hold it against Howler. He was a damn good SEAL and an asset to their team. He might not be the most tolerant of men, but when shit went down, he was a great person to have at their backs.

Kevlar watched as Blink settled himself at the bar.

Jessyka headed over with a beer in her hand, setting it in front of him before leaning on the bar and speaking to him for a few seconds, then heading away to make a drink for another patron.

"When do you leave for Hawaii?" Smiley asked, turning Kevlar's attention away from the lone SEAL at the bar.

"This weekend. Bertie bought business-class seats, so at least I can get some sleep on the plane."

"Sweet. Good for you. I hope you have a great time. You deserve it, Kevlar," Flash told him.

"Yeah, you work damn hard, and this is gonna be a great break for you," Safe agreed.

"I hope so."

"Just go with the flow and you'll be fine. This isn't a life-or-death mission, so enjoy it," Smiley offered.

"You gonna try to see Baker while you're there?" MacGyver asked.

"Yeah. Although now that he's got himself a woman, not sure what kind of time he'll have for me," Kevlar said with a shrug.

"Knowing Baker, he'll make time," Preacher said.

Baker was a former SEAL who'd made his home on the North Shore of Oahu. He was older, but still highly involved with SEAL missions. Kevlar didn't know all the details behind what he did for the government, but since he and his team had benefited more than once from the intel Baker provided, Kevlar didn't care. Baker was almost as much a legend as Tex...another former SEAL who'd made it his life's work to protect military men and women of all branches.

"Thank Baker for us," Smiley said. "For Nigeria."

Kevlar knew exactly what Smiley meant. That mission would've gone on twice as long as it had, if it wasn't for the info Baker had provided. "Will do."

"Well, this old man is going to call it a night," MacGyver said.

"Same here," Preacher agreed.

"I'll call Howler later, make sure he made it home all right," Safe said. "It's my turn, and I'm sure you've got things to do to get ready for your trip, Kevlar."

He did, and for once, Kevlar didn't feel an ounce of guilt for not wanting to check on his friend after yet another night at the seedy pick-up bar. "Thanks, man."

"No need to thank me," Safe replied. "Howler's an ass sometimes, but he's still family."

Warmth spread through Kevlar's chest. He'd wanted a close-knit team like this from the first day he'd gotten his Budweiser pin, and was so grateful he had one.

"If Bertie gives you too much shit, let us know," Flash said.

"And you'll do what?" Kevlar questioned.

"Don't know. But female or not, no one fucks with one of our own."

That warm feeling grew. "Thanks. But I can handle her. She's harmless." Kevlar actually wasn't certain of that last part, but his friends didn't need to know that. With every day closer to his trip, his ex seemed to come more unglued.

He didn't know what her problem was; *she* broke up with *him*, after all. But she seemed excessively upset that he was going to Hawaii instead of giving her the tickets. The sooner he left, the better off he'd be. With her chances of going on this vacation officially dead, she'd stop her bitching and leave him alone. He hoped.

Everyone reached for their wallets and threw some bills on the table to cover their drinks, then headed for the door, waving at Jessyka on their way out.

Kevlar looked back before he exited the bar and his gaze landed on Blink. He was staring down into his glass as if it was the most fascinating thing he'd ever seen. He'd tried to talk to the other SEAL a few times in the last three weeks, but Blink always shut him down. Kevlar wouldn't give up on him though; he was a damn good SEAL.

A bar wasn't the time or place to try again, but soon, Kevlar was going to sit Blink down and have a chat, whether the man wanted to talk or not. Kevlar didn't have it in him to let a fellow soldier suffer, so he was determined to make more of an effort.

Giving Jessyka a chin lift, Kevlar headed for the door. He needed to pack. For the first time since Bertie broke up with him, he was actually looking forward to the trip. It would be a good rest before he had to eventually head out on another mission.

Kevlar wasn't expecting anything life-changing to happen in Hawaii. He was simply going on vacation. He'd get some sun, play in the water a little, eat some good food, then come home re-energized and ready to get back to his life.

No matter how much he might want to find someone like his mentor's wife, he knew the odds of that happening were low as long as he was a SEAL. Too many nights away from home, too much danger and uncertainty. The sooner he came to terms with that, the better he'd feel.

CHAPTER THREE

Every time Marley or her parents texted, wanting to know how her trip was going and asking for updates, Remi was sure to send back nothing but positive comments. But the truth was...she was lonelier than ever.

Going on vacation by herself had sounded like heaven, but in reality, it was difficult. She was surrounded by happy families and couples. She'd gone to Duke's for lunch one day, and while the food was amazing, the staff welcoming and friendly, it kind of sucked sitting by herself, the other tables filled with laughing guests. She'd rented a car and driven up to the North Shore, but it was hard to look at the map on her phone and the sights at the same time. And while the Dole Whip at the Dole Plantation was to die for, in the end, she wasn't brave enough to try out the maze by herself.

So while the weather was amazing, her hotel was

perfect, and the views everywhere she looked were beautiful, Remi wasn't exactly thrilled with the trip. She'd spent more time than Marley would've approved of in her hotel room, sketching out cartoons, most of which would probably never see the light of day since they were somewhat depressing.

She was actually ready to go back home. Back to her condo in San Diego, where she could sit in her drawing chair and be the boring, introverted Remi Douchecanoe accused her of being.

Today was the snorkeling trip, then she had one more day on the island before she'd get on a plane and head home.

This excursion, at least, was one she was looking forward to more than any other activity she'd done so far. Mostly because she'd booked a semi-private tour. She wouldn't have to make small talk with large groups of smiling tourists. From what she understood from the email she received, there was only one other guest booked on the tour. Of course, if that person was annoying, he or she could destroy the trip just as easily as an overpacked boat filled with hyper, screaming tourists, so Remi kept her fingers crossed that whoever had booked the expensive snorkeling trip would be low-key.

She packed her sunscreen, hat, sunglasses, towel, mints for after she got out of the water, and debated for a moment about bringing a pad of paper and a few of her drawing pencils, but ultimately vetoed that idea. She was determined to live in the moment on this trip. To enjoy being on the water, and not have her head buried in her sketchbooks.

After putting on her swimsuit and the cute coverup Marley had convinced her to buy before the trip, Remi swung her bag over her shoulder and took a deep breath. Then she headed out of the hotel room to catch her ride to the pier, where she'd be meeting the boat.

* * *

Kevlar was having a good time on vacation, although it was strange to be alone. He spent most of his life around others. Even when he wasn't dating, he was with his team or around other Navy personnel on the base. Here in Hawaii, he was surrounded by people, but they all pretty much ignored him. No one spoke directly to him unless it was someone in the service industry, asking for his order or inquiring about what they could do for him.

Here, in Hawaii, he was almost invisible.

Chuckling, Kevlar shook his head. Had he really gotten so conceited that he wanted to be fawned over simply because he was a SEAL? No, it wasn't that. It was more that he'd gotten *used* to it. Used to the attention he received because of his profession.

This trip was good for him. A way to bring him back down to earth. To reflect on who he was as a person. He'd spent a lot of time watching the families who were staying in his hotel, interacting with their loved ones. He'd sat on Waikiki Beach one afternoon for more people-watching, and that had been fascinating. He liked having no idea who the men and women were who crossed his path. They could be clerks at a big-box store, or CEOs of multimillion-dollar businesses. But on the beach, it didn't matter. They were all just people, vacationers or locals, enjoying themselves in the sand and surf.

The experience humbled him. His training didn't matter here. He wasn't looked up to or looked down at. He was simply another tourist on the beach.

Chuckling a little at himself, Kevlar realized he was getting a bit too philosophical. He couldn't help but wonder how the trip would've gone if Bertie had been with him. Probably stressful. She'd have nagged him about one thing after another; bitched about the rain storm that moved through one afternoon that had soaked him and everyone else on the beach; would've spent her time shopping in the high-end stores instead of soaking in the atmosphere and culture of the island.

No, Kevlar had made the right decision to come to Hawaii on his own. Even if he *was* still getting pissed-off texts from her. It made no sense to him, but apparently him going to Hawaii had really struck a nerve. And now she was haranguing him from thousands of miles away, probably hoping to ruin his trip.

But that wasn't going to happen. Kevlar had two more days before he was scheduled to fly back to Riverton. Tomorrow, he was planning on driving up to the North Shore to visit with Baker and his wife, Jodelle. He was looking forward to meeting the man he'd only talked to on the phone and via email. He wasn't a very talkative guy, but ever since he'd gotten together with Jodelle, he definitely seemed more mellow.

Today, Kevlar was going on his scuba trip, the one thing he'd looked forward to the most. He was good in the water, obviously, but usually he was working. Today, he was going to take his time, take in the beauty that was Hawaii and the waters around the island.

Bertie had booked a private tour...probably hoping that he'd propose, even though they'd been nowhere near that level of commitment in their relationship. He wasn't upset in the least with the cost of this excursion, because it would be worth every penny. As much as he enjoyed people-watching on the beach, too many people diving would scare away the wildlife. The boat captain had sent an email with last-minute details about the trip and had informed him there would be just one other client on the tour, but she wasn't certified to dive, so she'd be snorkeling. Which was fine with Kevlar. He could be deep beneath the water and she could stay on top of it.

Smiling to himself, Kevlar hefted the bag with his gear onto his shoulder. It had been a pain to bring everything with him, but he was too anal to use someone else's gear. He knew his tank and the rest of the equipment like the back of his hand. He could troubleshoot without thinking twice, which had saved his life more than once while on a mission. If he truly wanted to relax and enjoy the dive, he needed to use the gear he was comfortable with.

Kevlar closed the hotel room door behind him and

headed to the lobby to catch a taxi to the pier. It was supposed to be a beautiful day, and he couldn't wait to get on the water...for pleasure instead of a mission.

Remi tried not to stare at the man who'd joined her on the small boat. He was ruggedly handsome. That was the only way she could describe him. He had a five o'clock shadow, as if he hadn't bothered to shave while on vacation. His light brown hair was short, and he had the most piercing blue eyes she'd ever seen. He wore a white T-shirt and a pair of black and blue board shorts that highlighted his muscular thighs and legs. Heck, even his toes were attractive...which was the most ridiculous thought in the world, because feet were gross.

At least Douchecanoe's were.

Remi shook her head. No, she wasn't going to think about that jerk today. She was on a boat skimming over the water, the sun was shining, and she was going to enjoy herself.

The other guest had introduced himself as Vincent, then he'd disappeared into the cabin of the boat with the captain, leaving Remi by herself in the back of the vessel... which was fine with her. It wasn't as if she would even know what to talk about with a man who was so obviously out of her league.

Still...her eyes were drawn back to the cabin, and she stared at the man—Vincent—as he talked with the captain.

He seemed confident in who he was, clearly had no problem holding his own in whatever conversation he was having with the other man. When he crossed his arms over his chest, the muscles in his forearms bulged.

Remi thought about how she'd sketch him. What kind of personality she'd give him in one of her comics. He'd be fun, a character everyone wanted to be friends with. But he'd have a secret, something that tormented him, which he never shared with anyone.

Taking a deep breath, Remi forced her gaze away from the stranger and purposely turned to look out at the waves as they motored out to wherever it was they were going to be snorkeling. Or scuba diving, in Vincent's case. Which was a good thing, because she had no idea what she'd talk about if they were swimming together. Remi just wasn't good in casual situations. Never had been. Marley was the outgoing one. The one who could charm everyone she met.

Remi was...Remi.

Sighing, she closed her eyes and lifted her face to the sun. She refused to think about anything other than having a good time today. Once they got where they were going, her fellow guest would go deep-sea diving and she'd do her float-and-breathe thing near the surface. After checking out a couple of different spots, they'd get back in the boat, eat the tacos the captain had promised would be waiting for them—which was ironic, really, considering what she did for a living—and go back to their respective hotels in Oahu.

She didn't need to impress him or anyone else. They were strangers sharing an excursion. That was it.

* * *

Kevlar had no idea why his gaze kept going back to the woman he'd met when he'd arrived at the pier. Maybe because she was unlike most of the women he met these days. Which made him mentally roll his eyes at himself. He was obviously hanging out in the wrong places if meeting a woman who politely shook his hand, gave him a small smile, and didn't immediately hit on him was unusual.

But for some reason, even while he was making small talk with the captain, his eyes kept straying to where she was sitting. Like now. With her head tipped back and a small smile on her face, Kevlar wondered what she was thinking. Why a beautiful woman like her was on a solo snorkeling trip. He guessed her age to be early thirties, and surely she had a husband and kids. He couldn't imagine why she wouldn't. Maybe they were off doing something she had no desire to do today, and her husband splurged and spoiled her with the private tour.

"She doesn't say much," the captain said, not missing where his gaze had gone. Again.

Kevlar turned to look at the man. He was pretty scruffy. He wore board shorts, just like Kevlar, but his T-shirt had a few sizable holes in it and the color was faded from the sun. If *he* ran a private excursion like this one, Kevlar would do his best to clean up for the guests, but what did he know?

"The chick?" he said, as if Kevlar hadn't heard him. "She don't talk a lot. Which is okay by me. I like 'em quiet and compliant." He chuckled at his own words.

Kevlar frowned. The man wasn't being completely inappropriate, but the sexual inuendo was there. It was a rude thing to say about one client to another, and this guy didn't even know him.

"I guess you being a SEAL and all, you're used to women throwing themselves at you. You'll have to work a bit to bring that one to heel, I'd guess."

Okay, so maybe he *did* know a little about him. Kevlar racked his brain trying to remember if he'd said anything about being a SEAL in their communications, and couldn't come up with anything. But then again, Bertie had been the one to set this trip up initially, so it was possible she'd informed him that, since he was a Navy SEAL, he'd be bringing his own gear.

"She's here alone," the captain went on. "No boyfriend. Like you, she was supposed to be here with someone, but she emailed last week and said it'd be just her." The man grinned. "So if you and her wanted to...you know...feel free. I'll keep my back turned and mind my own business."

This guy was disgusting. Kevlar hadn't missed the small camera aimed right at the seating area in the back of the boat. He wasn't going to have sex with the cute stranger sitting in the sun any more than he'd have done so with Bertie.

"Not cool, man," Kevlar said in a low growl. "You this much of a pervert to all your paying customers?"

Clearly hearing the disgust in Kevlar's tone, the man straightened and, when he answered, any inuendo in his tone was gone. "No, sorry. Of course not. I just thought..." His voice trailed off.

"You thought what?" Kevlar asked, getting more irritated with the man every time he opened his mouth.

"Nothing. You're right. That was rude and uncalled for," the captain said in an appropriately cowed tone.

Kevlar figured the asshole was just saying what he thought he should, but he did his best to calm down. "What's the plan for today?" he asked, wanting to change the subject away from the woman he couldn't seem to ignore. He'd rather discuss the details for their trip, so he'd know how much time he'd have under the water. He planned on spending every minute diving.

"We've got another half hour or so until we get to the first spot. I discovered it last year, and the best part is that none of the other tour boats have found it yet. So it'll be just us. There are a ton of sea turtles out this way and the coral on the bottom is untouched. There'll be plenty of wildlife to see and the fish are abundant."

Kevlar nodded. That sounded fantastic to him.

"We'll stay there for about an hour, then move to another spot. While you two are back in the water, I'll get lunch ready. Whenever you're done diving, you can come up and have tacos. I've got some beer or margaritas to go with it. Then we'll head back."

"Sounds good," Kevlar told him. He wouldn't touch the alcohol, not while on the water, but tacos sounded like a fantastic meal after diving. The captain went on to explain weather conditions and the types of fish he might see, but Kevlar's attention was drawn once more to the woman sitting out on the deck.

Her hair was pulled into a bun at the nape of her neck, but wisps had escaped and were flying wildly around her head in the wind. The locks had seemed brown back at the pier, but in the sun, the reddish highlights were more prevalent. Her lips were full and pouty, and even though she hadn't taken off her coverup, Kevlar could tell she was curvy all over. Exactly the kind of woman he loved.

Bertie took pride in staying slim. Too slim for Kevlar's taste, but he'd never said a word. Even he knew better than to comment on a woman's weight, no matter what it was. But he couldn't help but wonder what this woman, Remi, would look like when she took off her coverup.

He was being ridiculous, of course. He knew nothing about her. She could be a shrew. A total pain in the ass, which was why she was here by herself. Maybe no one wanted to come with her because she was a bitch.

But...he didn't think so.

She'd smiled at him when he'd introduced himself, in a sweet way that hit him squarely in his gut. He had no idea why; plenty of women smiled at him and he didn't feel a thing. Her gaze had dropped from his when he'd shaken her hand, but she'd peered up at him from beneath her lowered lashes in the next instant, as if she was as drawn to him as he was to her.

Which was stupid. Wasn't it? He'd just gotten out of a yearlong relationship and wasn't looking for a rebound.

Kevlar ran a hand through his hair and once again turned to face the ocean in front of him. He had to pull himself together. He wasn't here to indulge in a vacation fling, and even if he wanted one, there was no indication Remi would be up for that. Not that he'd go there, regardless. He wanted more than a one-night stand with a woman. Meaningless sex wasn't his idea of a good time.

But he couldn't deny he was attracted to the woman sharing the boat with him, even though nothing could come of it. As Bertie had proven, he couldn't even manage a relationship with a woman who lived in the same city, since he was gone so often.

Taking a deep breath, Kevlar decided the best thing to do was to keep his distance. Not because he didn't like her, but because he liked her *too* much, regardless of the fact he knew nothing about the woman.

It made no sense, this connection he felt. He'd do what he came here to do—scuba dive, and that's it. Tomorrow, he'd go up so see Baker and his wife, then head back to California and to his life.

When he got home, it likely wouldn't be more than a month or two before his next mission, and he needed to concentrate on that. As team leader, he had a lot of responsibility on his shoulders. To his country, the civilians who could get caught in the middle of something dangerous, and to his team. He had no time for a relationship, obviously.

Even with those thoughts rolling around in his head, Kevlar found himself turning to catch another glimpse of Remi out of the corner of his eye. She'd twisted on the bench so that one foot rested on the cushion, and her coverup had slid down, exposing a pale, curvy thigh.

Swallowing hard, Kevlar pressed his lips together and did his best to think about anything other than how badly he wanted to run his palm up that leg and see for himself if it was as smooth as it looked.

This was supposed to be a relaxing voyage, yet he had a feeling it was going to be anything but. He was a SEAL. The only easy day was yesterday, and he'd made it through Hell Week. He could survive a few hours on a pleasure excursion. No problem.

CHAPTER FOUR

Remi lifted her head, took the snorkel out of her mouth, and took in a deep breath. As much as she loved snorkeling, she didn't love clenching the plastic in her mouth and breathing through a tube.

She'd been following a sea turtle, enchanted and awed by its smooth movements and how it didn't even seem to notice her following. After tracking the turtle for what seemed like miles, but was probably only a hundred yards or so, she was thankful she'd gone outside her comfort zone and come to Hawaii by herself. This particular activity alone was worth it.

The man she'd been lusting over—and feeling embarrassed about, given how hard it was to keep her gaze off him while he'd put on his wetsuit and donned his scuba gear—had slid into the water as if he was born there.

Between one blink and the next, he was gone, under the water and off on his own adventure.

She'd been left on the boat with the captain, and she definitely didn't like the way he'd eyeballed her when she'd taken off her coverup before donning the cheap wetsuit provided by the boat rental company, along with the mask and flippers. She'd quickly followed Vincent's example and slid into the water, determined to enjoy herself and see some turtles.

The world under the water was beautiful and everything she'd hoped it would be. The captain hadn't lied, this area was teeming with wildlife. The fish were bright and varied, but it was the turtles that delighted her most.

Blinking water out of her eyes, Remi looked around for the boat. She was thirsty and tired and could really go for one of the tacos the captain had promised.

To her surprise, she saw nothing but water all around her.

Frowning, she spun in the other direction, only to see the outline of Diamond Head, what she thought was the extinct volcano on the coast of Oahu, in the distance—the very, *very* far distance.

"Oh, shit," she mumbled disbelievingly.

She'd missed the boat! Or had it left without her?

Either way, she was screwed.

Remi wanted to laugh. This was completely typical of something that would happen to her. She was constantly late to things back home. Marley was always bitching about her showing up anywhere from minutes to an hour or more late to outings. It wasn't that Remi *wanted* to be late, she just got caught up in her work and lost track of time. Kind of the way she'd done with that turtle.

Surprisingly, she wasn't freaking out. She didn't know why. Maybe because she was already thinking up how to use this ridiculous situation in one of her upcoming cartoons. Drawing was how she dealt with most things in her life. When she was sad, that always came out in her characters. If someone pissed her off, they'd show up in a cartoon doing something stupid or embarrassing. It was cathartic for her, and being left in the middle of the ocean during a snorkeling excursion was definitely something that needed to be immortalized in a cartoon.

A sound behind her had Remi shrieking in fright and spinning quickly. She imagined a huge blue whale lunging at her with its mouth open, ready to swallow her down. Or a Great White shark coming for her. Or even the turtle she'd been so distracted by, laughing at her predicament.

For a moment, Remi seriously thought she was having a heart attack and was about to come face-to-face with a sea monster from the deep. A black head appeared with huge bug eyes. It took a moment for her brain to understand what she was seeing. It wasn't a sea creature, but a man. A very specific man, at that.

Relief swam through Remi's veins. The first thought was, thank God she wasn't alone. The second was...oh crap. She didn't enjoy making small talk in the best of situations. In the middle of the ocean when they'd been left by the boat that brought them there? Even worse.

Then again, this situation wasn't exactly one where small talk was important, so maybe it didn't matter.

Vincent lifted his face mask and took the scuba regulator out of his mouth. His brow was furrowed and his lips drawn down in a frown. But even with that foreboding look on his face, the man was gorgeous.

He was utterly beautiful, in fact...and for a second, Remi was lost in a daydream where he'd take one look at her and fall madly in love and they'd run off and get married and have beautiful babies together. Then she snorted, and he looked at her in surprise, and all her dreams died.

Why would this man look twice at her? She had frizzy hair, carried too much weight to be considered attractive by society's standards, was an extreme introvert, and she tended to say the most inappropriate things at the worst times. And...she snort-laughed.

"Where's the boat?" Vincent asked gruffly, bringing her back to the present with a jolt.

"Gone," she said with a small shrug.

"Shit."

She couldn't help it; Remi laughed again.

"I'm not sure this is funny," Vincent told her, arching a brow in her direction.

"It's not," Remi told him. "But then again, it kind of is. I mean, think about it. What are the odds? It's not like he could've accidentally counted wrong before he left. It was just the two of us. How hard is it to count to two?"

To her surprise, Vincent actually seemed to be considering the question. “I should’ve seen this coming,” he said after a moment.

Remi was intrigued. “Why? Can you see the future? Can you read minds?”

Vincent chuckled this time, and as inappropriate as it was, Remi felt her nipples harden. How in the world could she think about anything other than how they were going to get back to land?

“My ex wasn’t happy that I decided to go on this trip without her.”

Remi’s eyes widened. “You too?” she blurted.

He stared at her as if she was the only person on the planet. As if they weren’t treading water in the middle of the ocean and would probably die out there if the captain didn’t come back.

“Yeah,” Vincent said after a moment.

“Wow. That’s a crazy coincidence,” Remi said, shaking her head.

“When Bertie and I broke up, she wanted me to transfer the reservations into her name so she could come out here with one of her friends,” Vincent said.

“When I refused to take him with me, Douchecanoe wanted me to give him half of the money spent on this trip. Except, he didn’t pay for any of it,” Remi said wryly.

Vincent’s lips twitched. “When I told Bertie I was actually going to go to Hawaii without her, I swear I saw fire shoot out of the top of her head.”

“When I depicted Douchecanoe as a money-grubbing asshat in my latest cartoon, he threatened to sue me for defamation, even though I hadn't used his name and there was no resemblance to him whatsoever."

Vincent's head tilted, and Remi swore he'd drifted closer to where she was treading water. "Cartoon?"

Remi was proud of her little comic strip. She worked hard to come up with funny and creative story lines each week and was paid well for her trouble. But it was still hard to believe her penchant for doodling had led to an actual career. That she was paid money for doing what she loved. "Yeah. I have a weekly comic strip that's published online, on about a hundred and forty different websites. And I just signed a contract for someone to turn my drawings into live-action clips for TikTok. The first one went up a week or so ago and already has two million views." She wasn't bragging, not really. It was still a little unbelievable, but she was proud and thrilled that she could entertain so many people with her drawings.

"What's it called?"

"Shouldn't we be trying to figure out how to get back to land?" she asked.

"Probably," Vincent said, staring at her expectedly.

His attention was heady. Most people looked *past* her, when they bothered to look in her direction at all. She wasn't exactly tall, blonde, and stacked. Having this man's complete attention was making her tingle in places she hadn't tingled in a very long time.

"I'm sure you haven't heard of it."

"Humor me," he ordered.

And there was no mistaking that his words were an

order. For a split-second, Remi wondered what he'd do if she refused. She decided not to push him. "Pecky the Traveling Taco," she told him, a touch defiantly.

She'd had every reaction under the sun when she told people the name of her comic strip. Laughter, disbelief, eye rolls, condescending remarks...you name it, she'd experienced it. So she was ready for just about anything from Vincent—except what she got.

"Are you *kidding* me? You're fucking with me, aren't you?" he asked with wide eyes.

"Nope. I know it's silly, but tacos are one of my favorite foods, and I was eleven and eating out with my grandparents one day. They took me to this hole-in-the-wall taco place near their house, and I got lost in my head imagining my taco standing up and walking around the room and deciding he wanted to go on an adventure to meet people."

Remi stopped talking and pressed her lips together. Shoot, she hadn't meant to admit that part. Usually when she told others how she came up with the name and idea for her comic, she kept things vague. But for some reason, maybe it was the situation, she'd gone and told Vincent the real story.

"That's one of my favorite comics! My friends and I talk about it all the time."

Remi rolled her eyes. "Whatever," she said, turning her head and looking in the direction of the mainland. She hated when anyone patronized her about her work. She didn't meet a ton of people who'd even heard of Pecky, but there were enough that didn't think too highly of what she did for a living. It might be just a comic strip, but she loved it.

"My favorite is the one where Pecky and his friend, Torty the tortilla, decide to go to an amusement park, and while they're on a roller coaster, his lettuce flies out and sprays all the people in the cars behind them, and they have to get the park employees to find all his missing parts and everyone screams when they see him 'naked'," Vincent told her.

Remi turned back to him, *her* eyes wide this time. "You've really seen my stuff?" she asked in awe.

"Seen and loved," Vincent reassured her.

Then he surprised her by holding out his hand above the water. "I know I introduced myself earlier, but in case you forgot, I'm Vincent. Vincent Hill. My friends call me Kevlar."

She barely refrained from snort-laughing again. As if she'd forget his name. Nope, it was burned into her brain. But she was impressed with his manners. Even if they were ridiculous, because they were in the middle of the ocean after having been left by the man they'd hired to take care of them for the day.

Remi reached for his hand. She grabbed hold and echoed, "I'm Remi. Remi Stephenson. My friends call me Remi."

Vincent smiled at her teasing reply, and the feel of his hand in hers made sparks shoot from her fingertips to her toes...and everywhere in between.

To her shock, he pulled on her hand until they were

almost touching chest to chest. Her flipper-covered feet brushed against his. "Are you okay, Remi?" he asked seriously.

She frowned. "Yes. Why? Are you?"

"I'm good. But you aren't freaking out."

"Would it do any good?" she asked seriously.

"Well, no, but that doesn't usually seem to matter in cases like this."

"You find yourself marooned in the middle of the ocean a lot?" she quipped.

His lips twitched again. She actually wasn't trying to be funny, but if he thought she was, she'd take it.

"Honestly? Not this exact situation, but ones like it, yes."

Remi couldn't help but be intrigued. "Really?"

Vincent sighed lightly. "I'm a Navy SEAL."

"Of course you are," she said with a roll of her eyes. She should've guessed that. She'd seen his body, he didn't have an ounce of fat on him. And he'd arrived with his own diving gear. She could totally see him as some sort of badass special forces soldier. Sailor. Whatever.

She was very aware that he hadn't let go of her hand, but she was in no hurry to let go of his either. The truth was, the longer they were out here, the more worried she was getting. She was a good swimmer, but there was no way she could swim all the way back to the island.

"I am," Vincent insisted. "I'm on leave at the moment, as you could probably guess. This vaca had already been planned and scheduled, so my commander encouraged me to go. You know...to relax."

She chuckled. "And here you are. Relaxing."

He returned her grin. "Something like that. Anyway, I've participated in my fair share of jungle rescues, kidnapping extractions, not to mention covert operations all over the world. So trust me when I tell you that you aren't reacting like most people who found themselves in your situation would."

It was Remi's turn to sigh. "I know...I'm weird." She'd been described that way more than once in her lifetime.

"No. You're perfect," Vincent said gently.

Kevlar stared at the woman bobbing in the waves in front of him. He'd decided earlier, on the boat, that he was going to stay away from Remi. Tried to convince himself that he wasn't interested. But the disappointment he'd felt after forcing himself to leave the vessel before she'd taken off her coverup had simmered within him the entire time he'd been scuba diving.

Was she as lush as he'd imagined? Did she have one of those adorable pooches on her stomach that always drove him crazy with lust when he'd been with women in the past? Was her bathing suit cut high on her thighs or more conservative? It had taken an extreme battle of wills for him to stop thinking about what she might look like and concentrate on the fish and turtles swimming around him.

When he'd surfaced and hadn't seen any sign of the boat, his first thought was, "Oh, shit." But he'd immediately suspected what might've happened. Bertie had threatened that if he went to Hawaii instead of letting her go, she'd make him sorry. Somehow, she must have arranged for him to get left out here in the middle of the ocean. Paid off the boat captain or something. He supposed she thought this was a perfect punishment for a SEAL, a man who was more comfortable than most in the water. It wasn't fair that Remi had gotten dragged into her malicious plot as well.

He should be planning, figuring out how to get to shore, but instead he was completely focused on the woman in front of him. She didn't respond how he'd expected. To anything. From their current situation, to him admitting that he was a SEAL. She intrigued him, just as he knew she would, which was why he'd stayed away. But his willpower was currently useless, given they were stranded together.

Now he wanted to know everything about her. Even in this dangerous situation, he couldn't stop himself from touching her, from asking questions.

He'd already found himself attracted to her physically, but now that he knew she wasn't one to get hysterical when things didn't go her way, *and* that she was the talented artist and brains behind Pecky the Traveling Taco, the cartoon he and all his teammates loved, he was pretty much a goner.

"I'm not perfect," she snorted in response to his earlier comment.

He was still holding her hand, and Kevlar was thrilled beyond belief that she hadn't let go.

"Prove it," he challenged.

"What?"

"Prove it," he repeated. "Tell me something about you that isn't perfect."

"Ha. How long do you have?" she retorted.

Pretending to look around, Kevlar shrugged. "I'm thinking we have some time."

"Shouldn't we be doing something? I don't know, like swimming toward shore maybe?" she asked.

"Can you swim the eight miles, give or take, to Oahu?" he asked.

"Can *you*?" she immediately returned.

"Yes," he said without hesitation.

"Of course you can," she mumbled.

"Come on, Remi, tell me something you think isn't perfect about yourself. We'll take turns sharing info."

"Fine. My grandmother can fart on command. She takes great pride in farting at the most inappropriate times."

Kevlar burst out laughing. "That's not something about yourself, but okay, I'll bite. Seriously?"

"Yup," Remi said with a grin. "Your turn. Why is your nickname Kevlar?"

"It was early in my career, my first mission as a SEAL. We were pinned down, surrounded by tangos...er...bad guys. It wasn't good. We were fucked, basically. I looked around and saw the same expression on all my teammates' faces—resignation. No one was going to give up, that's not in our DNA, but I got mad. Like, *furious*. That was my first mission, and I didn't want to die before I'd even gotten a chance to experience everything it was to be a SEAL."

"What'd you do?" Remi asked with wide eyes.

She was hanging on his every word, and it felt good. Really good. "Something stupid," Kevlar said with a small huff of laughter. "There was a truck parked not far from where we were pinned down. Still running. I figured I had one chance to get to that truck, blow it up, cause a distraction so my team could get the hell out of there...so I took it. I yelled 'cover me!' and took off before my team leader could even question what I was doing. I felt the bullets whizzing by me, but I didn't stop. I don't even remember much about what happened after that, but apparently I got to the truck and managed to stuff a rag into the gas tank and blow that sucker to smithereens."

"Holy crap!" Remi breathed.

"Yeah, well, before you go thinking I got all sorts of accolades for that, I actually got a reprimand."

"What? Why?"

She seemed offended on his behalf, which again made warmth spread through Kevlar's chest. "Because I was an idiot."

"But you saved your team, right?"

"Yup. But if I'd waited sixty more seconds, the backup my team leader had radioed for help would've arrived."

"Okay, but I don't understand why you have the nickname Kevlar."

"Because I didn't get hit by any of the bullets that were flying around when I ran toward that truck. It was as if my body was made of Kevlar, like they bounced off me or something. The name stuck."

"Wow. Okay, that's impressive, I guess."

Kevlar chuckled. "Trust me, I don't take chances like that anymore, and I'd be pissed if any of the guys on my team did. They know I play things by the book, and they trust me because of it."

"You sound close to them."

"I am. They're my brothers in every way that matters. I trust them with my life."

"That's awesome."

"Yeah."

"Am I allowed to ask where you're stationed? Here in Hawaii? There are SEALs here, right?"

"Yes. But no, I'm based out of California right now."

Remi blinked. "Really?"

"Yeah, why?"

"I live in California too."

Kevlar's heart beat just a little harder. "I'm in Riverton. Where are you?"

"San Diego," she said softly, with a small smile. "Right next door."

Kevlar closed his eyes for a beat. He was overwhelmed with...

Gratitude? Thanks? A sense of rightness? He'd

convinced himself that he couldn't have anything to do with this woman despite his immediate attraction, because he didn't want a fling and a long-distance relationship wouldn't work. And yet...she lived practically in his backyard.

Fate was a funny thing.

He opened his eyes. "Right next door," he repeated, and squeezed the hand he was still holding.

"So...if you could have anything to eat right this moment, what would you choose?" Remi asked.

Kevlar was surprised at the abrupt change in subject and didn't answer right away. He was still stuck on the fact that he might have a chance to get to know this woman better once they went home. And he had no doubt they *would* get home. They weren't dying out here in the ocean, no matter who'd decided that was what they wanted to happen.

Remi's cheeks pinkened. "Sorry. Ignore that. I'm awkward in the best of social situations, which this isn't. We need to figure out what we're going to do. Do you think that guy will come back for us?"

"Thin Mints," Kevlar blurted. He should be reassuring Remi that they'd get back to shore, but holding this woman's hand, treading water, and getting to know her was more important at the moment.

"Really? Aren't they seasonal?" Remi asked.

"For most people, yes. But back home, when I'm there, I volunteer with a Girl Scout Troop. I teach them things like tying knots, boating, safe water practices, and I take them camping...in return, I get paid in cookies." He grinned at the surprised look on Remi's face.

"I bet you're great with them," she said in a sincere voice.

"They're awesome," Kevlar said with a shrug. "They have an unending well of curiosity, and it's fun to see them get excited about the things I'm able to teach them."

"I've never been camping," Remi commented.

"I'm sorry," Kevlar said.

She shrugged. "My parents are rich. That's not usually something I tell men I've just met, but I'm thinking this situation isn't exactly normal. We didn't spend time camping or getting dirty when I was growing up...much to my grandmother's dismay. She always told my parents that I should be running around like a heathen, getting into trouble and playing in the dirt. But they disagreed."

"Your grandmother was right."

"Well, she also likes to shoplift packs of gum from her local market, so I'm thinking my parents might have had a reason to dismiss her life lessons."

Kevlar burst out laughing. "I want to meet this grandma of yours," he said.

"She'd love you," Remi told him with a smile. "And before you think too badly of her, the manager knows she does it, but he doesn't say anything because she also tips really well every time she's there. I personally think it's weird that almost every place these days has tip jars, but whatever. Your turn. Tell me something else about yourself."

Kevlar racked his brain to think of something interesting he could tell her. "I'm allergic to seafood," he said with a shrug. It wasn't a terribly exciting fact, but it was all he could think of at the moment.

Remi stared at him for a minute, then grinned.

"What?"

"It's just...here you are, surrounded by water, the only thing to eat for miles is seafood...and you can't eat it."

"We aren't going to have to eat fish, or any *other* creature swimming around us."

Remi frowned. "You don't know that. And I'm not exactly ready to give up and die."

"We definitely aren't dying," Kevlar reassured her.

She tilted her head and stared at him for a beat. "What aren't you telling me? What do you know?"

Kevlar shrugged. "You'll probably think it's creepy," he said.

"If it's something that will get us out of this water, put a taco in one hand, one of those awesome lava flow drinks in the other, and end with me in a dry bed, I'm not going to think it's creepy."

The only thing Kevlar could think about was her lying on a bed...preferably with him. But now wasn't the time or place for that kind of thought. "Right, so...you know I'm a SEAL. I have friends with connections. One in particular is a former SEAL who's taken it upon himself to keep others safe. He's a one-man stalker...and I mean that in a good way. He's made these tracker things. My team wears them when we're on missions. It's comforting to know if we're ever taken prisoner, this guy will know where we are and will send in the cavalry to get us out.

"Anyway, this wetsuit I'm wearing...well, it's the one I wear on missions. I forgot that I still had one of those trackers in the pocket. I activated it the second I realized we'd been left out here."

"Wait, wait, wait—are you telling me that there's a guy somewhere out there," she gestured toward Oahu with the hand that wasn't in Kevlar's, "who'll see that you're floating out in the ocean and will notify someone to come get you?"

"That's what I'm hoping," Kevlar told her.

"How will he know it's you? That you're not out here on a boat or something? Who will he contact? Will he come himself?"

Kevlar chuckled at the rapid-fire spate of questions. "Each tracker has its own code, the one I have is associated with a number that's uniquely mine. He might think I'm on a boat, that maybe I activated it accidentally or just in case. But he'll ask questions to make sure. That's what he does. He's got contacts on Oahu that he can reach out to, and no, he won't come himself."

"Someone's really going to come get us?" Remi asked quietly.

"Yes," Kevlar said with conviction.

Remi closed her eyes, and for the first time, Kevlar could see how stressed she was. Her jokes and the back-and-forth info-gathering was a way for her to cope. He frowned, making a mental note to look beyond her calm personality in the future. To make sure he helped her deal with stress if he thought she was hiding it from him.

He wasn't even freaked out about the "in the future" thing. Now that he knew she lived only a few short miles away from him, he wanted to get to know her. Wanted more time with her.

"We just have to stay relaxed. They'll come for us," he said.

Remi's eyes opened and she met his gaze. Her hazel eyes swam with tears as she nodded, but she refused to let them fall. She'd hidden her trepidation a little *too* well for Kevlar's liking.

He pulled on her hand without thought, and wrapped his free arm around her, holding her snug against his chest.

It didn't take much to keep them afloat; he'd always been extremely buoyant and the saltwater helped even more. Remi buried her face against his neck and held on tightly. He had the sudden urge to feel her against him without their wetsuits between them. To feel her curves against his body as they lay together in bed after making love.

"I'm sorry," she mumbled against his shoulder.

"About what?" he asked.

"For putting you in this situation."

Her words surprised Kevlar. He pulled back slightly, trying to see her eyes, but Remi refused to look at him.

"What are you talking about?" he asked.

He felt more than heard her sigh as they bobbed in the gentle waves. "Douchecanoe did this. I *know* he did."

"Did what?" Kevlar asked.

"Arranged for me to get left out here in the middle of the ocean. He called more than once before my trip. Swore I'd regret not giving him half of the trip's costs, even though he didn't pay for a single thing. We'd pre-planned this excursion, and I just know that he somehow convinced the captain to leave me. He even *said* something about hoping I got left in the ocean—just like we are now. You just got caught in his evil plan."

"Bertie threatened me too," Kevlar told her. "She arranged this dive for us under duress. She didn't understand why I'd want to go scuba diving on vacation, saying I spent so much time in the water as it was, why would I want to spend my free time doing the same thing I do when I'm working. But this is nothing like work. I can take my time and look at the wildlife and plants and stuff. When I'm on a mission, that's the last thing I'm thinking about. It could've just as easily been *her* who set this up, and you were caught in *her* evil plan."

Remi looked up at him then. "Why are people so... horrible?" she whispered.

"I don't know."

"Well, Bertie might hate you—which is ridiculous; how could someone hate *anyone* with a butt as nice as yours?—but my ex probably thinks he'll get millions of dollars if I end up dead."

Her compliment felt ridiculously good, but it was the last part that had him blinking in disbelief. *"What?"*

"My parents are Claire Crown-Stephenson and

Fernando Stephenson. They started their own company when they were in their twenties. They were already wealthy when they were bought out a few years ago by a huge manufacturer in a five hundred-million-dollar deal. And that was a low bid."

Remi was staring at him as if waiting for him to grow two heads and turn into some sort of sea monster. "Good for them," he said after a beat.

Her lips twitched. "You have no idea who they are, do you?"

"No."

"Crown Condoms," she said matter-of-factly.

Realization dawned. "Wow," he said.

"Yeah."

"So...you're a condom princess. Cool."

She snort-laughed again, and Kevlar couldn't help but think it was the most adorable sound he'd ever heard.

"That's all you're gonna say? Vincent, I'm the heir to a condom dynasty. I'm worth millions. I mean, *millions*. Plural times a gazillion."

"And Douchecanoe thinks he's gonna get that money *why*?" Kevlar asked, liking the sound of his real name on her lips.

Remi shrugged. "There was a time when I thought we'd get married, and we briefly talked about listing him as my beneficiary on my investments. I think he was conceited and stupid enough to think I'd already done it, even though we weren't married or even engaged. For the record, of *course* I didn't."

"Right. Well, when we get rescued, we'll figure out who's responsible. Right about now, it doesn't matter if it was your ex or mine who orchestrated this little adventure. All that matters is keeping calm until the Hawaii Navy SEALs arrive."

"You're not what I expected when I first saw you," Remi admitted.

Kevlar grinned. "I like keeping you on your toes."

"Or flippers," Remi said.

"That too."

"This is *so* going in a comic," she informed him.

Kevlar squealed dramatically. "My teammates are gonna be *so* jealous that I'm in a Pecky the Traveling Taco cartoon. I'm going to rub it in their faces all the damn time."

His heart swelled in his chest when Remi laughed, then lowered her head back to his shoulder and clung to him a little tighter. He held her against his body and couldn't help but sigh in contentment. This situation could've been a hundred times worse than it was. The weather could've been crap, Remi could've been a complete bitch and a pain in his ass, he could've decided to rent a wetsuit instead of using his own.

Someone would be coming for them. Tex would come through, he had no doubts whatsoever.

CHAPTER FIVE

Remi had no idea how long they'd been bobbing in the ocean, but she was getting tired. And extremely thirsty. And a little nauseous. She'd wanted to ditch her face mask and snorkel, but Vincent insisted on her keeping them... just in case.

It was that "just in case" that was making her uneasy right about now. The only thing keeping her from freaking out was Vincent's calm presence. How sure he was that someone would be coming to get them. But now the sun was beginning to set, and the thought of being out here in the dark wasn't a pleasant one. She'd never been afraid of sharks and other marine animals before, but this situation was changing her mind.

She'd never been the clingy type either, but she couldn't seem to let go of Vincent. His arms felt so warm and assuring around her, and he'd proven more than capable of keeping them both afloat.

They'd talked about everything from their favorite books, to foods they liked, to more serious things like their political leanings, terrorism, and the state of the world in general. He was funny, but he could be serious and deep at the same time.

"Hear that?" he asked suddenly.

Jerking in his arms, because she'd actually been on the verge of falling asleep, Remi lifted her head. She followed his gaze to the horizon...and saw what she thought was a boat coming straight for them.

"Holy crap, you were right!" she exclaimed.

"You doubted me?" Vincent teased.

She had but was too ashamed to admit it. "Of course not. You're one of the few and the proud."

He chuckled. "That's the Marines, honey."

"Right, sorry. Army Strong?"

"Remi," he warned.

She giggled. "Oh, I know! Born Ready."

"How the hell do you know all the military slogans?" he asked with a shake of his head and a grin on his lips.

"Love me a man in uniform," she quipped.

"The only easy day was yesterday," he informed her. "That's the SEAL motto."

"Well, they aren't wrong," she said dryly. "Yesterday, I was sitting on the beach with a drink in my hand and my tablet in my lap, drawing Pecky sitting on a beach with a drink in *his* hand."

She smiled at Vincent, but saw that his eyes were glued on the horizon...and he was frowning. "Vincent?" she asked nervously.

He turned his attention to her, and the intensity of his gaze made her suck in a breath. "Don't panic," he said firmly.

"You know saying that makes me *want* to panic, right?" she asked.

"I'm not sure the boat coming toward us is my friends."

"How can you tell? I mean, it's too far away for me to see much of anything."

"I just can. I need you to trust me."

"I do," Remi said immediately, without thought. It was weird, but she totally trusted this man. If she'd been stuck out here on her own, she would've been in a heap of trouble. But having him here, his calm demeanor, his belief that his friend would track him and send help, had been a lifeline.

"We need to go under the water. If this is my friends, they'll stop right where we are because they'll have the tracker coordinates. If it's not, they'll go by and we'll know."

Remi saw his lips say the words, heard them, but they didn't make sense. "I'm not sure how long I can hold my breath," she whispered.

"We'll share my air," he said, as if suggesting they were going for an after-dinner walk on the sand.

"I don't know—"

"I'm not going to let anything happen to you. You know why?"

Glancing at the boat, which was still heading for them at a fast clip, Remi found she was having a hard time breathing.

Then Vincent's finger touched her chin and gently forced her to look into his eyes. "You know why?" he repeated.

Remi shook her head.

"Because I want to meet your grandmother. I want to thank your parents for starting their condom company because I've used Crown condoms many times over the years. I want to share my Thin Mints with you and introduce you to my Girl Scouts. I want to watch you draw your Pecky cartoons. I want to introduce you to my teammates. I want a future—with *you*, Remi. It can't be a coincidence that we live in practically the same city and met thousands of miles away. And I can't have any of that if I don't keep you safe right now. Understand?"

Remi couldn't have looked away from Vincent if someone paid her. She wanted all that too. Desperately.

This was the craziest meet-cute ever. No romance novelist would ever write about this because it was so unbelievable. And yet, here she was. Falling hard for a Navy SEAL who'd just said they had to go underwater to be safe and he'd share his tank of air with her.

All she could do was nod.

"Good."

Then Vincent shocked the shit out of her by covering her lips with his own.

Even though the odds of them getting away from whoever seemed determined to see them dead weren't great, her nipples hardened and her inner core tightened. The kiss was rough and desperate on both their parts.

When he lifted his head, his pupils were dilated and he was breathing hard for the first time since she'd met him.

"I want you, Remi Stephenson."

Holy shit. This man was *intense*. And Remi was there for it.

"I want you back," she said simply.

He grinned. The intense look disappeared from his face, and he stared at her as if they were the only two people on earth in this tropical paradise, instead of two people about to be run over by a boat moving way too fast toward them.

"Right. Take a deep breath, sweetheart, and put your mask down. We're going under. We'll pass my regulator back and forth and take turns breathing. I've got you."

Remi nodded, although she definitely wasn't sure about this.

Vincent fiddled with something on the vest he was wearing, pulled down his own mask, and way before she was ready, they began to slip beneath the surface. Luckily, she'd taken a breath when he'd told her to. Even as they sank deeper beneath the waves, he held out his mouthpiece for her.

For a second, she didn't think she'd be able to get her body to obey what she was telling it to do. Breathing in while underwater wasn't natural, even with the regulator in her mouth. But then Vincent squeezed her waist, he hadn't let go of her even for a second, and she forced herself to relax.

She took two breaths, then nodded at Vincent, and he brought the mouthpiece to his own face and took a breath. Vincent held them steady several feet under the surface, and they took turns breathing in the air as the sound of the boat grew louder and louder. Looking up, Remi saw the vessel zip over their heads seconds later, going just as fast as it had when she'd first seen it.

So Vincent had been right. These weren't his friends. It wasn't someone coming to rescue them. It was probably whoever had left them out here in the first place, wanting to make sure they were dead.

The thought made her shiver, and Vincent's arm tightened around her once more. Reassuring her. Keeping her calm.

How long they stayed under the water, sharing the air in the tank on Vincent's back, Remi didn't know. But when he tapped her shoulder and pointed up, she wasn't sure she wanted to surface just yet. If whoever had come back for them was still nearby, he could spot them and finish what he'd started.

She shook her head.

Vincent palmed her cheek and stared at her through his face mask. He wasn't rushing her, would give her all the time she needed...well, all the time they had left in the tank. She wasn't stupid; she knew they had to be getting low after all the diving he'd done earlier in the day. But the patience Vincent showed gave her the bravery she needed to nod.

Without hesitation, he turned a knob on his vest and air bubbles burst forth, heading for the surface, just as they did.

Remi looked around frantically as their heads broke the surface. She saw nothing. No boat.

Vincent didn't hesitate to push the mask off her face to the top of her head. He gently took the mouthpiece from her and pushed his own mask up. Then he took her face in his hands and pulled her roughly toward him. She let out an *oof* as she made contact with his chest, then his lips were on hers once more.

And this time, Remi didn't hold back. She kissed him deeply, almost frantically. Showing him without words how much he was already beginning to mean to her. How grateful she was that he was with her. How much she admired him. It was crazy, she'd just met this man, but somehow she felt more herself around him than she had with any other guy she'd dated.

Their tongues twined together, just as their legs did. She wrapped her arms around his back, trying to get closer.

"Easy, sweetheart, you're okay," Vincent crooned.

It wasn't until she heard him speak that Remi realized she was breathing way too fast. Almost hyperventilating.

"They're gone. You're okay."

"I can't believe we just did that," she panted against his neck as she held onto him as tightly as she could.

"Kiss?"

She huffed out a breath. "No. *That* was awesome. Stupendous. Amazing. I mean, sharing your air thing."

"*You* were amazing. Are you sure you haven't done that before?" he joked.

Remi pulled back. "Not even close," she said.

At her tone, his smile died. "I mean it," he told her. "There aren't many people I'd trust to do that with."

"Will they be back?" she whispered, referring to whoever was in the boat.

"No."

Frowning, she said, "You can't know that."

"Then why'd you ask me?"

"I don't know."

"They aren't coming back. They came out to make sure we were well and truly gone, so they could report back to either Douchecanoe or Bertie. The next people we see will be my Navy SEAL friends. I give you my word."

"Okay," Remi whispered.

"Okay," he echoed. Then added, "I was serious, you know."

"About what?"

"About wanting to be with you once we get on dry land."

"Your hotel or mine?" she quipped.

"Don't care. But I want more than that, Remi. I can't believe you actually live near me. This feels like it was meant to be. I want to introduce you to my team and show you around Riverton. There are lots of SEAL wives there who I think you'd really love. My mentor's wife, Caroline, is a lot like you. Smart as hell, a little introverted, but as sweet as she can be. And Wolf couldn't love her more."

He was talking fast, too fast for Remi to be able to get a word in.

"And you can come camping with me and my Girl Scouts. I can even put in a good word for you and get you in the Thin Mint supply line. Anything you want, I'll bend over backward to make happen. Just please tell me you'll give me a chance."

When he paused to breathe, Remi asked, "You done?"

"Um...maybe?" he said a little sheepishly. "No, actually, I'm not. My job...it's intense. I'm gone a lot. It's why Bertie broke up with me. She said that I was never around when she needed me. I love being a SEAL, but I can promise you that I'll do whatever I can to make your life easier when I'm not there. I probably didn't do enough of that with Bertie, but Caroline can help you. She and her girl posse will love to take you under their wing."

"She knew what she was getting into when she agreed to date you," Remi told him sternly.

"What? Who?"

"Bertie," Remi said in a tone that was more calm than she felt. "I'm not an idiot. I've read books, seen movies, watched the news. I know that military people are deployed. And since you're special forces, you're probably sent off more than a regular sailor or soldier. I can handle it, Vincent. The truth is...I'm not a very outgoing person. I'm happy with my own company and I'm home alone more often than not. That doesn't mean I wouldn't miss you, but I have my best friend Marley, who lives nearby. And my parents aren't far away. I'm also sure you have lots of friends and connections who could help me if something came up that I couldn't deal with."

Remi paused and scrunched her nose.

"What was that for?" Vincent asked. He had a tender smile on his face, and Remi wanted to pinch herself that he was apparently as interested in a relationship as she was.

"Just that...this is all so...*fast*. I'm not the kind of woman men fall for instantly."

"Then they're idiots. From the first second I saw you on that pier, I fought with myself over wanting to get to know you better. There's something about you that's..."

Remi practically held her breath, waiting to see what he'd say.

"...calming," Vincent finally said after a moment. "Because of my job, I've had to become really good at reading people at a moment's notice. I've had to figure out if they're going to pull a weapon and try to kill me and my team, or if they're willing to assist. I didn't realize how stressful my relationship with my ex was until we were over. For as long as we dated, every time I knocked on her door, I always had a knot in my belly. I never knew if she'd be sweet and happy, or a total shrew. I've known you for mere hours, but with every minute that passes, you've shown me how brave, even-keeled, and strong you are."

"Vincent," Remi whispered, overwhelmed with his assessment of her. For as long as she could remember, she was the odd duck out. She didn't fit in with her fashionable and outgoing parents, though they adored her exactly as she was. She didn't make friends easily, and boyfriends were few and far between. But here was this amazing Navy SEAL, a true-life hero, telling *her* that he thought she was brave and strong.

"I'm not," she blurted. "I'm scared to death. Even though you've said you're sure someone is coming to get you, I'm afraid we're going to have to spend the night out here in the ocean. I'm thirsty and hungry and trying not to think about either. I also can't help but think about sharks and stingrays and piranhas feasting on my toes and going up from there.

"I'm worried that if we do get rescued, you're going to take one look at me and my frizzy hair and my definitely-eaten-too-many-malasadas-on-this-vacation body and wonder what the hell you were thinking. I'm wondering how long it'll be until you're trying to politely take back everything you said about wanting to get to know me. And on top of it all, even if we *do* get out of this stupid ocean, I'm worried that Douchecanoe is going to try again, to get rid of me once and for all."

She was practically winded by the time she was done talking.

Vincent hadn't taken his gaze from her. He was completely focused on her and what she was saying. That was a novelty. She always had the impression that

Douchecanoe was thinking about anything *but* her when they were together.

"Being strong even when you're scared is the very essence of bravery," Vincent told her firmly. "We aren't going to have to spend the night out here. I'll make sure you get all the water you can drink and those tacos you love so much as soon as we're rescued. And there aren't any piranhas in these waters."

He smirked a little when he said that, and Remi suddenly had another idea for a Pecky the Taco cartoon. It involved Pecky on vacation, floating on a raft in the ocean, and being surrounded by lost piranhas who only wanted to get home to their river in the Amazon. She forced herself to pay attention to what Vincent was saying.

"...think I've missed what you look like, you're wrong. Your hair is a lot like you, bursting at the seams with energy. And your body...it's *perfect*, Remi."

It wasn't, Remi knew that. But somehow, the way Vincent said the word made her believe that he was honestly attracted to every inch. She didn't know what she'd done in her life to deserve the interest of this man, but she was extremely thankful.

"And as for our exes, I don't know which one set us up like this, but you have my word that I'm going to do everything in my power, use all the connections I've got—and I have a lot of them—to figure this out and make sure we're both safe from anything like this happening again."

"Okay," she said after a moment or two.

"Okay?" Vincent asked, raising a brow in question.

"Uh-huh."

"There you go, being all calm and strong again," he murmured.

"You want me to scream, thrash around, cry and pout?" she asked.

Vincent mock shivered. "No way. I'll take you exactly how you are, sweetheart."

Remi knew he meant that he was relieved she wasn't panicking. But for some reason, his reply felt like more. Like a promise of some sort. His words were a balm to her soul, because for so long she'd felt as if she'd always had to be someone she wasn't in order to impress a man.

"How'd I get so lucky?" Vincent asked after a moment.

Remi couldn't hold back the snort-laugh. "Lucky? Vincent, we're still stranded in the middle of the ocean, in case you've forgotten."

"I haven't forgotten. But my SEAL friends will be here in less than three minutes and we'll have blankets, water, and food. How could I be anything *but* lucky?"

Alarmed, Remi looked toward the mainland—and saw another boat headed in their direction. She inhaled sharply.

"Relax. That's the Navy," Vincent said, sounding completely confident.

"How do you know? It could be that other boat coming back!" she exclaimed.

"I can tell by the motor. It's definitely the Navy," he replied.

Remi looked at the man she was still holding onto almost desperately. "Are you sure?"

"I'm sure."

Taking a deep breath, Remi nodded. "It's almost over."

"No, it's only the beginning," he countered.

"Are you always this...reasonable?" she asked. "Because I have to say, it could get annoying."

Vincent grinned. "Yup. It's a hazard of being a SEAL. I just can't get worked up over most things after what I've seen and done."

"That's fair," Remi had to admit. "I'm thinking Pecky needs to meet a Navy SEAL and have adventures with him."

The boyish grin that came over Vincent's face was adorable. "Everyone will be so jealous if I get written into a Pecky the Traveling Taco cartoon. I can't wait to brag about it." Then he kissed her again, and the next time he lifted his head, the boat was much closer.

Remi tensed involuntarily. Vincent had said he was sure this was the good guys, but the memory of looking up as the other boat raced over their heads was still too clear.

Vincent raised his arm, his hand in a fist as the boat neared.

A shout came from the boat, and it slowed, coming at them much slower.

"Told you," Vincent said, smiling at her.

"Yeah, you did."

"Hey! Tex called and said you might need a ride. Looks like he was right." An older man with hair much longer than Vincent's and a graying beard smiled at them as he maneuvered the large black rubber boat closer.

"Baker!" Vincent exclaimed. "Never thought I'd see *you* out here. Couldn't wait for our get-together tomorrow to see me, huh?"

"Well, Mustang and his team are on a mission right now. They're gonna be pissed they missed out on fishing you out of the ocean for sure. And for the record, you owe me. I was minding my own business, watching my woman hang out with her high school surfers, when I got word that you needed assistance."

"Appreciate it. I'll make it up to both of you tomorrow, if we're still on."

"We're still on," the man in the boat, Baker, replied. "Now how about we get you into this Zodiac and the hell out of the ocean."

"Absolutely. Remi first." Vincent turned to her. "Come on, sweetheart, let's get you out of the water."

She looked up at the boat and shook her head. She hadn't known the boat had an official name until Baker mentioned it, and she filed that information away, having a feeling she was going to draw a cartoon in the not-so-distant future with Pecky in a Zodiac, his lettuce flying away in the breeze and a huge smile on his face. But for the moment, she had to get into the thing. From a distance, the boat didn't look that big, but floating right next to it, she knew there was no way she was going to be able to climb into it on her own.

Almost as soon as she had the thought, Baker grabbed

her arms and pulled upward at the same time Vincent placed his hands on her ass and pushed.

She was sitting in the bottom of the Zodiac before she had time to take a breath. And then Vincent was there next to her. He'd pulled himself up and over the side of the boat as if it was child's play. He immediately ripped off his face mask, shrugged off the air tank on his back, and sat next to her on the bottom of the boat. He put his arm around her and pulled her tight to his side.

Baker passed him an emergency blanket folded into a small square, and within seconds, Vincent had wrapped it around her shoulders.

"Water?" Baker asked, holding out a bottle.

Remi grabbed it and began guzzling the best-tasting water she'd ever had in her life. It was Vincent's low, "Easy, hon," that made her slow down.

She looked at him sheepishly. "Want some?" she asked.

Vincent grinned. "I've got my own. Just don't want you throwing that up from drinking too fast," he told her.

Baker had already turned the Zodiac around and was headed back toward Oahu at a much slower pace than he'd arrived. "You want to tell me how the hell you ended up floating in the middle of the ocean when you were supposed to be on a diving trip?" he asked.

"Seems we both have exes who are pissed enough at us to try to make us regret going on vacation without them," Vincent said almost nonchalantly.

Remi couldn't believe he was as unfazed as he sounded.

"I'll do some digging tonight. Will let you both know

what I find out, if anything, when you come up to see me tomorrow."

Wait, what? Remi looked from the hot man at the wheel back to Vincent. As good-looking as Baker was, and there was no doubt he was a silver fox, she couldn't take her gaze from her SEAL. The man who'd made the worst experience of her life almost feel like an adventure instead of the attempted murder it actually was.

"Tomorrow when we see him?" she asked Vincent.

"I had plans to head up to the North Shore to visit with Baker and his wife tomorrow. Come with me?"

She'd already been to the north side of the island, but the thought of experiencing it with Vincent wasn't something she could turn down. Besides, she still kind of thought maybe all his sweet words were a result of the situation they were in. That once they were rescued, he'd come to his senses. If he wanted to spend more time with her, she was down with that.

"Remi?" he asked, looking concerned when she didn't answer right away.

"Yes, I'd like that."

"Good. You been to the Dole Plantation yet?"

It was almost surreal that they were talking about being tourists minutes after being rescued from the ocean. "Yeah, but I didn't do the maze, didn't want to risk getting lost and not getting out before they closed."

"We won't get lost," Vincent said. Then he reached over and took the hand that wasn't holding her water bottle. "I didn't even ask how much longer you were going to be here. In Hawaii."

"My flight leaves the day after tomorrow."

Vincent smiled. "Mine too."

What were the odds? Goose bumps broke out on Remi's arms.

Of course Vincent noticed, but luckily he misinterpreted the reason they'd appeared.

"Hang in there, we'll be back before you know it," he said, squeezing her hand reassuringly. "We'll get you warm soon."

Nodding, Remi realized she should be nervous about what might happen next. If Vincent would perhaps drop her off at her hotel and not contact her again. Or if she should be worried about Douchecanoe. About Marley's reaction to what happened to her. Her parents' reaction. About a million different things. But, surprisingly, she wasn't.

She was more excited about tomorrow. About spending time with Vincent outside the ocean. About getting together when they got home to California.

She just hoped everything he said he wanted was true. That he wouldn't figure out how big of a nerd she was, and change his mind about wanting to spend time with her.

* * *

The captain was sitting at a hole-in-the-wall, open-air bar near the marina when he saw the Zodiac approaching.

Fuck!

He'd thought the man and woman were dead. He'd even gone back to check to make sure, and when he hadn't found any sign of them, he was satisfied that he'd done what he was paid to do. Seeing the man and woman climbing out of the boat, looking none the worse for wear, wasn't going to please the person who was paying him a shitload of money.

Double fuck!

He pulled out his phone and shot off a text.

A minute after it sent, his phone rang.

Knowing who it was, the captain considered not answering, but that would only make things worse. "Hello?"

"You asshole! I can't believe you fucked up such an easy assignment!"

"Hey, I did what you wanted. I left 'em in the middle of the fucking ocean. Even went back to make sure they were dead and didn't see anyone out there. It's not *my* fault he somehow got in touch with someone to come and get him."

"Shit! What'd the person who picked them up look like?"

"Old. Gray in his beard. Tattoos."

"Fuck, fuck, *fuck*! This isn't good. Not at all."

The captain didn't like the sound of that. "What now?"

"Well, *obviously* you can't call the cops and inform them your customers disappeared during your charter, like we'd planned. *You* need to disappear instead. Go underground."

"That takes money," the captain protested.

"I already paid you."

"Half. I want the other half of the money you promised me. I did what I was hired to do. If I don't get what you owe me, I'll go to the police and let them know you're behind this whole thing." The captain was bluffing, of course. If he went to the cops, he'd be arrested too. But he was desperate. Living in Hawaii wasn't cheap, and if he had to hide out for an extended period of time, he needed cash.

"And admit your part in attempted murder? Not likely," the man growled, as if reading his mind.

"I can't go underground unless I have some cash."

"Fine. Get rid of your burner phone. It won't be traceable back to you. Go home. I'll send my guy to you tonight with the money. Then you need to be a ghost."

Relief swept over the captain. The ten thousand bucks coming his way should be enough for him to hole up off the grid for a while. "I will."

"Don't contact me again. *Ever*. Our business is over from the second we hang up. I'm getting rid of this number and you need to destroy that phone. Understand?"

"Yes."

"Fuck, this is a disaster," he muttered. "I'm gonna have to reassess. Make sure my name is kept out of this."

Then the line went dead.

The captain took a deep breath and powered down the burner he'd been using. Thanks to all the competition, his charter business had gone downhill in the last few years. He'd taken this job because he was desperate for money, and everything had been planned out carefully. The cops would interrogate him, of course, when his client disappeared into the ocean. But he'd been ready for all the questions, and had been reassured that even though there would be suspicions, he'd be cleared eventually. No body meant no proof he'd actually done anything wrong.

But now that both passengers had been found, alive and well, everything was going to hell.

Powerful and extremely smart people would be looking into him, his business. Scrutinizing everything, down to what size underwear he fucking wore and what he'd eaten for breakfast this morning. And those survivors would immediately tell their side of the story. How he'd simply left them in the middle of the ocean.

Fuck!

He tipped his bottle of beer to his lips and guzzled the rest down. He nodded at the bartender, putting the cell into his pocket to dispose of later, then turned and walked away, slipping into the sunset as the ghost he now needed to be.

"Thanks, man," Kevlar said, shaking Baker's hand after they arrived at the small marina. Baker had called in a favor, and a sailor was waiting in the parking lot to take them wherever they wanted to go—along with the police. He and Remi had both given their statements...not that there was a lot to tell. Now the police were tracking down the boat captain, and Remi was standing about twenty feet away, waiting for him, giving him space and privacy to say goodbye to his friend. She didn't have to do that, but he appreciated her consideration anyway.

"No thanks needed," Baker told him. "And you should know, Tex is already on this. When he realized something was hinky, he hacked your email. Found correspondence about the charter booked for today, hacked the captain's site and found Remi's name. He knows all about your girlfriend being the heir to the Crown Condom business, about her ex...and yours too. He's looking into the owner of the boat you chartered. And I'll see what I can dig up as well, as promised."

Kevlar could only laugh. He shouldn't be surprised that Tex had hacked his email and already knew about Remi, but somehow he still was. And hearing Baker call her his girlfriend felt...good. Really good. "You'll let me know if it was Douchecanoe or Bertie?" he asked.

"Of course. But does it matter which one it was?"

"Not really. Although I'd like to know to be prepared for any surprises in the future."

"There won't be any surprises if we can help it. Tex and I don't like to leave loose ends."

"Right. Again, thank you."

"Whatever. What time you comin' up tomorrow? If you're going to stop at the Dole place and do the maze, you gonna be later than we planned?"

Kevlar thought about it for a moment. "Lunch-ish? That should give us time to get to Dole and then to the North Shore without having to get up at the ass crack of dawn. I'm sure Remi's gonna be exhausted tonight and she'll want to sleep in."

Baker glanced over at Remi, standing with an emergency blanket still around her shoulders. Her hair had dried from the wind as they were coming back to shore, and it was currently in a crazy tangle around her head.

Kevlar thought she looked adorable, and he couldn't wait to run his hands through that wild hair. But he didn't like how unsure and lost she looked, standing by herself while he and Baker spoke.

"My gut's screaming that something is off," Baker said when he turned back to Kevlar once again.

"What do you mean? About Bertie?"

Baker shrugged. "About this whole situation. I mean, we both know you would've had no problem making it back to shore, even if you had to swim the whole way. Seems more likely you were caught in an attempt on *her* life. Are you sure you want to get involved?"

"Absolutely," Kevlar said without hesitation. "I wish you could've seen her, Baker. When she realized we'd been left, she didn't panic. There were no tears. She was determined to stay strong and calm. That asshole captain came back too."

"He did?" Baker asked in surprise.

"Yeah. I wasn't feeling warm and fuzzy vibes with how fast he was coming toward our location. He obviously wasn't out there to save us, as if he suddenly realized he left the only two people who'd been on the boat with him earlier. I went under and buddy-breathed with Remi until he was gone."

"And she didn't freak out?"

"No. Not at all."

Baker stared at him for a beat. Then said, "Buddy-breathing with someone you just met isn't easy. She must be special."

Kevlar wasn't surprised the former SEAL understood the magnitude of sharing his air with someone else. It wasn't as if he had a choice; that boat was coming straight for them and if whoever was driving realized they were still alive, things could've gotten dicey. But if Remi had panicked when they'd gone under, things could've gone just as bad. Buddy-breathing was the ultimate act of trust with another human.

"She is," he said firmly, acknowledging Baker's comment.

"Go," he ordered. "Get your woman warm. And feed her while you're at it. Make sure she drinks plenty."

"I will. See you tomorrow."

"Later," Baker said, jumping back into the Zodiac and preparing to head away from the dock.

Kevlar didn't know where Baker was going, but his attention wasn't on the legendary former SEAL anymore. It was on Remi. She was still wearing the shorty wetsuit. Her cheeks were red from the sun and probably the salt and wind as well. He'd never seen anyone as beautiful as she was at that moment.

He strode up the wooden deck toward her and pulled her into his embrace the second he was close enough.

"Everything all right?" she asked as her hands rested on his chest.

"Yeah. Are we going to your hotel or mine?" he asked, not beating around the bush.

She blushed a little, but didn't question him. Simply lifted her head and asked, "I don't know. Where are you staying?"

"The Holiday Inn on Waikiki."

She wrinkled her nose, and it was all Kevlar could do not to kiss her again. "Mine then. I'm at the Hilton. I have a corner suite with an ocean view."

Kevlar chuckled. "Yours it is."

"But we can stop by your hotel so you can get your stuff if you want."

"I don't need anything."

Her brow rose. "Um, Vincent, you're wearing a wetsuit."

"And I've got my board shorts under it. But if I need more to wear, I can pick something up at an ABC store along the way. They're everywhere and it won't take long."

"And it won't take long to stop at your hotel so you can get your own stuff," Remi said firmly.

Kevlar liked that she didn't back down. That she didn't just go with everything he said. It was funny, because Bertie was notorious for disagreeing with him, and he hated it—but the difference was, Remi was contradicting him on something that would be a nuisance for *her*, but would benefit *him*. He couldn't even imagine Bertie being in the situation Remi had faced today. And if she had, right now, his ex would definitely be insisting she be taken immediately to her hotel without any side trips.

"You okay with me coming back to your hotel with you?" he asked. They'd been in an intense situation together, and she might be having second thoughts about being with him now that they were safe and on dry land again.

In response, she grabbed his hand and turned toward the man waiting for them in his SUV. She towed him toward the vehicle and opened the back door. "In," she ordered.

Kevlar grinned. "Yes, ma'am," he said obediently.

Once they were in the backseat, she thanked the sailor who'd come to chauffeur them to their hotel, and politely asked if he wouldn't mind going by the Holiday Inn before heading to the Hilton.

Even with the short exchange of pleasantries, Kevlar could see that Remi had the young sailor wrapped around her little finger. Her kindness, even in the face of what she'd been through, was charming and endearing, and Kevlar couldn't blame the sailor for staring and smiling in a way that hinted he was slightly besotted with the bedraggled woman in his backseat.

Kevlar had no idea what time it was when they finally arrived at her hotel. But it was fully dark and he was tired. And if *he* was this tired, Remi had to be exhausted. Even though she was obviously flagging, she was still friendly and kind to the hotel staff. She'd had to go to the front desk to get a replacement key and she struck up a conversation with the clerk about the beautiful flower in her hair.

While Remi chatted up the employee, Kevlar opened his favorite food-delivery app and arranged to have dinner delivered to Remi's room. Comfort food. Stuff that wasn't too spicy—so tacos would have to wait. After spending the day in the water, they both needed carbs and protein. Easy-to-digest stuff that would be gentle on their stomachs.

When Remi opened her hotel room door, Kevlar couldn't stop the low, impressed whistle from escaping.

She giggled. "It's a bit much for just me, but this view is worth every penny." Then her nose scrunched up again, something he'd already realized was a habit. "I mean, I thought that before, but now...staring at that huge expanse of ocean has a different meaning for me." Her voice wobbled on the last few words.

Kevlar couldn't stay away from her if his life depended on it. It was the first true crack in her iron strength he'd seen all day. He dropped his bag—he'd quickly packed a change of clothes at his hotel, leaving his scuba gear behind—and strode toward her. Without hesitation, he pulled her into his arms.

She melted against him, and nothing had ever felt better to Kevlar. Had Bertie ever felt this good against him?

No. She hadn't.

Remi was soft and yielding, and she snuggled into him almost as if they'd done this a hundred times before. She wasn't that much shorter than him, only around four inches or so. Her hair brushed against his face as she rested her head on his shoulder, and he couldn't stop himself from lifting a hand and sinking his fingers into the unruly strands.

How long they stood like that, Kevlar didn't know. All he knew was that he didn't want to let her go. Although he hadn't been scared when he realized the boat had left them in the ocean, the day hadn't been without its stressors. He needed this hug as much as Remi did. As a Navy SEAL, he was supposed to be Superman. Plenty of people thought men like him didn't feel strong emotions, that he wasn't affected by the things he saw and did. But he was.

At that moment, his brain flashed to Blink, the SEAL who'd lost some of his teammates and was having a hard time coming to terms with what happened on his last mission. Kevlar wondered if having someone like Remi to come home to would've made a difference in how he coped with his trauma. Not Remi herself; she was taken by *him*. But someone like her.

Thoughts of the traumatized SEAL were set aside as Remi pulled back and smiled up at him a little self-consciously.

"I should shower."

"Yeah," Kevlar agreed. But he didn't drop his arms from around her.

"I'm okay," she said quietly. "I admit that I had a...a moment. Seeing the ocean and realizing if you weren't with me today, I'd still be out there. Probably trying to swim back to shore, and we both know how that would've ended up. But I'm good now. I can't wait to get out of this wetsuit and into something warm and soft. Not to mention, my hair is probably never going to recover from the salt, wind, and sun."

"I like it like this," Kevlar told her.

She snort-laughed.

It should've turned him off. Instead, it made him smile.

"Yeah, right. The Medusa look is so attractive."

He hadn't taken his hand out of her hair, and he tightened his fingers around her scalp as he pulled her closer.

Her eyes widened, but she didn't pull away. Satisfaction swam through Kevlar's veins. He leaned in and smiled when her chin tilted up, giving him easy access to her lips. But he couldn't kiss her right now. If he did, he wouldn't want to stop. And he was keenly aware of the large bed behind them. He wanted to lay her down and peel off that wetsuit to discover all her hidden secrets. But she was exhausted. Now wasn't the time.

He kissed her forehead instead, holding her against him, keeping his lips on her skin. She tasted slightly of salt and sweat. Even that didn't turn him off.

Kevlar inhaled deeply, then regretfully took his hand out of her hair. He put both hands on her shoulders and turned her toward the bathroom. "Take your time, sweetheart. I need to make some calls to my team. If dinner arrives, I'll get it."

Remi nodded, licked her lips, then walked toward the bathroom.

Kevlar felt like a voyeur, but he couldn't tear his eyes away from her ass. That wetsuit she had on showcased every inch of her body, even as it covered her. It was a tease that, at any other time, would've driven him out of his mind. But with tiredness pulling at him, he was content to simply admire her curves.

He didn't move until the door shut behind her. Then Kevlar took a deep breath and headed toward the balcony. He needed some air. Being this close to Remi was both torture and heady at the same time.

Thankfully, he'd left his phone back at his hotel that morning before he'd headed out to the pier. He pulled it out of his bag and stood on the balcony as he dialed Safe's number.

"Hey, Kevlar. How's Hawaii?"

"Interesting." Kevlar quickly summed up what happened that day.

"Holy shit, seriously? That bitch!"

Kevlar couldn't help but smile. He loved how supportive his teammates were.

"Yeah, if you'd've asked me a week ago if I thought Bertie could ever do something like this, I'd have said no way, but now...I just don't know, man."

"What do you need from us?" Safe asked.

"Nothing right now. I'm meeting with Baker tomorrow. He picked up Remi and me today and he said he was going to look into things. See if he could find any hint that Bertie had set this up. He'll also look into Remi's ex. And of course, Tex is going to be in on things too."

"Good thing you had your wetsuit with the tracker on," Safe commented.

"Yeah, made things move a lot faster than they would've otherwise. I'll talk to Tex tomorrow and thank him for being on the ball."

Safe chuckled. "Oh, he'll love that. You know Tex hates being thanked."

"Well, he's going to have to put up with it this once," Kevlar said.

"And Remi?" Safe asked.

Kevlar swore he could hear the smirk in his friend's voice. "Yeah. She's...unlike any woman I've ever met."

"You think a long-distance relationship can work?" Safe asked.

"That's the thing. She lives in San Diego."

"Holy shit, *really*?"

"Yeah."

"Wow! That's crazy lucky, man."

Kevlar thought it was more than luck. It was fate. But he kept that to himself. "It is."

"You gonna see her again?"

Kevlar couldn't keep the smile from forming on his face as he turned to look back into the hotel room. "Yeah."

"Cool. Try not to be too much of an asshole and maybe she'll give you a chance."

Kevlar chuckled at that. "Thanks for the vote of confidence."

"Anytime," Safe said with a laugh.

"What's happening there? Everyone enjoying their time off?" Kevlar asked.

"Pretty much."

There was a note of...something in his friend's tone. "What's wrong?" Kevlar demanded.

"Nothing really. Everyone's kind of restless. You know we don't do well with downtime."

"And?"

Safe sighed. "Howler's been hanging out at The Golden Oyster more than usual. Talking smack."

"About what?"

"Not about what—*who*," Safe admitted.

Kevlar frowned. "About me?"

"I guess. But he's full of shit. It's the alcohol talking."

"What's he saying?"

"Stupid shit."

"What's he saying, Safe?" Kevlar repeated.

"Just the usual...stuff about how you could've canceled your trip and gone on that mission to Syria. How if he was team leader, he would've put his team and country first."

Irritation swamped Kevlar. He loved Howler like a brother, but he got stupid when he drank, which was more and more often lately. There was a time when Howler *had* expressed interest in being team leader, but their commander had put Kevlar in the position instead. He and Howler had a long talk about it, and he'd thought his friend was all right with everything, but apparently there was still a bit of resentment there.

Kevlar made a mental note to have a long chat with his

teammate when he got home. If Howler really wanted to run his own team, it might be time to encourage him to do just that. SEALs switched teams all the time. He'd miss his friend, but he wanted the best for him at the same time.

"I'll talk to him," he told Safe.

"I figured you would."

"Everything else all right?"

"Yup."

"Good."

"You still coming back this week?"

"Of course."

"Cool. I'll see you in a couple of days. Try to stay out of trouble until then," Safe teased.

"Whatever."

"Kevlar?"

"Yeah?"

"Glad you're all right. If I hear anything from the gossip network here, I'll let you know."

"Appreciate it. Talk to you later."

"Later."

Kevlar hung up and stared off into the ocean, his mind spinning. He was going over everything that had happened today, his call with Safe, worrying about Howler and what the hell was going on with him.

A noise behind him had Kevlar turning, all the heavy thoughts going up in a puff of smoke as his gaze landed on Remi.

The bathroom was full of steam behind her, and she was standing at the door in nothing but a towel. Her skin was flushed from the hot shower and there was still water beaded on her shoulders and upper chest, above where the towel was barely covering her lush body.

"I forgot to grab some clothes," she said, sounding embarrassed.

Kevlar stared at her for a long moment, before he realized he was adding to her discomfort. He spun around and stared back out at the ocean, his heart thumping in his chest as he did his best to control his body's reaction to seeing Remi practically naked.

"I'm really sorry. I'll be out in a minute or two," she said from behind him.

Kevlar could hear drawers opening and the sounds of her shuffling things around.

"It's okay," he managed to say. "Take your time."

When he heard the bathroom door shut, he let out the breath he'd been holding. He'd never been this affected by a woman, especially one he'd just met. It was disconcerting and exciting at the same time.

A knock at the door distracted him and he headed over, relieved to have something to keep himself busy.

He was setting the delivery bags on the table in the room when Remi appeared again. Her hair was streaming around her shoulders, and he could see little beads of sweat on her forehead from the hot shower and the steamy bathroom.

"I'm done. Your turn," she told him with a small smile.

"Food's here," he said unnecessarily.

"I see," she said, her smile widening.

Of course she did. Kevlar was rarely tongue tied. But here he was, sounding like an idiot. "Go ahead and dig in, I'll be out in a few minutes."

"No rush," she told him.

Kevlar took large strides toward the bathroom, picking up his bag along the way. There was no chance he was going to make the same mistake she had. He couldn't be in the same room as her wearing only a towel. He didn't have that kind of willpower.

It was a relief to close the bathroom door behind him, but that relief only lasted a moment because the entire bathroom smelled like her. She was using the hotel's lotion and body soap, something that smelled like coconut and flowers combined. He itched to smell it on her body.

Instead of the hot shower he'd planned, he ended up getting under a cool spray, willing his body to behave. The cold water did the trick, forcing the blood out of his cock. He quickly washed himself and his wetsuit before dressing as fast as he could.

It was crazy how eager he was to be back with Remi. He'd just seen her a few minutes ago, and yet he was acting like a smitten kid, desperate to see his crush again.

When he opened the bathroom door, he could only stare in surprise. While he'd been showering and changing, Remi had taken all their food out of the bags and arranged everything on the table. Complete with napkins under the silverware.

"I didn't want to eat without you," she admitted.

Kevlar didn't know what he'd expected her to do. No...

that was a lie. He'd thought she'd dig into the food because it was obvious she was starving after everything that had happened today. But she hadn't. She'd waited for him. The simple gesture touched him in a way that was so unfamiliar.

He walked over to the table and slowly sat next to her.

Remi gave him a small smile and picked up a fork. "I know this is just mac and cheese, but it smells ridiculously good," she told him.

Kevlar couldn't take his eyes off her as she put the fork full of gooey, cheesy noodles into her mouth. The way her lips pursed and closed around the fork was almost erotic, and she wasn't even trying to turn him on.

The moan that left her throat had him just as hard as he'd been before his shower.

"Oh my God, this is so good. I thought tacos were my favorite food, but I lied. This mac and cheese is my new fave." Then she looked at him. "You aren't eating. Are you okay?"

Absently, Kevlar dug into the plate she'd made for him. She was right, the cheesy concoction was exactly what his body was craving.

They ate in silence, but it wasn't an awkward one. They were both concentrating on getting calories into their bodies and enjoying the feeling of their bellies being full. Kevlar made sure Remi ate some of the vegetables he'd ordered, to try to get as many nutrients into her as possible. There was also some delicious grilled chicken, which they shared.

By the time they'd finished eating, it was obvious Remi was hanging on by a thread. She'd yawned several times and her eyes were drooping. She was done for.

"You're exhausted. Go to bed, sweetheart," he told her. "I'll clean up here."

"It's not even that late," she protested, but Kevlar could tell it was halfhearted.

"So?" he countered.

Remi smiled. "True. I'm on vacation. I can do whatever I want, right?"

"Right."

"Are you staying?"

Kevlar paused. He wanted to. Badly. But he also didn't want to make her uneasy in any way.

"Please stay," she said quietly. "I know it's weird, and that we just met, but I'd feel better if you were here. It's not that I think Douchecanoe can do anything to me when I'm in my hotel room, but I also didn't think anything would happen on that snorkeling trip either."

She was babbling, and while it was cute, Kevlar could also tell that she was stressed.

"I'll stay," he reassured her.

He could see her shoulders droop in relief. Practically feel it radiating off her.

"Thank you."

She went straight to the bed and climbed under the covers without bothering to change. But then again, she'd put on a pair of leggings and a T-shirt after her shower, so she could easily sleep in those. She turned onto her side, and Kevlar could feel her gaze on him as he cleaned up their dinner dishes and put the leftovers, what little there were, in the small fridge in the room.

By the time he turned back to Remi, her eyes were closed and she was breathing deeply. She'd fallen asleep in seconds.

It struck him then how much trust she was putting in him. They were still practically strangers. Strangers who'd been through a very intense experience, but still.

He sat back down at the table and stared at Remi as she slept. He couldn't take his eyes off her. Had he ever been this fascinated with Bertie when she was sleeping—or any woman, for that matter? He couldn't say that he was. What was it about *this* woman that affected him so deeply, so fast? He had no idea. All Kevlar knew was that if he screwed things up between them, he had a feeling he'd lose something precious.

This was his chance at having a true partner by his side for the rest of his life. He had no idea how he knew that, or why he was even having those thoughts to begin with, but he didn't doubt his feelings.

As he watched, Remi curled her legs up and shivered in her sleep. That got him moving. He closed the balcony door, shut the curtains, and turned off all the lights in the room except for one on the other side of the bed.

Then he went to the small loveseat and sat in a position where he could still see Remi. For some reason, he needed to keep her in his line of sight. He wanted nothing more than to climb under the covers behind her, put his arm around her and hold on tight, but it was too soon for that. Even though he was thinking long term with this woman, he didn't want to rush anything. Didn't want her to wake up and be scared that she was in a strange man's arms.

So instead, Kevlar scooted down so his head was resting on the back of the couch and his legs were stretched out in front of him. It wouldn't be the most comfortable night's sleep, but he'd definitely slept in worse places in his life. Besides, he was watching over Remi, making sure nothing disturbed her rest. That made the position perfect.

CHAPTER SIX

Remi was a morning person. It used to drive Douchecanoe crazy. He always bitched that she was abnormal for being wide awake so early in the morning. And even though she was sore, and still tired, her eyes popped open bright and early, like usual.

She immediately sensed that she wasn't alone. But instead of freaking out about that, she relaxed when her gaze landed across the room.

Vincent had stayed, like he'd promised.

But then she frowned. He was sitting on the loveseat. His arms were crossed over his chest and his legs were straight out in front of him. He was using the seat back as a pillow, and while he looked relaxed enough, Remi knew that couch wasn't nearly as comfortable as the bed would've been.

A part of her couldn't help feeling confused about

why he hadn't slept in the bed next to her. It was big enough that they wouldn't even have touched. Was he simply being polite when he said he'd stay, but really didn't want to? Was he having second thoughts about her already?

Doubts swam through her as she lay there staring at him.

As if he felt her gaze, he stirred. His eyes opened and immediately zeroed in on her.

"Morning," he said, sitting up and stretching.

Remi could only stare. The man was truly beautiful. "Hi."

His gaze sharpened. "What's wrong?"

"Um, nothing? Why would you think something's wrong?"

"Because you sound...uncertain."

"I only said one word," Remi protested.

Vincent shrugged and his gaze never wavered. He sat forward, resting his elbows on his knees. "Are you uneasy with me being here? I can go."

"No!" Remi exclaimed. Then closed her eyes and sighed. "I was just thinking how uncomfortable that couch had to be and wondering why you didn't sleep on the bed. I mean, I know it's fast, but I wouldn't have minded."

"Look at me."

Remi didn't want to, wanted to put off his leaving as long as possible, but she couldn't deny him anything. She opened her eyes.

His blue gaze was intense in the morning light coming

through the crack in the curtains, which he'd obviously closed after she'd fallen asleep on him.

"I wanted to. You have no idea how badly I wanted to climb onto that mattress next to you. But I also don't want to do anything that might scare you or turn you off."

Remi scooted upward on the mattress and fluffed her pillows, sitting against the headboard. She kept the blanket pulled over her legs. She was well aware this kind of situation was how plenty of women had been conned. Scammed. Hurt. Or worse. Inviting a stranger back to her hotel room, trusting him, opening herself up to him...but this was Vincent. The man she'd shared a very intense experience with yesterday. One that he could've handled without a problem, but for her, could've ended in her death.

He was the only reason she was sitting in her hotel room right this moment. If she couldn't trust him to have her best interests at heart after all that, who the hell *could* she trust?

"I'm not afraid of you," she told him.

His head tilted a little, and Remi couldn't help but think he looked even more adorable. His hair was sticking up and his five o'clock shadow was a little deeper today. She'd refrained from looking too hard at the gray sweatpants he'd put on after his shower last night...but she hadn't missed the way he more than filled them out in the crotch area.

"I'm not a gentle man."

It seemed as if he was warning her.

Remi couldn't help it. She laughed. Did her usual snort-laugh, but she wasn't even embarrassed this time.

"I wasn't trying to be funny," Vincent told her.

"I know, I'm sorry. But, Vincent, if you think I've missed that about you, I haven't. You're a SEAL. I might not be completely sure what it is you do, but I'm not an idiot either. And while you might have a job that's dangerous, where sometimes it's kill or be killed, yesterday...you *were* gentle with me."

He just stared at her from across the room.

Remi took a deep breath and continued. "I wouldn't have asked you to stay last night if I was afraid of you. It might sound naïve but...yesterday changed me. Made me regret how much I've been missing in life by sitting in my condo and not venturing out more. Even here, on this gorgeous island, I've spent more time in my hotel than anywhere else.

"Snorkeling was the trip I'd looked forward to the most. And if you weren't there yesterday, there's a huge chance I wouldn't be *here* right now. So, no, you don't scare me. Spiders, yes. Drawbridges, yes. The fact that Douchecanoe didn't succeed yesterday and might try to kill me again, yes. But you? No, Vincent. You don't scare me."

In response, the man across the room slowly got to his feet. Remi didn't take her gaze from his. She couldn't. She felt frozen in place. As if she was watching what was happening from above.

Vincent crossed over to the bed and sat on the mattress by her hip. Remi scooted over a little to give him more room, but he didn't give her a chance to do more than that. He put one hand on the mattress by her butt and leaned into her. Remi held her breath.

"I'm on this," he said softly.

It was difficult to take her eyes off his lips, but Remi forced herself to meet his gaze. It was intense and emotion-filled. If she'd had any second thoughts about this man, they would've been shattered right then and there. It was corny, and ridiculous, but she swore she saw their future in his eyes at that moment.

"Okay."

"Okay?" he asked.

Remi nodded. "You told me I could trust you yesterday, and you were right. About everything. About staying calm, about someone coming for us, about going underwater and sharing air, about that boat not being your friend's...about everything. You made sure I was warm, fed, and that I drank approximately fourteen gallons of water. If you say you have this under control, I believe you."

Vincent closed his eyes and inhaled deeply through his nose. Remi didn't know what was going through his head, but it felt momentous. Life-changing. Excitement swam through her veins. She suddenly wanted to share her most private thoughts. To admit how disappointed she was not to have woken up in his arms. To tell him that she wanted him. Right here and now. Naked and deep inside her.

Instead, she blurted, "But trusting you doesn't mean I'm *not* writing Bertie and Douchecanoe into one of my cartoons and making Pecky humiliate the crap out of them."

Vincent's eyes opened, and he grinned. "Can't wait to see what you have planned for them." After a moment, he added, "This is going to work. You and me. It's gonna work."

"I hope so. I really hope once you get to know how... introverted I am, you aren't going to regret anything."

"I won't."

The two words were said with such conviction, Remi felt something deep inside, the part of her that always whispered she was too fat, too odd, too...everything, wither away and die. With this man, she was just Remi Stephenson. She could be exactly who she was already.

"I have a question," she said with a small smile.

"Yeah?"

"Can we find a taco truck today when we go to see your friend? I never did get those tacos the captain promised."

"We can do anything you want."

"Thanks."

They stared at each other for what seemed like minutes, but in reality was only seconds, before Vincent slowly began to lean forward. Remi's heart sped up. She lifted her chin as he got closer. His lips brushed over hers, and just when she was opening her mouth to invite him in, he raised his head.

Confused, Remi stared at him.

"I want you. I want to kiss you long and hard. I want to

climb under the covers with you and check out all your curves without anything in my way."

"Yes," Remi breathed. Wanting that with every fiber of her being.

Vincent's lips moved up in a sexy little smile. "But I can't," he said.

Remi frowned, and for a beat she had the horrifying thought that maybe everything she'd felt between them was a lie. But she dismissed that thought the second after she had it. No, this man wouldn't lie to her. She'd bet her family's entire fortune on that. "Why not?" she asked.

"Because I have morning breath."

Remi smiled. Huge. This man was perfect for her. "Me too," she admitted.

Vincent's hand came up and he smoothed it over her hair.

Wincing, Remi couldn't believe she'd forgotten how unruly her hair tended to be in the mornings. And she hadn't bothered to blow dry it yesterday after her shower, she'd been too hungry and too anxious to spend more time with Vincent. It had to be sticking out all over her head like she'd just stuck her finger in an electrical socket.

"I love your hair," he murmured as his fingers speared through the wild strands.

"It's ridiculous," was all Remi could manage. His hand on her felt so good.

"It's got a mind of its own. It's eclectic, stubborn, beautiful. Just like you."

Gah. This man.

His gaze came back to hers, but his hand didn't leave her hair. "What do you like for breakfast? A muffin and fruit? Pancakes and sausage? Nothing? Are you a coffee drinker?"

"At home, yogurt and oatmeal," Remi heard herself say, although it still felt as if she was in an alternate dimension. "But on vacation...here...malasadas, fresh pineapple and other fruit, and Kona coffee."

Vincent grinned. "Sounds perfect. I thought we'd get an early start on heading north. The traffic is always horrible, but if we can get in front of it, we'll have more time to spend with Baker and his wife, Jodelle, and maybe miss some of the crowds at the Dole Plantation if we get there when it opens."

"Okay."

"You've got some choices for how things go down this morning."

"Choices?" Remi asked.

"Yeah. I can head back to my hotel to shower and get ready for today. While I'm out, I can pick up some malasadas and coffee and meet you back in the lobby here, and we can head north."

"Or?" Remi asked when he paused.

"Or while you're showering, I can head downstairs and scrounge us up some breakfast. I can bring it back up here and you can eat while I shower and change."

"That one," Remi said without hesitation.

Vincent studied her.

"I thought we've been through this conversation

already today. I trust you, Vincent. Unless you're trying to give me an out and you don't want to stay."

"I want to stay," he told her immediately.

"Then stay," she whispered.

"Fuck," Vincent swore under his breath. Then he lunged, wrapping his arms around her and pulling her into his embrace.

Remi buried her nose in the space between his shoulder and head and inhaled as he held her tightly. They were both fully clothed, but for some reason, this felt extremely intimate.

"I don't deserve you, but I'm going to bend over backward to be the kind of man *you* deserve," he said into her hair.

Remi pulled back and stared at him. He hadn't let go of her, and his hands seemed to burn through the material of her T-shirt. "Don't you know? You already are."

She couldn't interpret the look on his face, but it was obvious her words meant something to him.

Vincent leaned toward her again, and this time his lips brushed against her forehead in a barely there kiss. Remi's nipples were hard under her shirt, and she felt her core clench. This unhurried seduction felt exciting. She would've slept with him right that second if it was up to her, but she couldn't deny she loved the slow build-up too.

Slow? She almost laughed. It had been *one day* since she'd met this man. Nothing about their relationship so far had been slow. But nothing had ever felt so right either.

"How hungry are you?" Vincent asked.

Remi shrugged. She didn't think he was talking about sex, because she was very hungry for that.

"The Dole place doesn't open until nine-thirty. We have some time to be lazy. Want to lay here and watch the sunrise for a while before we get up and start moving?"

"Yes!" She didn't have to think twice about her answer.

In response, Vincent stood and walked over to the massive floor-to-ceiling window in the room and pulled back the curtains. One of the best features of the suite was the balcony and the fact that, because it was a corner room, she had views of both the mountains and the ocean. As a result, she was able to see both the sunrise and the sunset.

The light outside had a pinkish hue, and the sun hadn't crested the mountains yet. To her delight, Vincent walked back to the bed, this time to the opposite side, and lifted the covers. He scooted toward her, then pulled her down until she was lying on her side in front of him. One of his large, muscular arms went around her waist, holding her against him. He'd propped his head up with a couple of pillows so he could see the sunrise too.

They lay there as the sun slowly made its way over the mountains. They didn't speak, simply enjoyed the moment. The fact that Vincent was the kind of man who could relax enough to take time to be in the moment said a lot about him. He hadn't immediately grabbed his phone to check messages or social media. He wasn't antsy about getting up and getting moving. He might be a big, bad Navy SEAL, but he was also a man who was worried about morning breath, who wanted to make sure she didn't feel coerced or uneasy about him staying in the room, and who was happy enough to spend their first morning together just...being.

Remi closed her eyes and smiled.

When she opened them, she felt Vincent looking at her. She turned her head and saw that indeed, his attention was on her, and not the beautiful morning show outside the window. "What?" she whispered.

"I've done some things I regret in my life. Morally gray things. But I've also done my best to be a good friend, son, and boyfriend the few times I've been in a serious relationship. I feel as if everything I've done, everything I've experienced, has led me to this point. Lying in bed with a woman I admire, who I want more than anything I've ever wanted in my life, and who I can't wait to get to know more about, simply watching the sun rise over a new day. It's surreal."

"I think that's my line," Remi told him, touched that he saw her that way. "I don't know where things will go for us. We might figure out after today that we were just drawn to each other because of the intense situation we were in. That we have nothing in common. But even if that's the case, I want you to know I'll never, ever forget you. And if things *do* work out, I'll be the best girlfriend you've ever had. I'll support you and your teammates. I'll never resent the Navy taking you away from me on missions. I'll be your cheerleader, your supporter, and I'll never take you for granted."

"Like I said before, this will work out. I'm gonna make

sure of it," Vincent told her. Then, as their gazes remained locked, he muttered under his breath, "Fuck it," before his head lowered.

His lips were on hers before Remi could blink. They'd shared kisses in the ocean, but this was different. Less desperate, more confident...more passionate.

Remi didn't think about morning breath. Didn't think about *anything* other than how good Vincent felt hovering over her while he made love to her mouth as if he couldn't get enough. The passion she felt with him was leaps and bounds more powerful than anything she'd ever felt before. Hell, even her fingertips and toes were tingling.

When he lifted his head, Remi felt almost dizzy. "Wow," she whispered.

Vincent grinned. "Yeah." His fingertips brushed over her cheek. "I'm gonna head downstairs and see if I can rustle up some malasadas for you. Anything you like in your coffee?"

"Just black, please."

His smile grew. "Another sign we were meant to find each other. How much time do you need?"

Remi shrugged. "Twenty minutes?"

"Twenty minutes?" he asked, a brow shooting up.

"Yeah, is that too long?"

"Bertie needed at least an hour."

"I'm not Bertie," Remi said firmly.

"No, you certainly aren't. Thank God." Then he leaned down and kissed her hard before lifting the covers and climbing off the mattress. "Take your time. I'll probably be gone a little longer than that. No need to rush, we have plenty of time this morning."

"Where are you going to get malasadas? There's a little coffee shop across from the lobby that has them. Or at least something close to them," Remi told him.

"I'm going to get you the real thing," he told her. "There's nothing better than Leonard's."

"Leonard's?" Remi asked excitedly, sitting up on the bed and pushing her hair away from her face. "But they always have a line."

"Yup. But it moves fast."

"You don't have to—" she started, but Vincent was already heading for the bathroom. He reappeared a couple of minutes later and came back over to the bed. He leaned down and kissed the top of her head and caressed her cheek.

"I'll be back soon."

"Okay." What else could she say? This man was willing to stand in line at Leonard's to get her authentic malasadas. If she wasn't halfway in love with him before, she would be now.

He smiled at her, strode toward the door, and then he was gone.

Remi took a deep breath.

Was she being stupid? Was she letting this guy play her?

No, she wasn't. She knew that down to her bones. If he wanted to hurt her, he'd had ample time last night, when she was passed out in the bed.

Letting out a little squeal, she flopped onto her back

and stared up at the ceiling. Who knew such a terrifying experience could end up literally changing her life for the better? If Douchecanoe knew how horribly his little stunt had gone wrong, he'd be *pissed*. The thought made her smile. She almost hoped he was the responsible party.

There was no telling what the future would bring, but Remi vowed not to regret a single moment. If she and Vincent didn't work out, fine. Until then, she was going to live in the moment for the first time in her life. She could practically hear Marley in her head, telling her to go for it.

Swinging her legs off the side of the bed, Remi stood and headed for the bathroom. She figured she had plenty of time, since Vincent would have to wait in probably the world's longest line known to mankind at Leonard's, but she wanted to be ready when he returned. She was looking forward to the day, to going to the Dole Plantation with someone instead of by herself, and even to seeing that hot older man again, who'd rescued them from the middle of the ocean.

She'd planned on spending her last day in Hawaii sitting on the beach, maybe sketching some new ideas for her comic strip, but she was more than happy to have her plans changed so drastically. She wasn't sure what would happen with Douchecanoe, or Vincent, or his ex, but for the first time in a long time, she was eager for whatever her future held.

CHAPTER SEVEN

The look on Remi's face when she'd opened the Leonard's Bakery box that morning and seen what he'd brought back for them had been priceless. Kevlar had gone a little overboard, getting both the regular malasadas and some filled versions. But he'd also picked up some Pao Doce wraps—Hawaiian sweet bread stuffed with Portuguese sausage—and some pineapple turnovers.

It had been a long time since such a simple gesture on his part had brought someone so much pleasure. He hated to keep comparing Remi to Bertie, but his ex would've rolled her eyes, told him how many calories the sweet treats contained, and refused to eat any of them. Remi's pleasure, and genuine surprise that someone would do something so simple for her, had Kevlar wanting to find more ways to make her feel good.

Their visit to the Dole Plantation had been fun. Since

she'd been there earlier that week, they didn't bother checking out the different kinds of growing pineapples on display, instead heading straight to the maze. Kevlar let her lead, and she'd gotten them so turned around they were well and truly lost. He'd never had a better time. Or laughed so much.

It was a revelation. He had good times with his friends, but as a SEAL, and as team leader, he felt a lot of pressure to always be on his toes. But Remi oozed happiness and a willingness to live life to its fullest. When he'd said as much to her, she'd rolled her eyes and adamantly disagreed, saying she was a socially awkward misfit who spent the majority of her time alone in her condo with only Pecky the taco to keep her company.

It was hard to reconcile in his head. She had no problem chatting up and laughing with the people they met while they were playing tourists. She didn't seem shy to him, seemed to revel in her interactions with others.

Not only that, but Remi was one of the kindest humans he'd ever met. She didn't seem to get irritated with the tourists who bumped into her in the crowded Dole Plantation gift shop, she smiled at everyone, and she'd even insisted on buying him a cheesy pineapple keychain as a memento.

All in all, Kevlar found himself being drawn to her more and more as the day went on. He hadn't found anything about her that turned him off. Granted, he'd just met her, but still, this didn't feel like a rebound kind of thing. He'd just broken off a long-term relationship, hadn't been looking to get into another one so soon, but being with Remi felt...right. He wasn't ready to marry her, of course he wasn't, but he knew he hadn't felt for Bertie in the year he'd been with her, even in the beginning, the things he felt for Remi after a single day.

As promised, they'd arrived at the house Baker shared with his wife, Jodelle, just past noon. It was a small house in a friendly neighborhood near the North Shore. They were sitting on plastic chairs on the back deck, and Remi was deep in conversation with Jodelle about the boy she'd adopted and how he was doing in college down in Honolulu.

Baker said in a low voice, only for Kevlar's ears, "I like her."

Kevlar smiled, pleased with the compliment. He didn't really know Baker, other than through the intel he supplied to their commander for some of their missions, but based on what the SEAL gossip network had to say, he wasn't a man who went out of his way to get into people's personal business.

"Me too," he told him.

Kevlar heard Remi snort-laugh, and it made him smile even wider. She might think she was a dork, but to him, she was simply adorable.

"I talked to Tex," Baker said in a much more serious tone.

Turning, Kevlar gave him all his attention. When he didn't continue, he asked, "And?"

"And from what we can tell, neither Bertie nor Miles were involved."

"Miles?" Kevlar asked.

Baker's lips twitched. "Douchecanoe."

Kevlar felt stupid. He didn't even know Remi's ex's name. In his head, he'd been calling him Douchecanoe, like she did. "Right. Are you sure?"

"Pretty sure. Miles is an opportunistic asshole. I'm guessing he had his eye on Remi's money the entire time. She makes decent money on her cartoons, but more importantly...did you know that she brings in seven figures a year from the interest on her trust fund?"

He *hadn't* known that. But honestly, it didn't matter to him. Kevlar shook his head.

"You know who her parents are though?"

"Yes."

"Right. So you know when they pass, she'll inherit even more millions."

Kevlar nodded. He didn't care about her money. He cared that she wouldn't have to worry about anything in the future, that she'd always have a roof over her head and wouldn't have to struggle, but as far as he was concerned, how much money she or her parents had wasn't any of his business. He wasn't interested in her because of her bank account, he liked her because of her personality. And he knew he'd only discovered the tip of the iceberg. He was excited to delve deeper and find out more.

"Her ex was trying to convince her to get a life insurance policy," Baker told him. "After some deep digging, I found an electronic copy of a completed policy he'd had drawn up with an agent, but it's not signed. I'm making an assumption here, but I'm guessing he brought it up to her and she refused to sign it."

Kevlar pressed his lips together. "Asshole," he muttered.

"Yeah. But Bertie wasn't much better," Baker went on.

Kevlar sighed. "I know. She'd been on me to change my own policy with the Navy. Wanted her name as beneficiary. Told me that I *owed* her for sticking with me through so many deployments and if something happened, I should want her to be taken care of."

Baker gave him a look. "She's a greedy bitch."

Kevlar chuckled, but the sound was flat. "Yeah."

"But I'm not sure she's smart enough to pull off what happened yesterday."

"Not sure it takes smarts. Just enough money in the right person's hands," Kevlar said dryly.

"That's true. I'm sometimes amazed at the things stupid people can accomplish when they have enough motivation."

"So she *could've* done it," Kevlar said. It was a question and a statement at the same time.

"It's possible, but until Tex and I find any concrete evidence, we think not."

Kevlar nodded. Then asked the question that instantly popped into his brain when Baker said he and Tex hadn't found anything to implicate either Bertie or Douchecanoe. "Then who?"

"That's what I was going to ask *you*. Piss anyone off lately?"

"Plenty," Kevlar told him honestly.

"Anyone who would want to get rid of you?"

He shrugged. "Would leaving me eight miles offshore, *with* my scuba gear, really be getting rid of me?"

"No."

The confidence in Baker's answer felt good. "Exactly."

"So that leaves us with someone wanting to kill Remi," Baker said.

The thought made Kevlar's stomach tighten. "Like who?"

"Don't know. That's why I'm asking you."

He hated to say it, but Kevlar admitted, "I don't know her well enough to know the answer to that question."

"You should get on that," Baker said.

"Workin' on it," he reassured him.

"So are we," Baker said.

Feeling better knowing that both Tex and Baker would continue to dig into this, Kevlar nodded.

"You takin' her home with you?" Baker asked.

Kevlar grinned. "Well, lucky for me, she already lives in San Diego."

"Lucky indeed," Baker agreed. "But that's not what I asked."

Kevlar looked at Baker with a brow raised.

"She reminds me of my Jodelle," Baker continued in a low voice that couldn't be overheard. Not that the two women seemed interested in the least in listening to their conversation. They were laughing and chatting as if they'd known each other all their lives. "My woman has a well of love inside her so deep, it engulfs anyone who's lucky enough to get through her shields and uncover it. You, your team, any unfortunate soul she thinks is in need. Once she opens her heart, that's it. It's a done deal. I have a feeling Remi's the same way. Be careful, Kevlar. Don't go there if you aren't willing to go all the way."

His first words made Kevlar feel good, but by the end of his speech, he was a little pissed. "I don't fuck around with women," he told Baker a little aggressively. "When I was younger, I was fine with superficial relationships. But I want more now. I want what Wolf and his teammates have. I want a woman I can come home to, who makes me feel as if I've left all my worries behind the second I walk through the door. Someone who can make the things I've seen and done fade away with a simple smile."

"And you think Remi is that woman?" Baker questioned.

"I don't know." Kevlar wouldn't lie to the man. "But after being around her for just a day, I feel closer to her than I *ever* felt to Bertie, who I'd been with for just over a year. She makes me laugh. Makes me think. Makes me want to be a better, kinder person. Want to bend over backward to make her happy. One thing I *do* know is that this isn't a rebound thing. It feels like a helluva lot more."

"Sounds like a good start to me," Baker said.

"Anyone hungry?" Jodelle asked, interrupting their conversation. "I'm not terribly hungry, as Baker and I had a late breakfast, but I can go in and make some sandwiches or something if anyone wants anything."

Baker smiled at his wife, and Kevlar felt a pang of jealousy shoot through him. The ex-SEAL was an extremely gruff man. His life had made him that way. But with his wife, it was obvious he was entirely different.

"I'm not eating if you aren't eating," Baker told Jodelle.

She laughed and looked at Remi. "One time, I made breakfast sandwiches for the high school surfers. I had one left, and I offered it to Baker. He refused to eat if I wasn't also eating. So to this day, when we're together, he refuses to put anything past his lips if I'm not also eating. It's annoying and sweet at the same time."

Baker simply shrugged. "Not happening, woman."

"I appreciate the offer, but I promised Remi I'd find her a taco truck," Kevlar said.

"That sounds awesome!" Jodelle exclaimed. "Most of the food trucks up here serve shrimp, but the Surf N Salsa truck has fish tacos to die for, and of course, their salsa is some of the best I've ever had. They also have burritos and a carne asada plate that's really good. Oh! I think the Pupukea Grill truck also has quesadillas, but the lines there are always usually pretty long. Wait! I almost forgot about Papi's Tacos! They have *amazing* street tacos. But, Kevlar, please don't leave the North Shore without going by Matsumoto Shave Ice. It's the best shave ice you'll get on the island, hands down."

"Got a preference, Remi?" Kevlar asked.

"Um...all of them?" she said with a small laugh.

"Done."

Remi raised a brow. "I was kidding."

"I wasn't," Kevlar told her. "You have any other plans today?"

"You mean other than rolling back to the hotel?"

Everyone laughed.

"And make sure you stop by to see the turtles at Laniakea Beach. There's no guarantee they'll be there, but they love to come up onto the shore and hang out in the sun. The locals take turns guarding them from asshole tourists who might feel the urge to sit on them to take pictures or other nonsense."

"Turtles? On the beach?" Remi turned to Kevlar. "Can we go? Please?"

"Of course," Kevlar said without hesitation. He felt Baker's gaze on him, but didn't want to turn away from the excitement and happiness he saw in Remi's eyes. She was practically vibrating.

"This is the best day ever!" she gushed.

It struck Kevlar once again that this woman was different than anyone he'd ever been with before. She hadn't once dwelled on the fact that someone had purposely arranged for them to be left in the middle of the ocean. He had no doubt she was still worried about who and why, but she wasn't letting that get in the way of her enjoying their last day on the island. And she didn't want to spend her time shopping, or dining in a Michelin-star restaurant. She was excited about tacos and turtles.

It was intoxicating, and Kevlar couldn't help but want

to soak in the happiness that seemed to seep from her every pore.

He wanted to always cultivate this part of Remi. Not hide any shit in life from her, but work hard to give her good experiences to make up for any bad. To see her smile at the thought of turtle-watching, or eating tacos, or getting lost in a maze. She brought out a side of him he didn't know he had. A nurturing side.

His friends would laugh at that. He wasn't a nurturing man. He demanded the absolute best from his teammates, pushed them hard. He didn't go out of his way to compliment or coddle, but each and every one of the men on his team knew without a doubt that he'd do what had to be done in order to bring them back home safe and sound.

But with Remi, he wanted to be...softer. Wanted to be someone who made her smile. Who was her rock when shit hit the fan, as it had yesterday. She hadn't hesitated to look to him when things got hard. He loved being that person for her, but he wanted to do the same when things were good too.

As they prepared to leave Baker and Jodelle's house, Kevlar watched as Remi hugged their hosts hard. She might claim she was a total introvert, but it was obvious to him that she actually enjoyed being around others. Her goodness was infectious, and he felt not one iota of jealousy when she hugged the taciturn Baker. That was just who Remi was. Friendly, compassionate. He had a feeling she could befriend the most gruff and belligerent grump out there. And probably earn his lifelong devotion in the process.

Hell, hadn't she already done that with him?

Kevlar put his hand on the small of her back as he led her to his rental car.

"I really liked meeting your friends," she told him as he held open her door.

"They aren't my friends," he felt obliged to say.

Remi frowned as she stood by the open door. "What? Yes they are."

"Sweetheart, I've only talked to Baker over the phone and via email before yesterday. I met him for the first time on that boat, when you did."

"What? That can't be true."

"It is."

"Oh...well, they're your friends now. And I thought they were lovely."

Kevlar could only smile at that. "In, Remi. It's warm out here, and I want to get the AC started so you don't overheat. Think about which food truck you want to go to first." When she sat, Kevlar shut the door and walked around the back of the car to the driver's side.

He looked at the small house and saw Baker still standing in the doorway. He gave him a chin lift and got one in return.

Smiling a little, and feeling deep down that Remi was right, he and the elusive Baker were probably now friends, Kevlar got into the car and started the engine, and the air conditioning.

If someone had asked him weeks ago what he thought he'd get out of his vacation to Hawaii, never in a million years would Kevlar have said a friendship with *the* Baker Rawlins, a more-than-he-bargained-for scuba trip, and finding the woman he wanted to spend the rest of his life with.

The latter part was ridiculous and so far-fetched, most people would scoff at the likelihood that he knew with such certainty that Remi Stephenson was meant to be his. But he knew how he felt. He just had to figure out how *not* to screw things up between them. Figure out who might have wanted her dead and mitigate the threat.

Then live happily ever after.

It wouldn't be easy, but then again, Kevlar was more than ready for the challenge. This might be the most important mission he'd ever undertaken in his life, and there was no way he would fail. The repercussions of doing so were far too high.

He looked over at Remi in the seat next to him. Her eyes were sparkling, her head was on a swivel so she wouldn't miss anything. She was happy to be here. Happy to be with *him*.

No, failing wasn't an option, not if it meant losing the bright, shining light sitting beside him.

CHAPTER EIGHT

"Don't be nervous."

Remi wanted to snort in reply, but she felt frozen. Yesterday felt like a dream. She'd enjoyed every second of the day she'd spent with Vincent. Loved meeting his friends, trying to find the food trucks Jodelle had recommended, chatting with people in line at the shave ice place, even sitting in the traffic jam they'd gotten stuck in on the way back to Waikiki.

To end the perfect day, Vincent had made reservations at Duke's. It felt like a completely different experience, sharing it with someone else.

He'd escorted Remi up to her hotel room afterward, and they'd watched a movie on one of the streaming services before watching the sun go down, along with the fireworks the hotel shot off every Friday night. She'd not wanted the day to end, and had been looking forward to what the night would bring. But Vincent hadn't torn off her clothes to have his wicked way with her, like she'd hoped.

They *did* make out, and she'd never felt so desired in her life, but Vincent had stopped things before they'd gone too far. And he'd done it in a way that didn't make her feel rejected. He'd said he wanted their first time to be special. That he wanted to get to know everything about her, her likes and dislikes, so he could make everything perfect the first time he made love to her.

Remi had never clicked with a man so quickly as she had with Vincent. She supposed she should be worried that this was some kind of unconscious need on her part to validate her appeal, especially after Douchecanoe. But deep down, she knew it wasn't that. Being with Vincent felt... right. As if she'd known him forever, instead of for a single day.

He'd left her hotel room around eleven, and had shown up at seven that morning with fresh coffee, sharing a breakfast of the Leonard's pastries they hadn't finished the day before.

It seemed like yet more proof that they were meant to meet when they discovered they were on the same flight back to California. Their plane didn't leave until around eight that evening, so they'd spent the morning snorkeling in the waters near the hotel.

Then they'd showered, packed, and done a little sightseeing before heading to the airport. She'd managed to upgrade Vincent's ticket to business class, so they could sit together on the redeye flight. He'd protested, but she'd done it anyway.

And now they were walking hand in hand through the San Diego airport toward luggage claim. His friends Wolf and Caroline were meeting them there. She'd arranged for Marley to come get her, but had texted before the flight and told her a little bit about Vincent, and how he was going to take her home...well, his friend was. Marley had warned Remi that they were going to have a girls' night soon so she could hear all the details about this new guy, which Remi was more than happy to divulge. She wanted her best friend's opinion. Valued it.

But first, she had to meet Wolf. The man Vincent had talked about on the plane. The man who was his mentor, who he looked up to, and whose opinion he highly valued. The thought of meeting someone who meant so much to Vincent was making her quake in her boots. Shoes. Flip-flops, whatever.

She felt grubby after a long flight. She hadn't had her coffee yet this morning, she definitely wasn't feeling at her best, and she wanted to make a good impression on Vincent's mentor. This was important to her, and she felt as if she was completely out of her league.

"Don't be nervous," Vincent said again, squeezing her hand as they stepped onto the escalator.

"I can't help it," she admitted.

As soon as they stepped off the moving stairs, Vincent pulled her aside and backed her against a wall. He leaned in until it felt as if they were the only two people in the world. She held onto his shirt at his sides and stared up at him.

He gently cupped her face. "You have nothing to be nervous about."

She snorted.

"You don't," he insisted.

"Vincent, this is a man you respect. I want him and his wife to like me. To think I'm good enough for you, even if I'm still wondering if that's true myself. It's the crack of dawn, my hair is probably sticking out in a million different directions, and I haven't had any caffeine yet." Remi closed her eyes at hearing the whine in her tone. She hated when her anxiety spiked like this. She hadn't worried as much about Baker witnessing it, as he'd literally seen her at her worst when he'd fished her out of the ocean. This was different.

"Look at me," Vincent ordered.

She didn't want to, but Remi was helpless to deny this man anything. She opened her eyes and stared into his beautiful blue orbs.

"I promise that Wolf will love you. Caroline too. You know how I know that?"

Remi shook her head, her mouth too dry to speak.

"Because he'll see in you what I do."

That didn't explain anything.

Vincent's lips twitched. "He'll see the goodness in you down to your toes. You don't even have to try, and it's there for anyone who cares to see it. But even more than that, he'll see how I look at you, and he'll know."

She couldn't stop the question from popping out. "Know what?"

"That you're mine."

Those three words should've sent Remi running for the hills. In what universe did a man claim a woman he barely knew? But instead, they sent a thrill shooting through her veins. "Okay."

Vincent pulled back a little and studied her, as if trying to read her mind. "Okay? You aren't freaked out about that? Don't want to protest and claim it's too early, that I'm being a Neanderthal?"

"It *is* too early. We're both fresh out of long relationships. But honestly, I feel the same way. You're mine, Vincent Hill." The last was said in a whisper, but the smile that spread across his face was all the validation she needed to know he hadn't been exaggerating; she wasn't alone in how she felt.

"All right then. When I tell you not to be nervous about Wolf and Caroline, believe me."

"I'll try."

"That's all I can ask."

Then Vincent leaned in and kissed her. He didn't care that they were in a crowded airport. Or that they just seemed to make some sort of long-term commitment to each other. But to be honest, neither did Remi.

The kiss was gentle and loving, and it only made her want more. Made her remember how his hands felt on her the night before as they'd made out in her suite.

When he pulled his mouth from hers, they were both

breathing hard, and Remi could feel his erection against her belly. He'd pressed her harder against the wall as they'd kissed, and she felt surrounded by him. Safe.

"I need a second," he said, when she looked at him in confusion when he didn't move.

Clarity dawned. "Right. Okay," she said with a small smile.

"You proud of yourself?" he asked. Then answered before she could. "You should be. I can't remember the last time I got a hard-on in public."

Her smile grew.

Vincent took a deep breath and eased away from her, and his hands slid down to her shoulders. "You good?"

"I'm good," she confirmed.

"Not nervous?" he pushed.

She couldn't lie. "Still nervous, but better."

"Good. You'll see I'm right. Ready?"

She wasn't, but then again, she was. She wanted out of this airport. Wanted to get on with her new life. Honestly, she really should thank Douchecanoe. If he hadn't been such a...well...douchecanoe, she never would've met Vincent. The thought of missing out on everything they were going to be together—she hoped—was too depressing to even contemplate.

Vincent turned and reached for her hand once more and they began to walk toward baggage claim. "Besides, this will be a good dress rehearsal for you meeting the rest of my team."

Remi nearly tripped over her feet at that. Shoot, she'd

forgotten how close he was to the rest of the men on his SEAL team. The thought of meeting more alpha men like Vincent made her tremble.

"And I need to meet Marley, your parents and your grandmother. If you think I'm not nervous about that myself, you're wrong."

Remi thought about that as they walked. He was right. If they were going to make their relationship work, they needed to introduce each other to the most important people in their lives. And she really had no doubt that *her* people would adore Vincent. He was so different from Douchecanoe.

Knowing Vincent felt some of the same trepidation over meeting her loved ones, though, actually took away some of her nervousness over meeting Wolf and Caroline. She knew Vincent would impress her friends and family, and if he had no doubts about her impressing *his*, she would believe him.

Then there was no more time to think. A man and woman were walking toward them, and she instinctively knew this was the couple who was there to bring them home. Wolf had a distinguished yet somehow still badass vibe about him, and Caroline was...

Remi silently sighed. She looked down-to-earth and normal.

She was momentarily ashamed of the immediate thought she had about the mysterious woman. For some reason, she'd pictured her being tall, willowy, perfectly made up—and completely out of Remi's league. But instead, she was kind of...plain.

"Kevlar!" the man said as he got close. He dropped his wife's hand and embraced Vincent in that way guys had. Sort of a half hug as he thumped his back a few times. Both men were smiling, and Remi stood off to the side watching.

"Glad you're all right!" Wolf said.

"Of course I am," Vincent retorted a little cockily.

Then Wolf turned to Remi. "And I'm glad *you're* all right too."

She was a little taken aback, but she smiled politely. "Thanks."

"I can't imagine what you went through. Well...I can, but that's a conversation for a different time. I'm very glad Kevlar was there with you," Caroline said.

Remi knew what she was talking about, as Vincent had told her a little about Caroline's story on the plane. About what made her so respected and admired in SEAL circles. It was hard to believe everything the woman had gone through, and hearing about it was partly what had made Remi so nervous to meet her. She was nothing like Caroline. Couldn't have survived half the things that woman had. But seeing the genuine welcoming look on her face made Remi relax a little.

As they walked toward the baggage carousel to wait for their bags, Wolf asked Vincent, "What do you need from me?"

Remi looked at Vincent when he said, "I need to borrow your girl posse."

Both Wolf and Caroline laughed, but Remi was confused.

"I'm already on it," Caroline told him.

"Aces Bar and Grill?" Wolf asked.

Remi wasn't sure who the question was aimed at, Vincent or his wife, but they both answered.

"Perfect!"

Then Vincent turned to her with a tender smile. "What do you think?"

"Um...about what?" Remi asked, completely confused.

"Kevlar!" Caroline said in exasperation, slapping him on the arm. Then she turned to Remi. "My friends and I are the girl posse. Kevlar wants us to take you under our wing. Answer any questions you have. Reassure you that dating a Navy SEAL isn't as horrible as some people like to make it out to be. Sure, it has its challenges, but the rewards are *so* worth it."

She looked at her husband with an expression so intimate, Remi felt a little like a third wheel. And when Wolf leaned over and kissed his wife's forehead, Remi blinked in surprise. How many times had Vincent done that same thing to her? Had he learned it from Wolf? Was it an innate thing that all these tough, capable men just did?

She didn't have time to think about it, as Caroline was still talking.

"If you'd be willing, I'd love to talk more with you at Aces Bar and Grill. It's a fun, low-key, safe place we like to hang out. One of our group owns the place, actually, and she's worked hard to make it less of a hook-up bar and more of a fun place to chill with no pressure or expectations as far as looks, what you wear, or having to deal with Frog Hogs."

Remi glanced at Vincent once more, and he came to her rescue.

"SEALs are sometimes called frogmen, and a Frog Hog is a woman who wants to sleep with as many of us as she can."

Remi screwed her nose up before she could mask her reaction.

All three of her companions laughed.

"Exactly," Caroline said. "Aces is laid-back, and there isn't any of that nonsense going on there. I mean, I'm sure there are still hookups and stuff, but it's not as blatant as it is at other bars. Anyway, if you're up for it, we'd love to have you join us for one of our get-togethers. We try to get out of the house at least once a week. We leave the kids to our husbands and we talk about nothing and everything. One of our favorite things is having women new to the SEAL scene join us, so we can tell them the truth—good, bad, and ugly—about dating someone in the special forces. What do you say? Please say you'll come!"

There was no way Remi could decline such a kind offer. And the truth was, she didn't want to. She *did* have a lot of questions, and it might be fun to hang out with Caroline and her friends. She'd certainly heard a lot about them from Vincent. "Can I bring my best friend?"

"Of course!" Caroline said without hesitation. "The more the merrier. Is she single? Because Kevlar's teammates are all single..."

"Ice," Wolf warned.

Caroline simply laughed.

Remi knew that Ice was Caroline's nickname, a moniker she'd gotten when she'd saved a plane full of people from terrorists.

"What? They *are*," Caroline said not so innocently. "Right, Kevlar?"

Vincent's lips twitched. "They're single."

"See?" Caroline told her husband.

"Marley's married. Has two kids," Remi interjected.

"Oh, well, that's awesome. She'll right fit in with our crew then."

And of course, that made Remi uneasy again. She didn't have children. Did that mean *she* wouldn't fit in?

"Start thinking about all the questions you have. I'll get your number when we're in the car and I'll text you a few dates and times to see what will work."

"Oh, my schedule is flexible. I work from home, so whenever you guys usually get together will work for me," Remi told her quickly.

"Cool. What do you do...if you don't mind me asking?"

"She's an artist. She draws the Pecky the Traveling Taco cartoon," Vincent answered for her. Remi felt his arm go around her waist, and when she looked up at him, saw a look of pride on his face.

"No way! Seriously? Oh my God, wait 'til I tell the girls!

There's no way any of them will miss our next Aces get-together!"

It was surreal that not only Vincent, but now Caroline knew of her little cartoon. As they waited for their bags, Caroline asked rapid-fire questions about how she came up with the ideas for her strips, how she got started drawing, and a hundred other inquiries related to Pecky and his friends.

By the time they had their bags and were all heading toward the parking garage, Remi felt as if she'd known Caroline forever. And she hadn't missed how Wolf was constantly keeping watch over his wife. Staying between her and the bulk of the crowd around them, putting his hand on her arm and pulling her out of the way of a man who wasn't paying attention where he was walking, keeping his head on a swivel as if he was constantly looking for possible threats, and placing a protective hand on the small of her back as they walked out of the airport.

Come to think of it, Vincent was doing the same thing.

She was hyper aware of every time he touched her, and she couldn't help but lean into him as they were waiting for their bags to come around. She was tired. She understood because of the time change, traveling overnight back to the mainland was the most reasonable way to make the most out of tourists' time on the islands, and she was thankful she didn't need to go into an office or anything and could adjust to the time change at her leisure. But she was even more grateful for the extra time with Vincent before she had to go back to her real life.

Despite all his assurances, a small part of her was still worried that once he got back into his normal routine, after he'd had time to reflect on everything that happened, he'd wonder what the heck he was thinking. After all, they really hadn't been apart since they'd lifted their heads from the water and realized they were alone in the ocean. That forced proximity might've caused feelings for her that weren't authentic. He'd had to take care of her, protect her, and maybe now that they were home, he'd come to his senses. Maybe after they parted ways, she'd never hear from him again.

He'd given her no indication that this was it for them. Exactly the opposite, actually. Even now, Vincent's hand was pressed firmly against her spine as they walked toward Wolf's car. It was just her own worries trying to undermine her confidence.

"I apologize in advance for Matthew's car," Caroline said with a laugh as they headed into the parking garage. "BABS is obnoxious."

"She's not that bad," Wolf protested.

"Big-Ass Black SUV," Caroline told Remi. "BABS for short. And the thing is huge. Ginormous. Could take on a train and win."

"Which is the point," Wolf said with a satisfied grin. "When you drive her, I know you're safe."

Caroline shook her head and rolled her eyes. She gave Remi a look that clearly communicated her amusement with her husband.

Secretly, Remi thought it was sweet.

When Wolf clicked the key fob he had in the hand that wasn't touching his wife, lights on an SUV blinked not too far in front of them. As they approached, Remi had to agree with Caroline, the vehicle was huge. She didn't know car models, but she recognize the Cadillac emblem on the back.

Wolf and Vincent got their bags put in the back while Caroline and Remi climbed into the car. As soon as Vincent joined her in the backseat, he reached for her hand. He squeezed it and lifted a brow, as if to ask if she was good.

Remi smiled back at him. Honestly, she'd been worried about meeting his friends, but she was relieved that he'd been right. They were down-to-earth and she felt comfortable with them almost immediately.

Caroline made small talk as they drove through the streets. The plan was to drop her off first, then they'd take Vincent home. With every mile they got closer to her condo, the more unsettled Remi felt. It would actually feel odd to be alone once more. She and Vincent had been together nearly every minute since they'd met.

Wolf pulled into the parking lot at her condo, and instead of feeling relieved to be home, Remi felt...sad. The vacation had been good, and then terrifying, and then fun. And now it was over and she had no idea what the future held, aside from an upcoming girls' night with Caroline's friends.

"It was so nice to meet you," Caroline gushed as she turned in the front seat to look at Remi. "I'll text you later today and let you know when we're gonna meet up at Aces, and give you the address. I really hope you and your friend will come, because the girls are gonna be *so* jealous that I got to meet you already. And remember to think of questions you have for us about military life and the Navy and SEALs and, well...anything!"

"Caroline, take a breath," Wolf said with a laugh. "You're gonna see her again, this isn't the last time you have to talk to her."

"I know, I'm just excited," Caroline told her husband with a huff. "I'd totally get out and hug you, but that would probably be weird. But expect a hug the next time I see you for sure. I didn't used to be a hugger, but being around all my friends and their kids has changed me into one."

"Give me a minute to walk her to her door?" Vincent asked, interrupting Caroline's gushing.

"Of course," Wolf said. "I'll just be here making out with my wife."

"Matthew," Caroline protested. Her cheeks were pink as she slapped Wolf's arm halfheartedly.

Remi was smiling as she climbed out of the large vehicle and met Vincent at the back. He refused to even consider letting her carry her own suitcase and instead gestured for her to lead the way.

She looked back at him once when they were walking up the sidewalk, and butterflies swam in her belly when she caught him staring at her ass. Smiling, she turned and unlocked her door. Vincent stepped inside and placed her suitcase in the small foyer.

Then he pushed her backward until she was up against the wall. The door was still open, but she couldn't see BABS or any of the other vehicles in the lot.

"Vincent?" she asked when he didn't do or say anything.

"I have things to do," he said strangely. "Need to call Tex, Bertie—to chew her ass out and see if I can suss out if she was behind what happened—my commander, my team. Check in with them, make sure they're all good, see if anything I need to know about happened while I was gone."

When he paused, Remi said, "Okay."

"But the thought of not being able to turn my head and see you is killing me already. Of not hearing your little hum of enjoyment when you have your first sip of coffee. Seeing your eyes light up when you see a box of malasadas. Not watching you wrap everyone you meet around your little finger with a kind word. In short, sweetheart...I'm gonna miss you."

Remi felt like she'd just melted into a pile of goo on her foyer floor at his words. Had anyone ever said anything that had made her feel so good before? No. The answer was definitely no. "Vincent," she whispered.

"I'm serious. You're already under my skin, Remi." His gaze roamed over her face, as if he was trying to memorize it or something. "And I like you there," he went on. "I sure as hell hope you were serious when you agreed to see me when we got home. Because I was. I *am*. I've never felt like this before. It's overwhelming and exciting at the same time."

She knew exactly what he meant, because he'd perfectly described her own feelings.

Then he lowered his head and rested his forehead against hers. They stood like that for what seemed like minutes, but was probably only seconds.

"I need to go," he said, but didn't move.

"I know."

"You need to get some rest."

"Uh-huh," she mumbled as her hands gripped his shirt even tighter.

Then he lifted his head. "You don't have to go out with Caroline if you don't want to."

"I want to," Remi reassured him.

"Good. She's...she's good people. As are all the women. They're good role models as SEAL wives. They'll tell you things as they really are. They won't sugarcoat anything. They'll tell you all the bad stuff that goes along with being a SEAL's significant other, as well as the good. I need you to be sure you want to be with me, Remi. Because if we do this...I'm one hundred percent in, and it'll break me if you're not. I've seen too many relationships crash and burn because of expectations not being met and misconceptions about being with a special forces operator."

"I'm really boring, Vincent," Remi blurted. "My idea of a good time is being in comfy clothes on my couch. Not going out. I'm not super social...like, *at all*. I'd rather sit at home and draw than go out. I forced myself to do the things I did in Hawaii because if I was going to be there, I figured I might as well see everything I could.

But I would've been just as happy sitting in my room, on the balcony, watching the ocean from afar rather than being in it." She huffed out a breath. "Would've been safer too."

"But then we wouldn't have met," Vincent told her with a smile. "And if you think I care that you'd rather be at home than out on the town, you're wrong. Honestly, that sounds like heaven. I do like hanging out with my teammates, and I hope you'll learn to enjoy that too. And Caroline wasn't lying about Aces. It's very low-key and almost like hanging out at home. But if you hate it, I'd never force you to do anything that makes you uncomfortable."

"Vincent?"

"Yeah?"

"I already know...I'm already sure. I'm one hundred percent in *now*."

He stared at her for a beat, then his head dropped and he crushed his lips to hers. Remi moved her hands from his waist to his back and held on as he kissed the hell out of her. She gave as good as she got. She might be an introvert nerd artist, but this man brought out a side of her she never knew she had. She wanted him. Needed him. Would do anything to have him yank her pants down right that second and take her against the wall.

"*Fuck*," he panted after he tore his mouth from hers. One of his hands was on her ass, squeezing, and the other had shoved up under her shirt. It felt like a brand on her breast.

In return, she'd been caressing his cock through his

jeans and was holding onto his bicep with her other hand, digging her nails into his skin.

They were both breathing hard, and Remi had never been as wet as she was right that moment. She wanted nothing more than to drag him up to her bedroom and get naked. But he had things he needed to do. And Wolf and Caroline were waiting for him.

He reached down and took the hand that was still holding his dick, lifting it up to his face and kissing her palm. He took a deep breath. Then another.

"I'll call you later. Give you time to take a nap. Make sure you eat something good when you get up."

"You mean not a doughnut?" she asked with a small smile.

"Exactly."

"Only if you do the same. I mean, it's been a week since you've had a Thin Mint cookie. Don't eat the whole box I know you've got stashed in your freezer."

He grinned at her, then sobered. "You know me better than most people, and it's been two damn days."

"Three," she corrected.

"Right. We're doing this," he said firmly. "I'll call you later. You want to have dinner together?"

"Yes." Remi supposed maybe she should put some space between them. Things were moving extremely fast. Marley would probably tell her to slow her roll, to be careful. But as she thought before, if Remi couldn't trust Vincent, a man who'd literally saved her life, who *could* she trust?

"I'll pick you up at five-thirty. We'll go back to my place. It's not as nice as this, but I want you in my space. That okay?"

Remi nodded eagerly. She wanted to see his apartment. You could learn a lot about a person by seeing where and how they lived.

"And tomorrow I'll take you to Aces. So you can get to know it before your girls' night. It'll make you more comfortable meeting the others if you aren't worried about your surroundings."

He was right. Of course he was. "Thank you."

"But to warn you, my team is gonna want to meet you. They might be there tomorrow night."

That made her nervous, but she wanted to meet the guys Vincent thought of as brothers. He'd talked a lot about them, and she felt as if she halfway knew them already. If they were going to have a relationship, one that worked, she needed to befriend the men who were most important to him. "Okay. And I'm guessing you might hear from Marley. She can be a mama bear. She already knows about you, and what you did out there in the ocean... keeping me safe and all...but now that we're dating, she's going to want to know a lot more."

"I'm all right with that."

"When I started dating Douchecanoe, she stole my phone and got his number, then texted him questions nonstop. He blocked her that same night."

"Give her my number, sweetheart," Vincent said. "I don't care if she has it, and she doesn't need to be sneaky in order to get it. I'll answer all her questions. I've got nothing to hide."

"So says the Navy SEAL," Remi quipped.

Vincent's lips turned up in a grin. Then he sobered. "There are things I can't talk about. Things about my job. My missions."

"I know," Remi reassured him. "All I care about is that you come home safe. I don't care where you were or what you did. Only that you and your friends don't get hurt."

Vincent stared at her for a long moment.

"What?"

"You're already the perfect SEAL partner and you don't even know it. Many women can't handle not knowing where their man is going or for how long."

"I'm not saying I'll like it, especially not knowing how long you'll be gone. But I get that it's a part of being with a military guy. I've never felt like this about anyone in my life, Vincent. So I'm willing to deal with the not-so-good parts of being with you in order to have the great ones. Because I have no doubt those will be completely worth it."

Vincent opened his mouth to reply when a loud honk came from the parking lot.

Remi blushed. "I guess Wolf's sick of waiting for you."

"He's just messing with me. I guarantee he's enjoying having a few minutes alone with his wife. Look at me, Remi."

She met his gaze.

"I'll call you later to make sure we're still on for dinner.

If you need anything, anything at all, don't hesitate to call or text. I'll get back to you as soon as I can."

"Okay. Same for you. I mean, I don't know what you'd need from me, as you're the badass SEAL, but still."

"I need your smile. I need your kindness. I need your adorable snort-laugh. I need *you*, Remi. Just you."

He was killing her. She didn't want to let go of him, but she knew she had to. A glimpse of their future flashed through her brain. Of the sadness of having to let him go on missions, but also the happiness and relief she'd feel when he came back to her.

Was she really going to do this? Get into a relationship with a man who willingly put himself in danger time after time, and just hope he came back alive and well after each mission?

Yes. Yes, she was. Because she'd never felt like this before, not with anyone. He made her come alive in ways she never expected. She'd do whatever it took to keep feeling this way.

She lifted her chin and kissed him, feeling brave and confident in their blossoming relationship. He returned her kiss and tightened his arms around her for a moment, before she was the one who stepped away. He needed to go. They both had things to do.

"I'll see you later."

"Yes, you will," Vincent said with such determination, goose bumps broke out on Remi's arms. She stood in the door as he strode down her walkway toward Wolf's SUV. He turned before he got into the backseat, and she waved.

He gave her a chin lift then hopped into the backseat and closed the door behind him.

As Wolf backed out of the parking spot, Caroline rolled down her window and called out, "I'll text you later with the details about girls' night!"

Remi yelled, "Okay!"

And then they were gone. She slowly closed the door to her condo and put her back to it. Silence greeted her. Sliding down until she was sitting on her ass, Remi wrapped her arms around her legs and rested her cheek on her knees. She'd never disliked being alone before, but now...it was discomfiting. It reminded her too much of coming to the surface in the ocean and realizing that she'd been left behind. That feeling of dread, of realizing no one knew where she was, or even that she was in danger. It was terrifying.

Taking a deep breath, Remi forced herself to get to her feet. She had things to do—laundry, putting in an online grocery order for delivery, cartoons to draw, phone calls to make, a nap to take. She didn't have time to break down. Besides, she was fine. Everything had worked out.

But a niggling thought deep down inside worried over what Douchecanoe might do when he realized his plan hadn't worked.

Vincent might think what happened was because of *his* ex, but Remi was sure he was wrong. And she might be an overweight, nerdy cartoonist and not a muscular Navy SEAL, but she'd do whatever it took to make sure Vincent wasn't in any danger because of her.

CHAPTER NINE

As it turned out, Kevlar didn't get a chance to see Remi the night they arrived back in California. Or the next one. As team leader, it was his responsibility to stay on top of the intel needed for their missions. And his commander had informed him that it was looking likely they'd be sent out in the next few weeks. Which was actually a lot of lead time. Sometimes they only had a few hours' notice before they were shipping out.

But it also meant there was a lot to do to prepare. The last thing Kevlar wanted was to go into a situation without as much intel as possible. It was the key to every successful mission.

And because he'd been gone a week, he had to debrief with his commander, find out what he'd missed while he was away. So that meant by the time he was done working for the day and able to get off base, it was late. Too late to spend the kind of quality time he wanted to with Remi.

He'd called her, feeling guilty when he'd woken her up, but she insisted on talking to him as he drove home from the base, then as he ate his late dinner. And it was...nice. She didn't bitch about the time, about how tired she was, about him working so much and breaking their dinner plans. She simply listened to him talk about the things he could.

That's what they'd done last night, as well. Though that call also included some unfortunate news. He told her about a conversation with Tex, who'd informed him Honolulu PD had found the boat captain dead of an apparent overdose. He was still looking into *why* the man left them in the ocean, but they'd missed any opportunity to question the captain himself.

He also loved hearing about her day. About her visit with her grandmother and the details on some of the senior's latest antics. About how happy her parents were to have her home safely. About how pissed Marley was when Remi finally told her everything about the ill-fated snorkeling trip.

Kevlar was upset that he hadn't been able to get her to Aces before the girls' night Caroline had arranged. He'd promised, and he hadn't been able to follow through, which was no way to start a relationship.

But Remi being Remi, she'd told him that life didn't always go as planned and she'd be just fine. Caroline had added her to a group text with all the other women, and they'd been talking back and forth since Remi had gotten back to California.

But tonight, he'd finally get to see her again. In person. Not just speak to her over the phone or on FaceTime. He couldn't wait.

Of course, he'd have to share her with Caroline and the other women, as well as her best friend and all of his teammates, but Kevlar would take time with her any way he could get it.

Caroline had texted him separately and made it clear that he wasn't to steal Remi away while she and the others were getting to know her. The text made Kevlar laugh—because he'd been planning on doing just that. Giving Caroline about twenty minutes before he came up with some excuse why he needed to talk to Remi, and then sneaking her out the back door so he could take her to his place and finally have the one-on-one time with her that he craved.

But he also wanted Remi to get to know everyone. She claimed she was an introvert who was more comfortable being at home, but he'd seen her in Hawaii. She charmed everyone she came into contact with—maybe except for the captain of the boat they'd been on, but since he'd most certainly been bribed with money to do what he did, he didn't count.

Remi actually seemed to thrive around others. She simply didn't realize it. Her goodness was like a shining beacon. People were drawn to her, and he was no exception. But he'd be a selfish asshole if he muffled that light, if he tried to keep it to himself.

Tonight he'd see if he was right. If Remi looked at all uncomfortable, or like she wanted to leave, he'd whisk her out of there. But he had a feeling she'd flourish in a friendship with the other SEAL wives. And he had no doubt whatsoever that she'd impress his teammates too.

They'd been highly skeptical when Kevlar told them he'd met the woman he wanted to spend the rest of his life with. Even more so when they'd heard the circumstances surrounding *how* they'd met. They'd insisted he was feeling some sort of "God complex" because he'd rescued the woman. But they were wrong. Kevlar felt it down to his toes.

And they'd see for themselves once they met Remi.

Kevlar pulled into the parking lot of her condo complex and smiled. She lived in a safe area and her condo was gorgeous. But he wasn't jealous. Wasn't threatened by her bank account. He was happy for her. Relieved that she didn't have to struggle to pay her bills. He would never be the kind of boyfriend or husband who got upset that he wasn't the sole provider for his family. But he'd provide for her in ways that money couldn't. With his support, his affection, doing things around the house that needed doing...taking out the garbage, painting walls, looking after their baby so she could draw.

He shook his head at how ridiculous he was being—it was way too soon to be thinking about babies with Remi.

Even if the thought made his dick twitch and a longing deep inside almost overwhelm him.

He parked his Subaru Crosstrek and hopped out, eager to see Remi in person again. He practically skipped up the walkway to her door, and to his delight, it opened before he got there. It was good to know Remi was just as excited to see him as he was her.

She was grinning from ear to ear and before she could even speak, Kevlar pulled her into his arms and covered her mouth with his. He kissed her with all the pent-up emotions he'd had in the last couple days. Frustration that he hadn't been able to see her, happiness to have her in his arms again, and the horniness that had rested heavily in his veins when he thought about their last interlude in her foyer.

He'd relived the feeling of her hand on his cock more than once. In his shower, in his bed, and at random times as he was going about his workdays. Her touch was burned into his psyche, and he couldn't wait to be skin-to-skin with her and feel her hands on him once more.

"Vincent," she moaned as he buried his mouth into the crook of her shoulder and neck. He inhaled deeply, loving the smell of her shampoo, or lotion, or whatever the hell it was. Beach. She smelled like the freaking beach. Sand, coconut, salt. He didn't know what the name of it was, but it made his dick hard with one whiff. Which was amazing, considering he didn't have the best memories of the beach because of Hell Week. But on her? He couldn't get enough.

"Hi," she said after a moment.

Kevlar forced himself to pull away from her and told himself to calm the hell down. The last thing he wanted was to scare her with his intensity.

"Hi," he returned.

She smiled a little self-consciously and ran a hand over her hair.

"You look perfect," Kevlar assured her. And he wasn't blowing smoke up her ass. She did. She looked great. She wore a pair of tight skinny jeans, Skechers on her feet, and a T-shirt that said Leonard's Bakery.

He blinked.

"Where did you get that shirt?" he asked.

Remi blushed a little and shrugged. "I went online and ordered it. I wanted a memento of that amazing box of malasadas you bought us for breakfast. I was bummed I couldn't order the actual pastries online, but decided to get a T-shirt. I was just going upstairs to change when you got here."

"Change? Why?" Kevlar asked.

"Because. I need to wear something...better for tonight."

"As I said before, you're perfect. This is what you should wear," he said firmly. "Jeans, T-shirt, sneakers. That's what everyone wears."

"Whatever," Remi said with a roll of her eyes.

"It is," he insisted. "I would *not* set you up to feel out of place or embarrassed the first time you met my friends," he told her. "Text Caroline, ask her what she's wearing."

"I can't do that."

"Why not?"

"Because!"

"Fine. I will."

"What? Vincent, no! What are you doing? Stop!"

But he wouldn't stop. Because he didn't want Remi to change out of the adorable outfit she had on. The jeans hugged her curves, making his mouth water, and that shirt...all he could think of when he saw the Leonard's logo was Remi sitting across from him at the small table in her hotel room, moaning deep in her throat as she sampled the different flavored malasadas.

"Get in here," she said after a moment, not letting him send the text to Caroline he'd started. She laughed as she grabbed his arm and pulled him into her condo. "Marley wants to meet you."

Kevlar stopped in his tracks. He'd been so intent on seeing Remi that he'd forgotten her best friend was coming to the condo, and he'd be meeting her for the first time. He felt as if he already knew the other woman fairly well—after all, they'd been texting back and forth for two days, since Remi had given Marley his number. And she hadn't held back either. She'd asked him about everything from how often he was gone, to his family, to his favorite color. He assumed she was thinking of any and everything to ask simply to see if he'd get annoyed and eventually blow her off. But he hadn't. He was more amused than irritated by her constant barrage of questions.

And knowing she was sharing each and every one of his answers with Remi made it all the more bearable. He'd learned Marley was sharing his responses when Remi commented on the coincidence that maroon was her favorite color, as well.

But...now he understood Remi's nervousness at meeting Wolf and Caroline that first time. He wanted to make a good impression. Marley was Remi's best friend. And if things didn't go well with this meeting, it was possible she could convince Remi that she could do better. Which Kevlar knew was true, but he was still hoping he could be the man she deserved.

Remi pulled him into her condo, and Kevlar had the humorous thought that this was the first time he'd been past the foyer, although some pretty darn good things had happened in that foyer.

Her place was nice. He got a brief glimpse of the kitchen as he entered the living area. Large space, up-to-date stainless-steel appliances, everything in its place. There was a small table next to the kitchen, with flowers in the middle and quilted placemats in front of each chair. Looking around the living area, Kevlar noted it was clean, but he was relieved to see it also looked comfortable. A throw blanket was tossed haphazardly over a recliner, magazines were strewn across a coffee table, and the leather couch looked very comfortable and well-used.

But he didn't have time to look closely at the books and pictures on the large bookcase, or the paintings on the walls, because a woman who could only be Marley was smiling politely as Remi towed him toward the couch. She was a few inches shorter than Remi, had thick red hair and green eyes, which were currently narrowed as if she was trying to read him before he'd even opened his mouth.

"Marley, this is Vincent. Vincent, this is my best friend, Marley. And you can only believe half of the things that come out of her mouth."

"Whatever, Remi. Hi, it's good to meet you," Marley said, holding out her hand for him to shake.

She was still smiling, but Kevlar could tell she was reserving judgement until he proved what kind of man he was. She had nothing to worry about, of course, but she wouldn't believe his word. She'd have to see for herself that Kevlar had no intention of doing anything that might hurt her friend.

He reached for her hand and shook it firmly, but didn't grip it hard enough to hurt.

"So...what are you doing about Douchecanoe?" Marley asked, once the pleasantries were over.

"Marl! What did I tell you about that?" Remi asked, sounding perturbed.

"You told me I wasn't allowed to grill him and I had to be nice. Screw that," Marley said. "I sat back and watched that asshole hurt you over and over. I'm not doing that again."

It was obvious Remi was embarrassed, and while Kevlar didn't mind Marley's protectiveness, he wasn't thrilled that the woman was making Remi feel uncomfortable.

"I've got a former SEAL buddy checking into his phone records and seeing what he can find. I'm planning on having a little chat with Miles as soon as I get intel back from my friend. Now, I'd appreciate it if you dialed things back a bit. You're embarrassing Remi, which isn't cool."

Marley blinked at him, and Kevlar could see that she instantly regretted making the moment feel awkward. She took a deep breath before turning to Remi. "Sorry."

"It's okay. You mean well."

Marley nodded, then turned back to Kevlar. "For the record, we don't use that name for Remi's ex. Ever. He's Douchecanoe. Always and forever."

Kevlar smiled. "Right. Sorry. My mistake."

"He admits when he's wrong. It's a good first step," Marley said as she winked at Remi. "I have to admit, Kevlar, you've been a good sport with all my texts," she added, sounding a bit friendlier.

"And *I* have to admit, you came up with some good questions," Kevlar returned. "That one about what I'd do if my SEAL team all had weights chained to their ankles and were in a sinking boat, while Remi was about to be eaten by a shark? Who I'd choose to rescue? That was classic."

"Seriously, I'm dying here," Remi said as she dropped her head into her hand as if trying to disappear.

"Don't you want to know his answer?" Marley asked, her eyes sparkling with humor.

Kevlar didn't wait for her reply. "You, Remi. Always you. My team can take care of themselves. Safe would've found a way to remove the locks on the chains, Smiley would've made a joke to keep the tension down, Preacher would've continuously yelled at me, letting me know where the shark was, if it was coming closer. MacGyver...well, he'd find some way to plug the hole on the leaking boat. Flash would use the chains Safe removed as a way to distract the shark, and Howler would step in to organize everyone while I was busy with you."

The look Remi gave him was so full of...he wasn't sure how to describe the emotion he saw on her face. Awe, disbelief, humor?

"Right, so...badass SEAL can save the world. All your friends will be there tonight, right?" Marley asked.

It was difficult for Kevlar to tear his gaze from Remi, but he forced himself to look at her friend. "Yeah. It'll be a full house. Between the girls' night, and all their husbands wanting to watch over their women, and my team being there, it'll be a little...chaotic."

"I thought Wolf and his friends usually stayed home on girls' night to look after the kids," Remi said.

"They do, but every now and then they all go out together. It doesn't happen too often anymore, because of the kids, but they enjoy having a few hours where they can all hang out and do adult things."

"Oh, that's nice," Remi said.

Kevlar didn't think it would be smart to admit that after Wolf told his team about Remi and Kevlar, and how they met, they all wanted to meet her too. It would freak her out, and that was the last thing he wanted to do. "Yeah."

"So, who are these women who're going to be there tonight?" Marley asked.

"Caroline, who Remi already met," Kevlar said.

"Alabama, Fiona, Summer, and Cheyenne. Jessyka will hopefully *not* be behind the bar all night. I'm not sure if Julie will be there or not, but Dakota could show up."

"Wow, okay, that's a lot of names to remember," Marley said, sounding unsure for the first time.

"Ha!" Remi exclaimed. "I tried to tell you, but you said I was just being my usual nervous self."

Marley rolled her eyes. "All right, I was wrong. Are you sure you're okay with going? I mean, with all the girls, plus double the number of guys, it's a lot."

"I was until you reminded me that all those people were coming to meet me and judge if I'm good enough to go out with Vincent," Remi said dryly.

But Kevlar shook his head. "You have it all wrong," he told her earnestly. "They're there to meet you, yes, but they won't judge. I mean, as long as you don't berate the employees or cause a scene by getting completely drunk and dancing on the tables—which I know you won't—they'll be cool. The guys'll be more interested in ribbing *me*, after meeting the woman who's got me so tied up in knots. I've been more distracted than they've ever seen me before. And the girls...they just want another woman to join their posse. Like Caroline said, the more the merrier with those guys. You won't be the one under the microscope tonight, sweetheart. I will."

Relief, a little skepticism, and anticipation were all easy to read on her expression.

"I could use some more friends," Marley said with a

shrug. "And my little heathens could use some new friends to terrorize."

Remi grinned. "My niece and nephew are angels, and I don't like you saying otherwise."

"That's because you don't live with them," Marley muttered.

Kevlar liked the dynamic between the two friends. "You ladies ready to go?" he asked, suddenly excited to get to Aces and show off Remi. Because there was no doubt that's what he was going to do. Remi was the best thing to happen to him in a very long time, and he was eager for her to meet the most important people in his life.

"Marl, Vincent claims what I'm wearing is fine for tonight, but I think I need to change into that outfit we picked out earlier. What do you think?"

Marley eyed Remi from head to toe, then turned to look at him. Kevlar prayed she wouldn't encourage Remi to change. He loved the shirt she had on, reminding him of the good times they had in Hawaii, and those jeans were crazy sexy on her.

"I think you should trust the man who saved your life out in Hawaii," Marley said after a beat.

Kevlar's shoulders sagged in relief.

"Are you sure? This is so...casual," Remi said, looking down at herself and running her palms up and down her thighs.

"You're going to a bar, Remi. Not a five-star restaurant," her friend retorted.

Thank you, Kevlar mouthed to Marley.

She nodded back, acknowledging his thanks, then said to Remi, "But maybe you could put on those new heels you bought before you went on vacation. It would dress things up just a touch."

"Oh! Good idea. I'll be right back!" Remi flashed him a little grin, then headed for the stairs.

As soon as she was out of eyesight, Marley turned to Kevlar, and he braced himself.

"So far, you haven't done anything to raise my asshole antenna. But I'm warning you—do *not* mess with Remi. She's good down to her soul, and she has so much love to give. But if you're only with her because of her money, or because you want some sort of post-vacation fling, end this now. I mean it. She's been shit on too many times for it to happen so soon again after Douchecanoe. And if you so much as raise your little finger against her, I'll break if off and shove it down your throat and make you choke on it."

Even though this was a serious conversation, and it was obvious Marley was completely serious, Kevlar couldn't keep the small smile from forming.

"This isn't funny," Marley warned. "I'd do anything for Remi. And that includes going toe-to-toe with you, even if I know I'll lose. She's my closest friend, and she deserves the best. And if you aren't that, if that freaks you out, you need to move the fuck on before she falls too hard."

Her words hit Kevlar hard. But not in the way Marley might think. He wiped all traces of humor from his face. "It doesn't freak me out. Remi is...she's different from anyone I've ever been with before, in all the right ways. Do you know that when we were out there in the ocean, and she realized we'd been left behind, she didn't panic once? She stayed calm, joked with me, and did everything I asked of her without hesitation. She got under my skin then, and every minute I've spent with her, talked with her, has only made me more and more intrigued.

"I'm not with her because of her money. I don't want a fling. And I'll never, ever hurt her. I'm not perfect, she probably deserves better than me, and my job will make a relationship extremely difficult, but I want this. Her. More than I've wanted anything in a very long time."

His gut tightened as he waited to see what Marley would say about his heartfelt response.

To his relief, she seemed to relax, and she even smiled a little.

"Good," was all she said, before they heard footsteps on the stairs.

"Perfection!" Marley said when Remi stepped back into the room.

Kevlar had to agree. The black heels she was wearing put her almost even with his six feet, and the confidence they seemed to give her was a massive turn-on. Her hair was pulled into a low bun at the back of her neck, and she'd added some lip gloss while she was upstairs. She looked completely out of his league, and Kevlar had never been prouder to have a woman at his side than he was right now.

"Right, so let's do this," Marley said. "I'll meet you guys there. I gotta get back to the little terrors right after dinner."

Respect for the woman increased. She had stuff she probably needed to do, but she was still taking time out for Remi. He was glad Marley would be there for moral support, even if he was sure she wouldn't need it. Caroline and the others would welcome both of them with open arms.

After the women grabbed their purses, they all left the house and headed to the parking lot together. Marley took off in her minivan, and Kevlar led Remi to his Crosstrek. Once they were inside, Remi put a hand on his arm.

"You okay?"

"Yeah, why wouldn't I be?" Kevlar asked in confusion.

"Marley can be... a lot. I'm sure she said something when I went upstairs, maybe even warned you off. She means well. We've been through a lot together."

Kevlar relaxed. "I don't mind," he told her honestly. "She's protective of you. I approve."

Remi rolled her eyes. "You guys act as if I'm ten years old or something."

"Not at all," he countered. "We just want to make sure no one hurts you if we can help it."

"I can take care of myself," Remi argued.

"Of course you can. You're an adult. Are you telling me if someone came at Marley, you wouldn't throw down for her?"

"I'd do anything for Marley," Remi replied.

"Exactly."

They stared at each other for a beat. "Right. Okay then. But you guys are good?"

"We're good," Kevlar confirmed.

"Whew," Remi said with a small smile, pantomiming wiping her brow. "Douchecanoe hated her."

"That's because he's a dick," Kevlar said matter-of-factly.

Remi snort-laughed, which made his cock twitch in his pants. He shouldn't be turned on by her unique laugh, and yet he still was. It was so...Remi.

He reached out and slid his hand behind her nape and pulled her closer. She came willingly, a smile on her lips.

"I've missed you," he said softly.

"It's only been two days since we saw each other, and we've talked every night," she protested.

"You haven't missed *me*?" he asked.

Her cheeks pinkened. "Maybe," she hedged.

"Guess I should remind you of what you've been missing then," Kevlar said, before dropping his lips to hers.

He was probably getting lip gloss all over himself, but he didn't care. She could be covered in clown makeup and he'd still want to kiss her. Making out with this woman turned him on more than the actual act of sex with past girlfriends. It was one more sign that she was meant to be his.

They were both panting by the time he forced himself to pull back. His hand in her hair had pulled her bun loose, and her out-of-control waves were now framing her face. He'd never seen anything more beautiful in his life.

"You messed up my hair," she complained with a small smile.

"Worth it," he returned.

Taking a deep breath, she sat back in her seat and reached up and pulled down the visor. "Better drive, Vincent. If Marley gets there too far ahead of us, there's no telling what she'll tell your teammates or the other women before we get there."

Kevlar chuckled, but dutifully reached for the key. He watched out of the corner of his eye as she smoothed her hair back and redid the bun. When she turned to look at him, she had a smile on her face.

"Vincent?"

"Yeah?"

"Thanks."

"For what?" he asked.

"Everything. For being you."

He reached for her hand and internally sighed when she held on tight. "If things get overwhelming for you tonight, just let me know and we can leave. Or take a break outside. Or something."

"I'll be okay," she reassured him.

"I mean it. No one will care if we leave before they do."

"I'm an introvert, but I can handle a night out," she said evenly.

"Never said you couldn't, but there are going to be a lot of people there."

"It's *okay*, Vincent. Promise. If it gets to be too much, I'll just go to the restroom, or find a quiet corner or something. I've had plenty of time to learn how to navigate social waters, even if I'm not fond of swimming in them. Don't worry about me."

"Don't you get it?" Kevlar asked. "I'll *always* worry about you. Doesn't matter if I'm ankle deep in the sand in the Middle East in the middle of a mission, or across town in a boring meeting on base. I have a feeling you'll always be on my mind, and I'll always wonder if you're okay."

"Vincent," she whispered.

He shrugged. "I'm intense, sweetheart. You should know that about me by now. If you can't handle that, can't accept it, then maybe *I* should be the one warning you off *me*. As I told Marley, this isn't a fling for me. There's something about you that drew me in the second I saw you. I want it all with you, Remi. If you don't want the same, I can turn this car around right now and we can go our separate ways, before things get too serious."

"I want it," Remi told him immediately as she squeezed his hand. "And it's too late anyway."

"For what?"

"It's already serious," she said a little cautiously.

Kevlar's heart flip-flopped. "Yes. Yes, it is," he agreed with a small grin.

"Best day of my life was being left in that ocean with you," she admitted.

He couldn't disagree, even if he didn't like the fact that her life had been placed in danger.

"And if *you* need a break, if tonight becomes too much for you, feel free to use me as an excuse and we can get out of there," she told him.

This woman. She was perfect for him.

"If I want to leave, I'll simply tell everyone that I'm done. I'd never use you as an excuse. Not like that. But if I decide I don't like my friends eyeballin' my woman, if I want to take you back to your place, or mine, and make out like teenagers, you good with that?"

She looked at him shyly but said without any guile, "Yes."

Kevlar's dick jumped in his jeans again.

"Good to know," he teased.

Remi giggled.

Somehow, being around this woman made all the things that usually haunted his memories disappear. She was worth everything he'd seen and done in his life. Sitting here next to her, holding her hand, made all the death and destruction fade into the background.

All too soon, he pulled into the Aces Bar and Grill parking lot.

"You ready for this?" he asked.

"Absolutely."

Reluctantly, Kevlar let go of Remi's hand so they could get out of the vehicle, but he claimed it again as soon as they met around the front of his car. They walked hand in hand to the door. Taking a deep breath, Kevlar opened it and followed her inside.

CHAPTER TEN

Remi had been nervous about tonight, but she was having a wonderful time. And Vincent had been right, her jeans and T-shirt made her fit right in with the other women and patrons of the bar. She and Marley were sitting at a table with Caroline and five of her friends, and from the moment they started talking, it was as if she'd known them her entire life.

She'd never clicked with a large group of women before. Being a loner all her life, she tended to make friends with one, maybe two people at a time. But every single woman was down-to-earth, friendly, and had no problem teasing each other—and Remi—as they talked about anything and everything. The topics ranged from the politics of the Navy, deployments, children, life after their husbands retired, and which alcoholic drinks were the best.

They'd willingly answered all the questions Remi posed about Navy SEALs, and more she didn't even know she had.

"Deployments suck," Jessyka told her without beating around the bush. "I used to dread those phone calls Benny would get, telling him they were going wheels up in three hours. He'd have to rush around to get packed and it was so hard to explain to the kids where Daddy was going and why. Mostly because I didn't know the answers."

"Yeah, the not knowing when they'd be back was the worst," Summer agreed.

"But when things got hard, we had each other," Fiona added.

Everyone nodded in agreement.

"Remember the days before we had kids, when we'd all go to Caroline's and hang out in her basement and be depressed together?" Alabama asked.

"That was the best!" Cheyenne agreed.

"Not the being depressed part, but having each other," Fiona clarified with a small laugh.

Caroline rested her elbows on the table and leaned closer to Remi. "Here's the thing. Our guys—SEALs and other special forces operators—they do what they do because they truly believe in serving their country. They don't do it for the awards or pats on the back. They do it so their loved ones back home can live their lives free and relatively safe. The most important thing I did for Matthew was letting him do what he loved, what he was good at, without having to worry about me back home.

"A woman who was faithful and strong was what he needed the most. And that wasn't a hardship for me. If I ever got worried, or thought I couldn't do it, I'd talk to my friends who were going through the same thing I was. We're here for you if you need us, Remi. Loving a SEAL isn't the easiest thing in the world. Our men, they were gone a lot. But knowing they were making the world a better place, a safer place, it was worth the sacrifice."

Her words settled deep inside Remi. She already didn't like the thought of Vincent being gone for long periods of time, but it wasn't as if he was off frolicking in the sun and sand. He was doing dangerous work. Important work.

"And it won't last forever," Summer added. "Eventually the younger guys, like Kevlar and his team, take over and the old farts are pushed out."

Everyone laughed at that.

"Then they're home all the time, getting in our way, being overprotective and ordering us around," Cheyenne agreed.

"Except you like it when Dude orders you around," Fiona teased.

"True," Cheyenne said without a shred of embarrassment. "He does it so well."

Everyone laughed again.

"I have to admit it's nice to be able to have help around the house, especially when it means I can go to the grocery store without the kids," Alabama said.

Remi listened as the other women talked about get-togethers on the beach with all the families, and it was obvious the hardships they'd gone through when their husbands were active duty were more than worth the good lives they were living now.

"Can we talk about Kevlar and his team now?" Summer asked, as she glanced across the bar to where the men had gathered.

Looking in that direction, Remi couldn't keep the smile off her face. Vincent and his team were hanging out with Wolf and his friends. It was a mix of silver foxes and their younger counterparts. Remi had been introduced to the other women's men earlier—Abe, Cookie, Mozart, Dude, and Benny—but didn't really know who was who yet. They were all still in very good shape, they'd obviously worked hard to keep their physiques lean and mean. Even in the short time she'd been observing them, it wasn't hard to see they were completely devoted to their wives. They'd left them alone to have their girls' night, but they'd checked on them often, making sure they had drinks and no one else in the bar harassed the table of women.

Not that anyone would. Jessyka was the owner, and she'd talked earlier about how hard she'd worked to change Aces' reputation from that of a rowdy SEAL hook-up bar, to a more laid-back place where men and women could come to simply have a drink in peace, without having to worry about being hit on or harassed.

"Seriously, every SEAL currently in this bar is so good-looking," Cheyenne said with a happy sigh as she took a sip of her wine.

Remi had to agree. Intellectually, she'd known

Vincent's friends would likely be fit and muscular because of their job, but she hadn't expected every one of them to be quite so handsome. They were all around the same age, late twenties to early thirties, and they ranged from around her height to six-three or so. They all had different distinguishing features...but honestly, they still kind of looked like a bunch of older, more muscular frat guys.

Though there was an air of subtle danger about them that was unmistakable. They were also hyper alert. Every time the door of the bar opened, everyone's gazes immediately sized up whoever entered, looking for any potential threats. Beyond a brief meeting, Remi hadn't had a chance to sit down and talk to Vincent's team, however, as she and Marley had been whisked away by Caroline soon after meeting everyone. But they'd all seemed friendly and happy for her and Vincent.

"I do feel bad for Blink though," Jessyka said softly.

"Who?" Marley asked.

"Blink. He's the guy sitting at the bar by himself. He's from another team. Comes in almost every day and nurses a beer all night. He doesn't get drunk, simply sits there and stares off into space, lost in his thoughts."

"Anyone know what happened?" Fiona asked.

"I do," Caroline said.

Everyone turned to her.

"But I can't say. Matthew told me the other night, and it's not my place to share."

"I heard some of his teammates died," Summer said.

"Yeah, they did. Others were medically discharged. That last mission...it wasn't good," Caroline admitted.

"I think he blames himself," Jessyka said.

"Looks like it," Caroline agreed with a nod.

"So...he's not on a team anymore?" Remi asked. "Is he on vacation, or leave, or whatever it's called?"

"Convalescent leave," Caroline explained. "I think thirty days, but I'm not sure."

"Then what happens?" Marley asked.

"He'll probably be assigned to another team. Will probably get PCS'd."

"Permanent Change of Station," Summer explained. "Which means he'll move to another Navy base and join a team of SEALs there."

"But he'll have to get cleared by psych first," Caroline said.

"He's not exactly Mr. Congeniality," Alabama added in a low voice. "He's kind of gruff."

"He's not that bad," Jessyka insisted. "He's just...sad."

"But he can be sad and not take it out on others," Fiona said. "He's snapped at a few people even while we've been here."

"Can you blame him? If people are being idiots, and he's thinking about what happened to the men on his team, he probably can't help but call others on their stupid behavior," Jessyka said with a shrug.

"True, but if he doesn't want to be around people, why does he come to a bar?" Fiona asked.

No one said anything, just stared at the red-haired man sitting at the end of the bar by himself.

"Anyway," Caroline said, sitting up straighter. "You and Kevlar are adorable together, Remi."

It was obvious she was changing the subject, which was all right with Remi, because she wasn't comfortable talking about the guy at the bar behind his back. It didn't seem right. She felt bad for him, but didn't know enough about the Navy or SEALs in general to know much about what his future might hold.

"Caroline said you and Kevlar were left in the middle of the ocean when you were snorkeling?" Cheyenne asked.

"But you don't have to talk about it, if it brings up too many bad memories," Fiona said quickly.

Surprisingly, Remi didn't mind discussing what happened in Hawaii. Because while being left in the water had been scary, spending time with Vincent gave her plenty of good memories as well.

"It's okay," she told her new friends. "Yeah, I'd been following this sea turtle, and when I finally lifted my head and looked around, the boat was nowhere to be seen. I didn't know what the hell was happening, and then Vincent was there. He kept me calm. Reassured me that he had some sort of tracker in his wetsuit and his friend would know he was in trouble and send help."

"Tex," Caroline and Fiona said at the same time.

Everyone laughed, except for Remi and Marley.

"Who's Tex?" Marley asked.

"He's a former SEAL who lives out on the East Coast

with his wife, Melody. He's obsessed with keeping track of his friends and their women," Caroline explained.

"He's awesome," Fiona said softly. "Truly cares. I don't know what I would've done without him."

"Me either," Cheyenne agreed.

"Same," Jessyka said.

"So this Tex guy was tracking Vincent? Why?" Marley asked, obviously still confused.

"Vincent said the tracker was in his wetsuit, the one he wears on his missions. He'd forgotten about it, but said Tex would know something was up when he was in the ocean, in one spot, for too long for a diving trip," Remi explained.

"You had to have been scared. I would've been," Alabama said.

"I was. But Vincent was...perfect. He was so sure someone would be coming for us. Of course, when the guy who left us came back to make sure we were dead or something—I'm still not sure what he planned to do if he found us; nothing good, probably—Vincent took us underwater, and we shared his air tank until the boat was gone again."

Marley's eyes widened. "You didn't tell me that part!" she scolded.

Remi had purposely not mentioned that part of the harrowing event with her best friend, because she'd already been pissed off and scared with all the other stuff she'd shared.

"It's not easy to do that. Buddy-breathe, I mean," Caroline said.

"You've done it?" Remi asked.

"Yeah. With Cookie. It's a long story, and it's scary as hell. You have to really trust the other person to give you the thingy to breathe when you need it."

Remi nodded. It *had* been scary. But staring into Vincent's eyes as they passed his regulator back and forth had made it a little less so.

"Anyway, so that jerk obviously didn't see you, and someone came to rescue you?" Cheyenne asked.

"Yeah. Baker. He was intense, but nice. We went to his place the next day and spent some time with him and his wife, Jodelle. It was fun."

"Wait, Baker? *The* Baker? I'm so jealous! I've heard a little about him from some of Benny's friends who are stationed out there in Hawaii," Jessyka said.

"Is that the hot surfer guy who lives on the North Shore?" Fiona asked.

"Yes! Him!" Jessyka exclaimed.

"I heard he walked across lava to burn up some bad guy."

"I heard that he knows all the mafia members in New York, and in other big cities."

"And *I* heard he's so good-looking that he secretly models for *GQ*."

"How could it be a secret if he lets someone take pictures of him for a magazine?"

"I don't know, but he's apparently a recluse who rarely goes out of his house except to surf."

Remi chuckled at the women's over-the-top conversation. She interrupted them to say, "I don't know about any of that. But I *will* say that I was ever-so-glad to see him pull up alongside us in the middle of the ocean. And that the visit I had with him and his wife was totally normal, and he was friendly and concerned about how I was doing after my ordeal."

"But he's good-looking, right? Tell me he's good-looking," Jessyka said, her eyes sparkling.

"Oh yeah, he's hot. He could totally be a model, but I have a feeling he'd be horrified if anyone even suggested something like that. He doesn't seem like the kind of guy who'd enjoy the spotlight. At all," Remi said.

"What else did you do while you were in Hawaii?" Alabama asked.

Remi went on to talk about some of the things she'd done on her own, "Before Vincent," as she now thought of the earlier part of her trip, and then what they'd done together on their last day.

Talk around the table turned to vacations, and where the other women wanted to go. Remi glanced over at the guys, and they were now involved in what looked like some sort of pool tournament. They'd taken over two of the tables and were laughing and joking with each other.

Then she turned her attention back to the man sitting at the bar by himself. She felt sorry for him. He'd probably been doing what the other SEALs did on every mission. And if he was anything like Vincent, he'd lost men he loved like brothers. It sucked. Hard.

"I'm going to head to the bar and get a soft drink.

Anyone want anything?" Remi asked during a lull in the conversation.

"I can get it for you," Jessyka said, and started to stand.

But Remi quickly said, "Oh no, stay. It's fine. I need to stretch my legs anyway. I'm good."

"If you're sure..." Jessyka said.

"I'm sure," Remi replied.

When conversation began flowing again, Marley leaned over and asked, "You okay? I know being around people like this isn't exactly your thing. You want me to come with you?"

"I'm good. Promise. I'll be right back."

Marley nodded, and as Remi stood, her friend was quickly drawn back into the conversation about which was better, a vacation somewhere cold where lots of snuggling with a husband could happen, or a tropical location that involved bathing suits and sun.

Remi caught Vincent's eye as she made her way through the crowded room, toward the bar.

He started to put his pool stick down, obviously intent on joining her, but Remi waved him off and mouthed, *I'm good.*

He tilted his head as if to ask if she was sure, and Remi nodded.

He gave her a chin lift, then turned back to his game, but she could feel his gaze on her as she continued toward the end of the bar. It felt good. Both that she could have an entire conversation with him from across a room, and that he was willing to drop everything to come to her if she needed him.

As much as she wanted to spend time with Vincent, the urge to talk to the man the others called Blink was stronger at the moment.

Her heart was breaking for him, this stranger, and she couldn't help but think about Vincent being in his place. What if it had been *his* team that had been on a horrible mission? And this guy didn't seem to have anyone else to lean on. She hated that. She felt as if she at least needed to make an effort to check on him. He might rebuff her efforts. Might be a jerk to her, as he'd apparently been to others. But she wouldn't be able to sleep if she didn't at least try.

Marley had called her a softie more than once. Was sure that's how Remi had ended up with some of her less-than-desirable dates. But it was just who Remi was. She didn't like when people were hurting. Even strangers.

There was an empty seat next to the man, which probably wasn't the best sign, but Remi was determined to at least say hello.

She hoisted herself up on the barstool, and the man behind the bar told her that he'd be with her in a moment.

Now that she was here, Remi wasn't sure what to say. The man next to her hadn't even glanced her way when she'd sat down.

Taking a deep breath, she blurted, "Hi. I'm Remi."

He didn't move. Didn't seem to even hear her.

"I'm friends with Vincent...um...Kevlar. You might

know him. I guess he comes here with his team, friends, all the time."

At that, he turned to glance at her. It wasn't exactly a friendly gaze, but it wasn't hostile either. And he hadn't told her to beat it, so she gave him a smile and kept talking.

"This is my first time here. It's nice. I wasn't really expecting a place called Aces Bar and Grill to be this upscale. And that's horrible and makes me sound like a snob, but I'm not much of a bar-goer. I mean, I like going to a chain restaurant and having a glass of wine with my meal, but a bar? No. Especially in this town. No offense, but having military guys hit on me when I'm trying to enjoy a drink isn't my idea of a good time. Not that anyone really hits on me anyway. I mean, I don't exactly exude 'hit on me vibes'...but still."

He didn't comment, simply continued to stare at her. But again, he wasn't telling her to get lost, so Remi continued.

"I'm here meeting Caroline Steel and her friends tonight. And Vincent's friends. And Caroline's husband's team. It's a lot. They're all very nice, but since I'm used to sitting at home and talking to the voices in my head, being here is...loud."

"Do they talk back?"

He spoke!

Remi couldn't keep the grin off her face. She couldn't tell if he was making fun of her or not, but it didn't matter.

"All the time," she said with a shrug. "I'm an artist.

Well, a cartoonist. *I* think that's an artist, but I'm sure there are lots of people out there who would disagree. But Pecky—he's my main character—doesn't care what others think. When he wants to go on adventures, he tells me in no uncertain terms and demands I draw him in the places he wants to go."

For the first time, Remi wondered how this man got his nickname. "Do people call you Blink because you win staring contests?" she blurted. On the heels of that thought, she got an idea. "Oh! Do you mind if I write you into one of my cartoons? I can see you and Pecky having a staring contest, but he'd win—sorry. Pecky's a taco, after all, and I'm thinking he could out-stare anyone, even you. He can win, but instead of getting mad, you simply give him one of those manly chin lifts Vincent and his military friends give people, then you go back to your drink."

To her amazement, she saw the man's lips twitch upward. She'd made him smile! Her embarrassing babbling was totally worth it.

"What can I get you?" the bartender asked, taking her attention from the man next to her.

"An iced tea, please."

"Long island?"

Remi frowned in confusion. "What?"

"Long Island iced tea?"

"Is that a brand?"

A small sound had Remi whipping her attention back to the SEAL beside her. Blink, the man everyone said was depressed and grumpy, had *laughed*. He wasn't laughing now, but she'd heard it.

"A Long Island iced tea is an alcoholic drink. It's pretty strong," he told her.

Feeling stupid, Remi blushed. "Right. I knew that. No, just a plain one. No alcohol. Sweet tea if you can, please."

The bartender gave Blink a long look, then nodded at her and turned around to make her drink.

"Kevlar's good people," Blink told her.

"Yeah. I like him. A lot."

"You should be careful though. Not everyone is as... loyal, as he is."

"What do you mean?" Remi asked.

But instead of answering her, Blink picked up the beer in front of him and took a sip, staring off into space again.

Taking a risk, Remi touched his arm. She felt his muscles twitch under her hand, but he didn't move. "I'm sorry about your team. I don't know what happened, but it had to be bad. There's nothing I can say that will bring your friends back. And it has to hurt even more because you were there to witness it."

He turned his head at that, but there was no humor in his gaze. He looked...blank.

Remi wanted to slip off the barstool and go back to the other women, but she was determined to say what she felt he might need to hear.

"I'm overstepping; I know I am. But it hurts my heart to see you sitting here by yourself being sad. You know, if I died, and Marley was moping around, being Grumpy

McGrumpster to those around her who just wanted to help, I'd be pissed at *her*. I mean, I guess I wouldn't mind her being sad, because she *is* my best friend, but I'd want her to get over it and live. For me. Do all the things we'd always talked about doing and never got around to. Renting a convertible and driving through the western states like Thelma and Louise did in that movie. Eating cotton candy until we wanted to barf, even though neither of us even like the stuff. Going to Texas and taking pictures in a huge field of blue bonnets. I don't know...all that stupid stuff that looks so awesome in movies but in reality, no one has time for.

"I didn't know your friends, and as I said, I don't know what happened, but you're a SEAL. And if I didn't have Vincent when the shit hit the fan while I was in Hawaii, I wouldn't be here today. You're a hero. I know you are. And I just want to say...thank you for what you do."

"I'm no hero," he growled. Honest-to-God growled.

"That's what heroes always claim. But you saying it, doesn't make it true."

"You're kind of annoying," Blink told her.

"I know," Remi said, nodding, not turned off in the least. She squeezed his arm. "You're allowed to be sad. Allowed to be pissed. You can feel any way you want to feel. But I'm guessing any team would be lucky to have you on it. That whatever happened taught you a lot. If mistakes were made on your mission, you'd never allow them to happen again. That in itself makes you a valuable person to have at someone's back. I'll go so far as to say, if Vincent was in trouble, I'd want you there with him."

Blink stared at her with an odd expression. One she couldn't interpret.

"Sorry. I'm talking out my ass again. But I am *totally* putting you in a Pecky cartoon. Maybe I'll have you win that staring contest after all, though. Because I have to say, you're really good at it."

She was rewarded with a few crinkles around his eyes, as if he was once more amused by her. She'd take it.

"Iced tea. Sweet. Unloaded," the bartender said as he placed the glass in front of her on a napkin.

"Thanks," Remi told him, reaching for the bills she'd put in her pocket earlier.

"Put it on my tab," Blink said.

"Oh, that's okay, I can—"

"My tab," Blink repeated firmly.

"Will do," the bartender said, then walked away.

"Thank you," Remi said softly.

He didn't respond.

Remi reached out and squeezed his arm once more, then slid off the barstool. She took a step away from him, but something made her stop.

She stepped up to Blink's side, leaned in, and kissed the side of his head, near his temple.

It was a totally spontaneous action, and she wasn't even sure why she'd done it, except that she couldn't stand the sadness that seemed to be oozing from every molecule of his body.

"It's a cliché," she said softly. "But I'm gonna say it anyway. Thank you, Blink. For your service. For what you do. For what you've seen and done. For your sacrifices. I appreciate them. And you."

Then she turned and walked away without looking back. She may not have made a difference to the man, but she felt better that she'd at least tried.

CHAPTER ELEVEN

"Your new girlfriend just kissed Blink," Howler said with a curl of his lip.

Kevlar turned toward the bar, where he'd already seen Remi sitting next to the other SEAL, and watched as she walked back toward the table with the women. "What?"

"His head. She kissed his *head*. Jeez, Howler, don't give the man a heart attack," Safe told him.

"A kiss is a kiss. If that was my woman, I wouldn't want her kissing another man. Especially one like *him*," Howler said.

"Leave him alone," Flash growled.

"He's been an asshole all night," Howler protested.

"And he has a good reason," Flash returned immediately. "Cut him some slack."

"Wonder what she said to him," Preacher mused.

"Because I'll be damned if he doesn't look less pissed off at the world than he usually does."

Kevlar studied the SEAL sitting in his usual spot at the bar and realized Preacher was right. Blink was still sitting there with his shoulders hunched, staring at nothing...but he had a sort of half smile on his lips that definitely hadn't been there before. Hell, hadn't been there since returning from his last mission.

It didn't surprise Kevlar in the least that his Remi had somehow gotten through the shields the broken SEAL had shored up around him ever since that mission had gone so fucking wrong.

"Still wouldn't want my woman kissing someone else," Howler grumbled.

But Kevlar dismissed his friend's words. He'd already had more than enough to drink tonight, and something was up Howler's ass lately. He wasn't going to take anything he'd said to heart.

Ever since Kevlar had returned from Hawaii and the team had begun to prepare for their next mission, Howler had been even more difficult than usual. It was always his job to play devil's advocate when they were strategizing. To point out the holes in any plans, to bring up points that were in opposition to what the others suggested, but for this upcoming mission, he seemed more...angry about his role. As if he was taking everything personally, which he'd never done in the past.

Kevlar had been thinking about asking Flash to take over Howler's role, to be the one to bring up alternate viewpoints and suggestions to make them one hundred percent sure what they were planning was absolutely best for the mission. Howler wouldn't like it, but if he couldn't keep his emotions or whatever was going on with his personal life *out* of the planning sessions, then things needed to change.

"She fits you," Smiley told Kevlar.

"She keeps checking on you, which is fucking adorable," MacGyver added.

"Yeah. Looks over here as if she wants to make sure you're all right," Safe agreed.

"As if Kevlar needs looking after," Howler said with a snort. "He's with a dozen freaking Navy SEALs. What does she think's gonna happen? A bunch of tangos are gonna break through the wall and take us out?"

"Maybe she just likes looking at his ass," Preacher suggested.

Everyone burst out laughing, and Kevlar couldn't help but like that thought.

"Maybe he should give her something to look at, then. Why don't you go over to the other side of the table and try to put the three ball in the corner pocket?" Flash said as he lifted one brow suggestively.

"You tryin' to show *his* ass off to *my* woman?" Dude asked, obviously overhearing the conversation.

"As if Cheyenne would look at anyone else," Cookie told his friend as he slapped him on the shoulder.

"She knows better," Dude said with a little smirk.

"Need to find me a submissive woman," Howler said.

"One who does *what* I want, *when* I want. Must be nice to have someone at your beck and call. Maybe I'll try ordering around the next Frog Hog I take home, put her on her knees where she belongs."

"Watch it, Howler," Dude said in a low, harsh voice that was nothing like the teasing tone he'd had a minute ago. "A woman's submission is a gift, not something to be forced on her."

"I was kidding, jeez. Take a chill pill," Howler retorted.

"What did you just say to me?" Dude asked, putting down the pool stick he'd been holding and taking a step toward Howler.

"Come on, Dude, enough," Wolf said firmly, stepping in front of his friend.

"How many drinks have you had, Howler?" Kevlar asked, blocking him from Dude as well.

"Always the team leader, huh?" Howler sneered. "Always in charge, even in a bar. I have news for you, buddy, you don't know everything. Not even close."

"Never said I did," Kevlar said calmly. Howler always got a little belligerent when he drank. That was nothing new. But tonight, he didn't like his nasty attitude. Not at all.

"Whatever. I'm done here. Met the new side piece like a good little teammate. She's not up to your standards, Kevlar. And I'm probably the only one brave enough to say it out loud. She's frumpy and plain and she was just hitting on another SEAL right in front of your face, but you're so hard up you didn't even notice or care. Mark my words—

once she's ridden your cock, she'll be gone. Just like all the other bitches who lust after SEALs."

"Too far," Cookie snapped as he wrapped a hand around Kevlar's arm.

Kevlar hadn't realized he'd taken his own threatening step toward his friend until Cookie stopped him. "Go home and sleep it off," he told Howler between clenched teeth.

"Or just get the hell out of here," Wolf barked, clearly pissed off. "Remi reminds me a lot of my Caroline. Women don't need to be on the cover of a magazine to be beautiful, you dumbass. It's what's *inside* that makes them that way."

"Figures *you'd* say that," Howler said. "I'm out of here. Going to The Golden Oyster, where at least the women are honest about what they want. One night with a big cock. Both of which I'm happy to supply," he said, slurring slightly. "Don't come crying to us when she leaves you after the first mission she has to deal with, Kevlar."

"I won't," he muttered, as he watched Howler weave toward the door.

"Is he driving?" Mozart asked.

"No. He always takes a taxi or an Uber when we go out now, because we always take his keys away from him, and he doesn't like having to arrange to get his car back to his place the next day," Preacher explained.

"At least that's something," Benny muttered.

"Wow, he's an *asshole*," Abe said, after Howler was gone.

"He's not always that way," Flash said, defending their teammate.

Kevlar didn't speak up to defend him. He was disgusted with his friend. They'd been through hell together, literally, and always had each other's backs. But hearing him disparage Remi made Kevlar want to pound his friend into the ground. He'd overstepped. Big time. Howler's words didn't make him think twice about being with her, but they *definitely* made him second-guess bringing her around the team.

Well, around Howler. And that sucked.

"Don't listen to him," Smiley told him.

"I'm not."

"She did kiss Blink—the side of his head, not a *kiss*-kiss—but I'm thinking if anyone needed a woman's compassion and kindness, it's him," Cookie said.

Kevlar didn't disagree, but after the confrontation and ugly words from Howler, the evening had lost its shine.

It seemed Howler's departure had also drawn the attention of the women, as they were looking over at them with concern.

"Looks like the ladies might be done with their girls' night," Dude said. "Think I'll take Cheyenne home."

"I'm sure April will be glad to see her mom," Mozart said, as he walked over to the rack on the wall to put his stick away.

The others did the same, and before Wolf passed him, he patted Kevlar on the back. "She's a keeper. I knew the moment I met Caroline that she was special. And I was right. When you know, you know. Don't let her get away."

"Don't plan on it," Kevlar replied.

Wolf nodded and headed for the table.

"Howler *is* being an asshole," Safe told him once the other men were gone. "He was way out of line tonight."

"I don't know what's crawled up his ass lately," Kevlar replied.

"I'll talk to him," Flash offered.

"Not sure it'll help," Preacher muttered.

"Fuck him," MacGyver said firmly. "Remi's awesome. We like her. She's good for you, Kevlar. Having a life outside missions and the Navy is a good thing. And it gives me hope that of all of us assholes, if you can catch the eye of someone as sweet as Remi, maybe we can too."

"Thanks," Kevlar said, feeling a little better but still wanting to get the hell out of there.

"Go," Smiley prodded. "Take your woman home."

His woman. That sounded amazing. He nodded at his friends and made his way to where Remi was hugging the other women goodbye at the table.

* * *

"Whatever happened, it was intense," Caroline said in a low voice in Remi's ear as she hugged her. "I don't know his teammates that well, but I know my husband. And if whatever was said was enough to put that pissed-off look on his face, your man's gonna need some soothing. So...go soothe him."

Her man. Remi liked the sound of that.

She hugged the other women and watched as their

husbands claimed them and everyone walked toward the door.

"Girl, tonight was fascinating," Marley told her. "Love the women, and their husbands are hot as hell. They've definitely aged well. And Vincent's teammates..." She fanned herself. "Whew. They should put them on a recruiting poster. Not sure about that dude at the bar, but I admire you for wanting to help him."

Remi wasn't surprised her friend knew what she'd done. She and Marley knew each other almost better than they knew themselves at this point in their friendship.

"Here comes Vincent. Take him home and rip off his clothes and tell me tomorrow if he looks as good naked as he does in his wetsuit."

"Marley!" Remi exclaimed, but she couldn't say anything else because Vincent was there, wrapping an arm around her waist from behind.

"Have fun!" Marley said with a grin. "I'm headed home to the husband. I'm thinking we'll put the kids to bed early. I've been...inspired by all the eye-candy tonight."

Remi rolled her eyes. "Drive safe. Text me to let me know you made it home all right."

"I will. Don't text me when *you* get home, because it'll be way too early in the morning for me."

Remi blushed, but Marley simply laughed and waved as she headed for the door. As she watched, Safe jogged toward her through the crowd, giving Vincent a chin lift.

"What's that about?" Remi asked him.

"He's gonna walk her to her car. Make sure she's good," Vincent told her.

"Oh, that's nice. Thank you."

"You don't have to thank me for taking care of the people you love."

It was amazing that he truly didn't think he was doing anything out of the ordinary. But he was. And Remi was grateful. Thankful. Felt blessed that he was with her.

"You ready to go?"

"Yeah."

Without a word, he turned her toward the door.

"Wait, I need to pay for my drinks."

"Already taken care of," Vincent told her.

"By who?"

"Me. I won the right to pay for drinks tonight."

"Wait, *won*? I'm confused," Remi told him as they made their way to the exit.

"When there's a girls' night out, the guys take turns paying. Since you and Marley joined them tonight, I got the privilege of paying."

"I'm not sure that's a privilege," she told him dryly.

"The hell it's not," he countered.

Remi didn't understand guys, not at all. But she couldn't help but feel a warm thrill move through her at being taken care of like that. At being a part of a group of such amazing people. It wasn't as if she couldn't afford to pay for her own drinks; she could pay for *everyone's* drinks. But it was nice not to have to for once.

Vincent led her to his car and once they were on the

road, she looked over at him. He looked...perturbed. But Remi didn't think it was at her. "Things looked intense with you and your friends there at the end of the night. Everything all right?"

Instead of immediately saying yes and dismissing her concern, Remi was impressed when he shrugged and said, "Not really."

"Anything you want to talk about?" she ventured.

Vincent sighed. "Howler was being a dick."

Remi thought about his friend. He looked to be the youngest on the SEAL team. Had blond hair and blue eyes and was extremely good-looking. Like the man could probably be a model if he wanted to be. He was muscular, but not overly so. He wasn't as tall as the other SEALs, but Remi had no doubt he could hold his own when it came to combat.

But the way he'd looked at her made Remi uneasy. As if he'd been sizing her up all night, and she'd come up short.

"He said something about me, didn't he?" she blurted.

Vincent turned to glance at her, and she knew with that one look, she was right.

He sighed. "Yeah."

One word, but Remi's respect for the man next to her rose even higher.

"Vincent, it's okay if one of your friends doesn't like me. That's normal. It doesn't bother me."

He raised a brow as he looked at her again.

Remi gave him a small smile. "I mean, of course I want all your friends to click with me, but the odds of that happening are low. I'm a little weird, and I can be standoffish when I meet people for the first time. That's a result of growing up and having people only want to be my friend or go out with me because of my family's money. And you can't imagine the number of condom jokes and sexual innuendos I've had to suffer through as a result of being the daughter of the man who founded Crown Condoms. If it's just my looks he took a disliking to, I can deal with that, because I am who I am. But if it was something I actually said or did, please tell me so I can try to fix it the next time I see him."

"It wasn't anything you did," Vincent said immediately. "Something's been up Howler's ass for a while now, and I can't figure out what it is and he's not talking to me. But I'll find out sooner or later. Preferably sooner, since we have a mission coming up and if he's still being a dick, the team'll turn on him. But no, you didn't do anything offensive or that needs fixing."

"Are you upset that I talked to Blink?"

"What? No. Why would you even ask that?"

"I don't know," Remi said with a small shrug. "He's just...No one went over to talk to him tonight, and he's a fellow SEAL. I just thought that maybe he'd done something so horrible that he was a pariah or something in your circles, and maybe me talking to him set Howler off."

She knew she was right when Vincent winced slightly.

"It *was* me talking to him that upset your friend, wasn't it?" she probed.

"Blink's not a pariah. We all feel bad for him, but we're

not sure what to say that will help him cope with what happened to his team. As I said before, Howler's got something going on, it's got nothing to do with you. And you can talk to whoever you want. I'm not the kind of man who doesn't want his girlfriend associating with anyone but him. As long as I know you're coming home with me at the end of the night, you can talk to anyone you'd like."

His words made her feel all warm and fuzzy. But she still wanted to clear the air about Blink. "He's hurting, Vincent. I don't know what happened, but it's eating at him. He's actually kind of sweet, in a grumpy-old-man kind of way. He looked like he needed a friend. I totally embarrassed myself, said all sorts of stupid things, but he *smiled*, Vincent. And even laughed once! Was probably laughing *at* me for being such a dork, but I don't care because I got him to smile. I wasn't hitting on him, I just felt the urge to talk to him a little. Let him know that I appreciated everything he's done for our country...even if I don't know what that is."

"You told him that?" Vincent asked.

"Yeah. He didn't respond, and I didn't really give him a chance. He didn't like that I called him a hero, but tough. He is. As are you and all your friends. No, don't shake your head, you *are*," Remi insisted almost fiercely. "If you hadn't been there in Hawaii..." Her voice trailed off and she shuddered.

Vincent reached over and took her hand in his and squeezed.

Remi took a deep breath to control her emotions. She

didn't want to cry. The night had actually been really good, and she'd enjoyed herself. She refused to think about what-ifs.

"I kissed him," she blurted. Then hurried on so Vincent wouldn't get the wrong idea. "I don't know if you saw me do that or not, but it didn't mean anything. I mean, it did, but not in the way it does when I kiss you. It was just on the side of his head. I just wanted him to know that no matter how alone he might feel, there was someone who cared about him. As a friend. Even though I'm pretty sure he was just tolerating me being in his space and talking to him. But that's all it was."

"Relax, Remi. It's fine. I know what your kisses do for *me*, and I have a feeling Blink needed your special brand of care more than most people."

Her muscles, which she hadn't realized were tense, loosened.

He pulled up to her condo, and Remi's eyes widened in surprise. The ride home hadn't taken nearly as long as she'd thought, hoped, it would.

Without a word, Vincent turned off the engine and reached for his door handle. "I'll walk you up," he said, making it clear he wouldn't take no for an answer.

Remi got out and smiled a little when he took her hand in his as they walked toward her door. She noticed that Vincent's head was on a swivel, looking around the area as they approached her front door.

"You should get the bushes around your door trimmed," he said almost casually. "Someone could hide in them and you wouldn't know they were there until you'd opened your door, and they came up behind you and pushed you inside."

She shivered at the vision his words created in her head.

He swore under his breath. "Sorry, didn't mean to scare you."

"No, you're right. I'd much rather be safe than sorry." Remi unlocked her door, then turned to him and asked shyly, "You want to come in?"

"Yes. But I'm not."

Remi frowned. "You aren't?"

Vincent stepped forward and took her face in his hands. He tilted it up to his and stared down at her for a long moment.

"Why?" she whispered. "I want you to." Later, she'd be embarrassed at how desperate she sounded, but right now she simply wanted to spend more time with this man. To take him to her bed and show him how much she wanted him.

"I want to come inside more than I want my next breath. But you know what I want more?"

"What?" she asked, trying not to let disappointment overwhelm her.

"You in my bed a year from now. You smiling at me across the breakfast table. You waiting for me when I return from missions. Your brand of kindness and goodness infecting all my friends. You being there for my fellow

SEALs when they're at the end of their rope and are struggling to find a reason to continue on.

"I want more than one night, Remi. I want it all from you. All your mornings, all your nights, your tears, laughter, hearing you babble on about anything that comes to mind, and seeing you look up at me exactly how you are right now, as if you're two seconds from ripping my clothes from my body and you'll die if you can't have me right this second."

Was that how she was looking at him? Remi wasn't exactly surprised. She licked her lips and loved how she felt his erection against her belly. "And you can't have all that if you come inside now?" she asked.

"I don't know, can I? I don't want you to be with me out of some sense of gratitude for what happened in Hawaii. I don't want to be some sort of rebound fuck because you're feeling emotional about everything. I want to be in your bed because you want what I want. A future."

Remi opened her mouth to assure him that she *did* want that. But he put a finger on her lips.

"All I'm asking is for you to be sure. To think about it. Really think about it. Being with a SEAL isn't a walk in the park. I'm hoping Caroline and the others made that clear tonight. I'm gone a lot. When you need me, there will be a lot of times I won't be there. You'll have to mow the grass yourself, fix the toilet when it breaks, wipe the tears off our little girl's face when she falls and skins her knee. Being with you tonight, then having you decide you can't do it, can't live the life of a SEAL's wife...I have a feeling it would change me in ways that wouldn't be good."

Remi could understand that. He'd just gotten out of a bad relationship, and she actually respected the fact that he didn't want just sex.

"You aren't a rebound," she told him. "I was over Douchecanoe way before I finally broke things off. You are *nothing* like him. And if the grass needs mowing or the toilet breaks, I'll call someone to take care of it or do it myself. And I'm strong enough to take care of our family until you get home to kiss our booboos, dry our tears, and celebrate any milestones you might have missed."

He closed his eyes as he struggled to control his emotions. She saw it in his face; what she'd said meant something. Remi slid her hands up his chest. She wrapped one around his nape, and the other she used to pull him closer. His hands dropped from her face and curled around her waist.

"I'm sure, Vincent. But I can wait until *you're* sure. I'm not with you because of your job or gratitude. I respect what you do and am damn thankful that you were the one on that boating trip with me. But I can feel gratitude and respect about other people, and still not want to invite them into my bed. I want you there because you're *you*. When you're ready, I'll be here. I've never felt about a man the way I feel about you."

His eyes opened, and he stared at her with such longing, it almost brought her to her knees.

"You make it extremely difficult to be a gentleman."

Remi snort-laughed. "You, Vincent Hill, are no gentleman. And I can't wait to experience every part of you. Just cut me some slack, because I have a feeling I'm not going to live up to your expectations at first." She was blushing now, but refused to look away from him.

"Are you kidding me? Being around you makes me feel as if it's my first time all over again."

Remi smiled. "Are you sure you don't want to come in?" she teased.

"I'm going to kiss you, sweetheart."

"You won't hear me complaining," she retorted.

Then his lips were on hers, and Remi swore she saw stars. He made love to her mouth, and every nerve ending in her body tingled to life. She wanted him. Deep inside, fucking her hard and deep with the cock she could still feel against her belly. The kiss wasn't enough. She needed more. Needed his hands all over her. His mouth.

She pulled back with a gasp and stared up at him. "How long?" she asked.

He frowned in confusion. "What?"

Remi felt a little better that he seemed as befuddled as she was. "How long do you need to wait before you're sure of my intentions toward you? A week? Two? A year? How long are you going to make me wait?"

He smiled. "I'm not sure there's a timetable to this, sweetheart."

She studied him. Then said, "Twenty-three phone calls, two more get-togethers with your team, four one-on-one dates, a third-base make-out session, an afternoon at my parents' house, and dinner with me at Marley's place. That should convince you that I'm serious."

"Fifteen calls, one more get-together with my team, two one-on-one dates, meeting your family and Marley's, and *three* third-base make-out sessions," he countered.

"Deal."

"Damn, you didn't even think about it," Vincent teased.

"Don't need to. I was the one who invited you in tonight, remember?"

More emotion passed through Vincent's eyes before he closed them and rested his forehead against hers.

"Just don't hurt me," Remi whispered. "I couldn't take it. My heart couldn't take it."

His eyes opened at that. "I won't. I promise."

"Thank you."

He kissed her again, and the electric currents once more shot through her system. He pulled back and stepped away from her way before she was ready. Remi licked her lips, still tasting him there. She wanted more, but respected him enough to give him what he needed. Namely, the reassurance that she was in this relationship for the long haul.

"In, Remi. Lock the door. I'll talk to you soon."

She nodded and backed into the doorway.

Vincent stood on her walkway looking so damn gorgeous, it made her heart hurt. It was still hard to believe he was interested in her. Nerdy Remi Stephenson, the cartoonist.

He grinned. "You going in?"

"Yeah." But she didn't move.

"Remi," he warned with a small frown.

She giggled, then slowly closed the door. Once it was shut, she turned the dead bolt, then peered through the security peephole. Vincent ran a hand through his hair, adjusted his crotch with a grimace, then finally turned and headed back to his car. Remi couldn't keep her gaze from dropping to his ass. He definitely had a good one. She noticed at the bar when he was playing pool, but up close and personal, it was even better.

Smiling, she turned her back to the door, still grinning like a fool. Her body was still humming from his kisses. Was she disappointed that she wasn't in her bed right now, rolling around with Vincent? Yes. But deep down, she was satisfied with how the evening had gone. The respect he was showing her, wanting to be sure that they weren't engaging in some short-term fling, felt amazing.

Her phone rang as she was still standing there replaying the evening, and Remi dug into her purse for her cell. Frowning when she saw it was Vincent calling, she answered. Not giving him a chance to say a word, she asked, "Are you all right?"

"Yes. This is one. Want to get them done."

"One?" she asked in confusion.

"One phone call. We agreed on fifteen."

Remi's lips curled up into a huge smile. "Right. One. Where are you?"

"Just pulled out of your parking lot."

"Oh."

"Miss you already."

"Well, I feel the need to point out that you could still be here."

"I'm questioning my sanity at this point," Vincent retorted.

"I think you did the right thing," she admitted.

He paused, then said, "Yeah. I think the fact that I want this relationship to work so badly has made me nervous," Vincent said. "Made me cautious."

"Cautious isn't a bad thing," she told him.

"What's your schedule for tomorrow?" he asked.

"I really need to get some drawing time in. I have a deadline coming up, and I've got a ton of ideas rolling around in my head for Pecky and his friends. What about you?"

"More meetings for that mission that's coming up."

"But it's Sunday," Remi protested.

"Lesson number one of being with a SEAL...there's no such thing as weekends."

"Right," she said with a nod.

"I don't know how long we'll be tomorrow. But if I get off base early enough, you want to have dinner? With me?"

Remi grinned at how nervous he sounded. "Yes. I can cook for us."

"How about if I pick you up and bring you to my place? It's nothing fancy, but I can grill up some chicken, or steaks, or veggies if you'd prefer."

"Sounds perfect."

"Which one?"

"All of it."

Vincent chuckled. "All right. I'll text you tomorrow to check in and let you know what the plan is."

"Okay."

"Remi?"

"Yeah?"

"Thank you."

"For what?"

"For understanding. For being awesome. For being there for Blink tonight. I've tried to talk to him in the past, with no luck. But it's obvious I should've tried harder. All of us need to step up and make sure he knows that he's not alone. That we're there for him."

"You don't have to thank me for that," Remi protested.

"I do. And I did."

"You're welcome."

"I'll talk to you tomorrow. Sleep well, sweetheart."

"You too. Drive safe. Will you let me know when you get home?"

"Yeah. Thanks for a good night."

"Thank *you*. Talk to you later."

"Later."

Remi clicked off the phone and realized she had a goofy smile on her face. Didn't they always say that anticipation made things better? She didn't know who "they" were or what "things" they were talking about, but she prayed in her case, in regard to being intimate with Vincent, *they* were right.

* * *

Brandon "Howler" Starrett stared up at the ceiling as the Frog Hog he'd picked up at The Golden Oyster bounced up and down on his cock. He didn't remember her name, not that it mattered. He needed to get off, and she wanted to fuck a SEAL. They were both getting what they wanted. But Howler's mind wasn't on what the bitch was doing.

He couldn't stop thinking about how unfair things had become at work. He'd worked his goddamn ass off while Kevlar was fucking around in Hawaii. He'd researched the situation in Chad, where they were heading for their next mission. He'd done what he could to get the information their commander wanted, and yet as soon as Kevlar returned, everyone had conveniently forgotten his hard work, turning to Kevlar for intel instead.

He was sick of being overlooked. Of Kevlar getting all the attention and accolades.

"Oooh, baby, you're so hard. So big. Touch me, squeeze my tits," the woman moaned from above him.

Fuck that. He did what he wanted, when he wanted. *He* was in charge, not her. He didn't want to hear her voice. All he wanted was to fuck.

He grabbed her hips and pushed her off him. His dick popped out of her pussy with a loud squelch, and he immediately climbed to his knees and pushed her face into the covers. He yanked her ass up and smacked it hard. He could see his handprint bloom on her white skin. He lined his cock up and shoved himself back into her pussy.

She moaned into the sheet and arched. She was loving this. Loving his domination.

Howler held her hips tightly as he rocked in and out of her willing body. But even as good as she felt, he was a long way from getting off. He was getting more out of being in charge than the actual fucking. He craved the control.

Because he had no control whatsoever as a SEAL. He was a grunt. Just another warm body to carry a weapon and do what someone else ordered.

He wanted to be the one in charge. The one ordering everyone else around. The one planning the missions. He was just as good as fucking Kevlar. He'd been through the same training. Hell, he'd *carried* Kevlar through Hell Week, more than the man had helped him.

So why had *he* been chosen as fucking team leader over Howler?

He thrust harder into the woman, getting angrier and angrier about his fucked-up life. He barely heard her moans, which were probably fake anyway.

He'd thought he'd taken care of this problem. It was why he'd worked so hard for months to show his commander that he'd be just as good, *better*, as team leader —he'd assumed Kevlar wouldn't return from Hawaii.

Because he'd done everything in his power to make that happen.

How was he supposed to know the asshole would bring his wetsuit on vacation? And that he'd have that fucking tracker Tex used to watch over them?

The trackers were fucked up. Howler didn't want or

need someone babysitting him. When he was in charge, he'd order his team to leave that shit at home. He didn't need some old fart in his basement in Pennsylvania watching his every move. It was a pussy thing to do, and it figured that the damn guy and his trackers ruined his plans.

He'd hoped Kevlar would die in that ocean. The captain was supposed to bring him *twenty* miles offshore and leave him behind. He'd known Kevlar was a goddamn SEAL. Instead, Howler had learned the captain got lazy and greedy, not wanting to use all his fuel. He'd dropped him eight miles from Oahu.

He'd waited impatiently that day, expecting to get a call from his commander that Kevlar was reported missing. He'd been ready to fly to Hawaii immediately to put on a good show of organizing the search for his friend and teammate, to prove to everyone that he was able to be team leader...

But instead, he got the call that the asshole had been *rescued*.

Not only that, but the passenger on the boat with him, who should've just been collateral damage, was actually from the area—and now Kevlar fancied himself in love.

Everything had gone wrong.

Howler wasn't the new team leader. He was still a fucking grunt.

Kevlar wasn't dead. He was very much alive, and happier than ever with the new bitch in his life.

It wasn't fucking fair!

Howler *deserved* to be team leader. He was so angry

and jealous, he couldn't fucking see straight. He was just as smart as fucking Kevlar, and yet, everyone still looked to *him* for guidance. Even now, the others on the team were bending over backward to please him. So frickin' happy for him that he'd found some new pussy. It was disgusting.

But more important than any of that—Kevlar had Tex and that old-ass former SEAL in Hawaii trying to figure out who'd hired the captain to leave his ass in the middle of the ocean.

They couldn't discover it was him. If they did, his SEAL career would be over. And that wasn't acceptable.

Howler had covered his tracks, he was too damn smart to leave any trace that he was the one who'd arranged for Kevlar to fucking disappear. And he'd taken care of the one loose end that could link him to the events in Hawaii.

The captain.

Tex had surely known who'd piloted the boat before Kevlar was even rescued. And when the captain called to tell Howler that Kevlar and Remi had been grabbed from the ocean by Baker, he knew what had to be done.

He'd immediately called the man who'd delivered the burner phone to the captain...but instead of delivering the rest of the money for the job, as the captain demanded, his contact had gone to the man's shitty apartment and silenced him—permanently.

As planned, the police had ruled his death an accidental fentanyl overdose. The asshole wouldn't be talking to Tex, or Baker, or *anyone*, ever again.

And Howler's contact in Hawaii? No one would find him. He was a ghost. Disappearing into the wind.

Smiling at the thought, Howler glanced down. He didn't know how long he'd been screwing the Frog Hog, but she was no longer faking any moans. In fact, she looked uninterested as he pounded in and out of her. Fucking bitch.

Howler grabbed a fistful of her hair, and she yelped as he yanked her head up. "Bored?" he sneered.

"No! You feel great. Awesome. Oh, baby!" she crooned.

She was a big fat liar. Saying what she thought he wanted to hear. Just like everyone did with fucking Kevlar. Sucking up to him.

If Howler couldn't kill him, he needed to take him down a peg. Hurt him in a way that would put him out of commission, that would allow Howler a chance to show the commander and everyone else that he could lead the team just as well.

Breaking a leg would be perfect, his back or neck even better, but Howler wasn't sure how to do that without getting involved personally.

He thought of their evening at Aces...of Kevlar's new woman kissing that pathetic loser, Blink...

He'd watched the asshole for a couple of weeks now. Seen how broken he'd become after one bad mission—which made him a sorry excuse for a SEAL in Howler's eyes. If he couldn't handle the dark side of their job, then he shouldn't be in special forces.

But the man gave Howler an idea.

He realized that breaking Kevlar *emotionally* would be just as effective as breaking him physically.

Even Howler could see just how far Kevlar was already gone on his latest pussy. He could use that fact to his advantage...

His lips curled, and he felt his balls draw up against his body as he considered options in his head. A kidnapping, maybe. Kevlar would be consumed with finding the bitch he thought he loved. He'd get thrown off his game, wouldn't be able to function in his role as a SEAL. But the mission in Chad would still need to continue.

Howler would volunteer to take over the team and lead them into Africa.

Satisfied that he could use Remi to take out Kevlar, even if he'd have to strike quickly, Howler pulled out of the bitch on her knees and jerked his dick frantically as he imagined himself kicking ass as the SEAL in charge in Chad. The accolades would pour in, he'd get the respect he deserved, and Kevlar and the rest of the team would finally see how badly they'd underestimated him.

Remi Stephenson would be collateral damage. But all was fair in love and war, and Howler would claw his way to his rightful position at the top of the heap no matter who got hurt in the process.

Grunting as his orgasm finally hit, Howler watched as his come sprayed all over the Frog Hog's ass and back. As soon as he was done, he shoved the woman and she fell onto her side.

"Get out," he growled.

"What?" she asked, looking at him in confusion.

"Did I stutter?" Howler asked. "I said, get out."

"Asshole," she muttered.

Howler moved before the woman could blink. He grabbed her around the neck and pressed her into the mattress. "What did you call me?" he hissed.

She scratched at his hand, trying to pry his fingers off her throat. "Nothing," she croaked.

He loved the look of fear in her eyes. "That's right, bitch. I'm in charge. I could do anything I wanted to you right now and no one would know. No one would care about a whore like you. You bagged a SEAL, now get the fuck out. And if I hear the slightest whisper of you complaining about what happened here tonight, you'll regret it. You got exactly what you came for. You begged me to take you home. You begged for my cock. Don't pretend it was anything other than what it was. Understand?"

He loosened his grip enough for her to nod. Feeling on top of the world, and loving the feeling of power he had over the bitch, Howler backed off.

He lay on the mattress and smirked at her as she scampered away from him and fumbled with her clothes. He loved that his stare was making her uncomfortable. Loved watching her tits bounce as she tried to put on her shirt. His come was still on her ass and back, and Howler felt a dark thrill at the fact that she'd have his mark on her until she got home and showered.

She didn't look back as she left his room. He heard his

front door slam, and Howler smiled as he rolled onto his back. With one hand behind his head and the other resting on his belly, he realized he felt amazing. Energized.

He had a lot to figure out, to plan, and little time to do it, but he'd get it done. Kevlar would be taken down, Howler would get the promotion he deserved, and everything would work out the way it was meant to.

His time to be in charge was coming, and he couldn't fucking wait.

CHAPTER TWELVE

Kevlar ran a hand through his hair in frustration. It had been a full week since he'd seen Remi. Since he'd dropped her off at her door and kissed the hell out of her...and since he'd lost his mind and refused to go into her condo. He didn't know what had come over him, it was obvious she was inviting him in to do more than talk. But as he stood there, he'd had the overwhelming urge to slow things down. To not rush into being intimate with her.

The last thing he wanted was for her to think they were having a short fling. A one-night stand. That wasn't the kind of man he was any longer. With Remi, he wanted more. He wanted it all.

Seeing her with his teammates, with Wolf's wife and her friends, with Blink, he'd realized that he was on the cusp of something special, and he didn't want to do anything that might mess it up. So he'd come up with the asinine idea to put off having sex, so she'd know for certain that wasn't all he wanted from her.

But now, a week later and with the universe conspiring against him, he was regretting not taking what she'd offered when he had the chance. He knew better. Knew his schedule was unpredictable. Knew the bad guys of the world could act out at any time and screw up his well-planned intentions.

Fifteen calls. What a joke. He'd talked to Remi at least double that by now. But he'd made no headway toward the other items they'd agreed on before taking the next step in their relationship. It was hard to meet her parents and her best friend's family when he couldn't get away from work other than way late at night or too early in the morning.

He was frustrated, and missing Remi, and tired, and sick of the petty arguments Howler kept initiating in their planning and intel meetings. He'd been almost insubordinate throughout the last week—and Kevlar was done. He needed to find out what was up his friend's ass. *Now*.

Sighing, Kevlar looked at his watch and winced. Eight-thirty. He'd had no idea it was so late. He'd gotten to work around eight that morning and was still there. This was the first time he'd had a chance to breathe. He and his teammates were wrapping up their intelligence gathering for the mission to Chad. Their commander, along with a couple of captains and even a rear admiral, had been included in their briefings today. Kevlar hadn't even had more than a few moments to text Remi and let her know he was thinking about her.

The longer he went without seeing her, the more worried he got that she'd rethink everything between them. Being told he would be gone a lot and experiencing it firsthand, before they'd gotten a chance to really cement their relationship, were two very different things. And the last thing he wanted was her calling it quits before they'd barely even begun.

He couldn't help but recall all the things Bertie had said when she'd broken up with him. How she'd felt abandoned. How he hadn't been there when she'd needed him the most. The echoes of her words rattled around in his head, and it was almost enough to make him throw in the towel and forget about attempting a relationship with *anyone*.

"We've been at this for hours. Take tomorrow morning off," their commander said after the rear admiral had left the conference room. "We'll meet up again after lunch. Maybe then we'll have better evidence on where the HVT is holed up and we can make concrete plans."

The break was much needed. Kevlar wondered if he could somehow manage to see Remi in the morning before he had to get back to the base.

As if his thoughts had conjured her, his phone rang and her name appeared on the display.

Smiling, Kevlar answered. "Hey, I was just thinking about you."

To his surprise—and concern—all he heard for a moment was yelling. Then Remi said his name in a shaky voice. "Vincent? Are you done with your meetings for the day?"

"What's wrong? Who's yelling?" Kevlar asked.

"It's Douchecanoe. He's here. And he's really mad."

"He's where?" Kevlar asked.

"Here. At my condo. He wanted to come inside and talk but I wouldn't open the door. Now he's pissed and won't go away."

"I'm coming. Do *not* open that door." Safe and Howler were the only two members of his team still left in the room. He put his hand over the phone and said urgently, "I need you guys."

To his relief, both men immediately nodded. Things between him and Howler had been strained, so Kevlar was a little surprised when he didn't even hesitate to have his back, no questions asked.

"I'm not planning on opening the door, but he's pounding pretty hard," Remi said.

Kevlar could hear the pounding loud and clear over the phone line. He could also hear the fear in Remi's voice. He was already on the move, his friends at his heels. "What's he mad about?" he asked, needing some answers.

"He's claiming I called the cops on him. Says they came to his job and accused him of trying to kill me. He says if he gets fired, it'll be my fault."

"All right, take a breath, honey. Did you call nine-one-one?"

"No, I called you first."

It felt incredible that the first person she wanted to call for help when she felt threatened was him, but he was too damn far away. It would take at least ten minutes for him and his friends to get to her condo. "I need you hang up and call the police," he told her. It was one of the hardest things he'd ever done. He wanted to keep her on the line, know that she was all right. But he needed her to be safe more.

"Okay." She sounded lost. And so very far away.

"I'm coming, Remi. Hear me? I'm coming. I'll be there soon, but the police can get there faster."

"Yeah," she agreed.

"If you need to hide, do so. Do you have somewhere you can hide?"

"Not really. The bathroom maybe."

"Then go there. Lock the door. Stay low." He wanted to tell her to grab a weapon, but he didn't want to think about her having to use it. Didn't know if she *could*.

"Right. I'm taking a knife from the kitchen too."

So much for him thinking she couldn't defend herself. To his relief, however, being told what to do seemed to give her confidence. Now that she had some sort of plan, her brain seemed to be kicking in.

"I'm sorry I bothered you. I wasn't sure what to do."

"You could *never* bother me, sweetheart," Kevlar told her firmly. "Now get upstairs. Call the police. I'll be there as soon as I can."

"Okay. Drive safe."

He wanted to laugh. There she was, scared out of her mind, with her ex yelling at her and pounding at her door. She felt threatened, worried enough to call him for help, and she was telling *him* to drive safe. "Hang on, Remi. Stay strong."

"I'll try," she whispered, then she hung up.

He'd jumped into Safe's Jeep Wrangler while he'd been talking to Remi, and Howler had gotten into the back. Safe was driving like a bat out of hell, which Kevlar appreciated.

"Sitrep," Howler said as soon as Kevlar lowered the phone from his ear.

"Remi's ex is at her condo, not pleased that the cops came to question him about Hawaii," he said succinctly. "She's calling nine-one-one now."

"She called you before the police?" Safe asked, taking a second to glance at Kevlar.

"Apparently."

"You're so in there," he said with a small grin.

"Don't give a shit about that, just want her to be safe," Kevlar said between clenched teeth.

"When we get there, we should split up," Howler said. "I'll go to the front with the ex. Kevlar, you and Safe can head around the house to make sure he doesn't try to get away. Maybe there's a back door that's unlocked, so you can get inside and deal with Remi's hysterics. Once the tango's out of commission, we can figure out our next steps."

"No fucking way," Kevlar told his teammate. "There's no need to go around the house if Douchecanoe is at the front. And there's no need for you to confront him alone. I don't know shit about this guy. I don't know if he's a fighter, if he's armed. The three of us can take him down easier together.

Then I'll call Remi when it's safe, so she can come downstairs and unlock the door. But I'm hoping the police will already have the situation under control by the time we get there."

"And if they don't?" Safe asked.

"Then we'll assess at that point. There's no fucking need to skulk around the house like a bunch of bad B-movie actors. I have a feeling when he sees us, this asshole will just piss his pants and try to get the hell out of there."

He hoped. The closer they got to Remi's condo, the more nervous Kevlar became. He had no idea what they'd find when they arrived. He hoped like hell the cops would already be there, as he'd told Howler, and have things under control.

Safe made a hard turn onto Remi's street and, to Kevlar's relief, they could see blue and red lights swirling in the dark night. They couldn't park close to Remi's condo because of all the cop cars, so Safe pulled into a parking spot near the entrance to the lot, and Kevlar was out and moving before he'd even stopped the vehicle.

"I'm on your six," Howler told him as they ran.

Kevlar barely heard him. All he could think about was getting to Remi. Making sure she was okay.

There was a man face down on the grass with an officer's knee in his back. Miles, he assumed. He was yelling that his rights were being infringed upon, that he hadn't done anything wrong. Even as Kevlar ran by, the officers hauled Miles upright, his hands now cuffed behind him, and led him toward one of their vehicles.

"Damn, we missed all the fun," Howler complained.

Kevlar wanted to protest that this wasn't fun, not at all, but he'd arrived at Remi's front door and didn't get the chance.

"Stop!" the officer standing there ordered.

"Where's Remi?" Kevlar barked.

"You can't go in there," the same officer told him sternly.

"Officer, that's my girlfriend in there."

"Yeah, well, that guy claims *he's* her boyfriend too," the officer said with narrowed eyes, gesturing toward the police car where Douchecanoe had been led.

"He's her ex. Please, I need to see her," Kevlar begged.

The officer must've heard something in his voice, because his next words were a little gentler. "We're clearing the house now. Making sure there aren't any perpetrators inside, just in case. When we're sure it's clear, we'll talk to the victim, see if it's okay to let you in."

Kevlar wanted to push inside and go to Remi, but he felt a hand on his arm, pulling him away from the front door. The urge to shrug his friend off was strong, but he knew he needed to stay calm. Remi needed him, and he couldn't risk pissing off the police officers and having them detain him as well.

"We totally could've taken him," Howler muttered from Kevlar's other side. "Wouldn't have been an issue if we got to him first."

For the first time in a week, Kevlar agreed with his teammate.

Time seemed to pass in slow motion as he waited for

the all clear. Finally, a policewoman stuck her head out of the front door of Remi's condo and asked, "Is one of you Vincent?"

"I am," Kevlar said, stepping forward.

The woman nodded. "Ms. Stephenson's asking for you." She gestured for him to come inside.

"We'll be here in case you need anything," Safe said.

"Why should we stay? She's good now, and tomorrow's our first morning off in ages. I was gonna head to the bar."

As he entered the foyer, Kevlar heard Safe smacking Howler's head, and normally that would make him smile, but all his concentration was on getting to Remi. Seeing for himself that she was all right.

He followed the officer into the main living area. Remi was sitting on her couch with a blanket around her, and she looked...small. Her shoulders were hunched and she had a blank stare on her face.

"Remi," he said.

She turned her head at hearing his voice, and the lost look was swept off her face, replaced by one of such relief, it made Kevlar stop in his tracks. She flung off the blanket and hurried toward him, throwing herself at him.

He wrapped his arms around her so tightly, he wasn't sure he'd ever be able to let go. "Shhhh," he murmured as he felt her shaking against him. "You're okay. You're safe."

But he couldn't get her look of relief out of his mind. As if she wasn't all right until the moment she saw him. He'd never been a harbor for anyone before. Had never been anyone's safe place. It was scary and heady all at the same time.

He felt her take a deep breath, then she nodded against his chest. She leaned back but didn't let go of him. "You came," she whispered.

"Of course I did," he told her. "If it's within my power, I'll always come."

She closed her eyes at that, and when she opened them again, she seemed to have a better hold on her emotions. "Thank you," she whispered.

He opened his mouth to apologize for all the times in the future that he wouldn't be able to be there when she needed him, but an officer behind him spoke before he could.

"We need to get a statement from Ms. Stephenson."

Remi turned, but Kevlar didn't let go of her. They walked back to the couch and, after she'd sat, he picked up the blanket and wrapped it around her shoulders.

"Tell me what happened tonight," the man ordered.

"I was hanging out, watching TV, when there was a knock on my door. I wasn't expecting anyone, so it startled me. I went over and looked out the peephole and saw it was my ex."

"His name?"

"Douchecanoe," Remi said without hesitation.

Kevlar's lips twitched, before he said, "Miles Barton."

He thought he saw amusement in the other man's eyes, but he banked it and gestured for Remi to continue.

"He said something about knowing I was home, which

is creepy because he had to have been watching me or looking in my windows, which I wouldn't put past him. Anyway, I told him to go away, that I had nothing to say to him. He kind of lost it, yelling at me that if I didn't open the door, he'd break it in. That he had plenty to say to *me*. Then he went off on some rant about the cops coming to his job to talk to him about what happened to me in Hawaii, how they were accusing him. He wanted me to call off 'my goons', said he knew they were watching him. I don't know what the hell he was talking about, because I didn't hire *anyone* to follow him. I just want him to go away."

"Hawaii?" the detective asked.

Remi sighed. Then she spent the next ten minutes telling the officer about breaking up with her ex, the trip they'd planned to Hawaii, how angry he'd been when she went without him, and finally, about being left in the ocean on the snorkeling trip.

"I was with her," Kevlar finally interjected. "We were both left. I have no doubt a detective probably *did* talk to him about what happened and his possible role in it—he did tell Remi he hoped she was left in the ocean on her snorkeling trip, which seems too specific to be coincidental. But as a Navy SEAL, I've got some connections who've been trying to find out if it was her ex, or mine, who was behind that stunt. So far, they haven't come up with anything concrete. I doubt my contacts would be careless enough to hire someone who would let themselves be spotted while following a mark, so I'm thinking Miles is simply paranoid. Pissed that Remi broke up with him. Lashing out at her as a convenient target."

The officer had jotted several notes as Kevlar talked. He finally looked up, his gaze studying Kevlar, then softening a bit as he looked at Remi. "Yelling isn't exactly a crime," the man said after a moment. "Did he threaten to hurt you?"

"No," Remi said with a small shake of her head. "But he was so angry. Kept ordering me to open the door so he could talk to me. Telling me if I didn't call the police and tell them he had nothing to do with Hawaii, he could lose his job and his reputation and it would be all my fault. He swore he had nothing to do with it."

"Do you believe him?" the officer asked.

Remi pressed her lips together. "I don't know."

"Right. So, here's where we're at. We can cite him for disturbing the peace and, if you'd like, tomorrow you can file a restraining order against him so he has to stay one hundred yards away from you at all times. But since he didn't specifically threaten to do you harm, we can't arrest him."

Kevlar stiffened. "Didn't threaten her? He was pounding on her door, trying to break it down. He outweighs Remi by at least fifty pounds. If he'd been able to get in, he would've hurt her, I have no doubt of that."

"But he didn't," the officer said calmly.

"It's okay," Remi said, putting her hand on Kevlar's thigh.

It wasn't okay. It was anything *but* okay.

"Stay alert, and call us if anything else happens. If he comes back tonight."

"I will. Thanks," Remi said softly.

The officer stood up from his chair, and Remi did the same. Kevlar had no choice but to stand with them. He walked with Remi to the door and was glad to see Miles was nowhere to be seen.

Howler and Safe were still there, along with a few other officers. Most of the neighbors had gone back inside, now that the excitement seemed to be over.

"What are they doing here?" Remi asked, looking up at Kevlar.

"Who?"

"Safe and Howler."

"Oh, Safe drove me here, and Howler was still in the conference room when I got your call and offered to come."

"Did I interrupt your meeting?" she asked, her brows furrowing.

"We were done," Safe reassured her, as he and Howler approached.

"And we have the morning off," Howler said with a grin.

"Oh. And you guys got stuck in my drama. I'm so sorry."

"We aren't stuck anywhere," Safe reassured her. "Nowhere else I'd choose to be. In fact, I'm guessing the other guys'll be pissed they hadn't still been there when you called, so they could be here for you too."

"I mean, I might rather be at the bar," Howler mumbled.

Kevlar stiffened, but Remi simply chuckled. "Well, I appreciate you being here anyway. You can go now, though. I'm okay."

Howler nodded and turned, immediately heading to the parking lot and to Safe's Jeep.

But Safe didn't budge. "You sure?" he asked.

"Yeah."

"Because I'm happy to hang outside, keep watch and make sure that asshole doesn't come back after all the cops leave."

Remi tilted her head as she frowned. "You don't want to go to the bar with Howler?"

He scoffed. "No."

"And you'd be willing to sit in your car, in my parking lot, for a few hours to watch for Douchecanoe?"

"Not a few hours. All night," Safe countered.

"Why?"

"Because you're important to Kevlar, so you're important to us. Besides, I don't like bullies. And your ex sounds like a big fucking bully."

"I...um...wow."

She stepped away from Kevlar and approached Safe. When she hugged him, Kevlar wanted to laugh at the look of surprise on his friend's face. He awkwardly returned her embrace, but she didn't even seem to notice that she'd shocked him. Remi backed away, and Kevlar pulled her against his side once more.

"I appreciate the offer, but you've been working really hard and have to be exhausted. I'm sure Douchecanoe is too freaked out to come back tonight. He'd be an idiot to do so anyway. Go home, Safe. Get some sleep. Enjoy sleeping in." She grinned. "You need to continue to plan to save the world tomorrow."

Safe chuckled, then sobered. "You sure?"

"I'm sure."

He looked at Kevlar. "You need me to stay?"

Kevlar shook his head. He was on the same wavelength as Remi on this one. Miles had been pissed while on the ground in cuffs...but more than that, he'd been completely freaked out. He wouldn't risk actually getting arrested by coming back.

Besides, Kevlar had no intention of letting Remi stay here. Miles might know where she lived, but he had no idea where *his* apartment was.

"We're good," he told Safe.

His teammate gave him a chin lift, then turned and headed for his Jeep, where Howler was waiting.

The officer told them once again that if they needed anything, not to hesitate to call, before heading to his car, along with the few remaining cops.

Kevlar locked the door behind him and Remi and took a deep breath before he pulled her into his embrace. He held on tight, probably too tight, and sighed in relief as she seemed to hold on to him just as desperately.

"You scared the shit out of me," he mumbled into her hair.

"I'm sorry."

"No," Kevlar said, pulling back so he could look into her eyes. "You need me, you call. You can't get in touch with me, you call Safe. Or Smiley, Preacher, MacGyver, Flash, or Howler."

"I'm thinking Howler might not like to have his latest booty call at the bar interrupted," she joked.

But Kevlar wasn't in any mood for teasing. "I mean it, sweetheart. As much as it pains me to say this, I won't always be here when you need me. But if my team and I are unavailable, I'll make sure you have the numbers of at least a dozen other SEALs who won't hesitate to drop everything to get to you."

"I'm okay. Really. I'm usually much more...unflappable than I was tonight. I just...after Hawaii...I think I'm feeling my mortality a little more. And since we don't know if it was Douchecanoe or your ex who arranged for us to be left in the middle of the ocean...I don't know. I got scared."

"You did the right thing. There's no telling what he would've done if he got inside."

"I know."

"We aren't staying here."

"What?" she asked.

"I'm taking you to my apartment. It's not as nice as your condo, but Miles doesn't know where it is. You'll be safe there."

"I don't want him to chase me out of my home," Remi argued.

"He's not. He won't. This is just for tonight. You need

to sleep, and if you stay here, every little noise will keep you awake. You'll wonder if it's him."

"That ever happen to you?" she asked, with a little too much insight into his psyche.

He could've lied. Made a joke. But he didn't. She was too important. "Yes. After intense missions, it's sometimes hard to come home to normal life and get used to the everyday sounds out my window. Loud bangs, kids yelling, dogs barking, they all mean different things when I'm safe in my apartment than when I'm in SEAL mode."

"I bet. Okay."

"Okay what?"

"I'll come to your apartment tonight. But if I refuse to leave tomorrow because I feel safe there, don't blame me."

Her words had a profound effect on Kevlar. The thought of her moving in and never leaving sounded...perfect.

The thought should've freaked him out. He normally didn't bring women to his place, period. Even Bertie had never stayed the night in the entire year they'd dated. Of course, the few times he'd had her over to his apartment, she wasn't impressed with the area and was visibly uncomfortable in his plain, utilitarian space. She couldn't leave fast enough. Kevlar spent most of their time together at her frilly, overdecorated apartment.

But the thought of Remi in his space, his bed, had a deep longing surging through him.

"Pack as much as you want, sweetheart. You want to stay a week, a month, forever, you won't hear me complaining." The words came from his soul. From his heart. From the place he'd thought had long since given up on finding someone to spend his life with.

"Vincent," she whispered, sounding overwhelmed.

"Stop thinking. Just go pack," he ordered.

She smiled at him before nodding and backing away.

Kevlar watched her until she disappeared up the stairs, then he took a deep breath. He had no idea what just happened, but there was a definite shift somewhere deep inside him. He'd been content to go slow. To wait. To see how things played out between him and Remi. But that changed the moment he'd heard her frightened voice on the phone. When he'd realized she was in danger.

Life was short, he knew that better than anyone. And it wasn't guaranteed. One day you could think you had your whole life ahead of you, and the next, you could be lying dead on the street.

He wouldn't rush Remi, but he'd let her know in no uncertain terms that he was ready to move their relationship forward. That he wanted everything she had to give.

CHAPTER THIRTEEN

Remi felt off-kilter. She was shaky and couldn't stop looking over her shoulder. She hated that Douchecanoe had gotten to her. She'd heard him yell before, but the threatening tone in his voice tonight was something new. If he'd managed to get inside, or if she'd opened the door to him, she wasn't sure what he would've done.

Her first call should've been to the police, but she hadn't thought when she'd clicked on Vincent's name. She wasn't thinking about interrupting an important meeting, or that he might not want to get involved with a fight between her and Douchecanoe. All she'd thought about was how safe she felt when she was with him. It didn't matter that the police had arrived first.

She'd heard him yelling her name as he'd approached her condo. And that meant the world to her.

He'd come.

As soon as he could, he'd come when she needed him.

The feeling in her chest threatened to overwhelm her. She'd begged the officers to let him inside. Needed to see him. To touch him. Needed him to ground her.

And the second his arms closed around her, she finally felt safe.

She was prepared to beg him to stay the night, but that became unnecessary when he told her he was taking her to his place. Hadn't asked. *Told* her.

She was completely all right with that.

She wanted this man. Everything within her screamed that he was the one. The man she'd been waiting and searching for her entire adult life. He didn't care that she didn't wear makeup. He didn't care that she snort-laughed. He respected her career, didn't call it a hobby or make fun of the fact that she made a living by drawing a talking taco. And he hadn't made a single snide comment about her parents being in the condom industry.

But it was more than all of that. It was a goodness she could sense oozing from every pore of Vincent's body. He was brave and protective. Yes, he was also a little rough around the edges and a lot blunt, but she didn't hold that against him. He'd learned to be that way because of being a SEAL.

His friends were the same way. She could sense a darkness in all of them, but that darkness was tempered by a strong need to protect. To slay dragons. It was no wonder they were all so close. Like was drawn to like, and Vincent and his teammates were all cut from the same cloth.

Safe was a good example. She hadn't asked him to stay. Hadn't even hinted that she might feel a little uneasy, wondering if Douchecanoe would come back. But he'd somehow known, and had volunteered to sit in her parking lot all night, keeping watch. He had to be tired, had to have wanted to go home to his own bed and enjoy the morning off. But instead, he'd volunteered to help keep her safe.

Honestly, it made her want to cry.

Well, maybe it was everything that had happened that was making her want to cry. But she wouldn't. She was stronger than that. She wasn't hurt, Douchecanoe hadn't touched her. And now she was going to Vincent's apartment. She'd been curious about where he lived ever since they got back to California. She couldn't wait to see it for herself.

As if he could read her mind, Vincent reached for her hand once they were on the road. "I hope you aren't expecting fancy," he said a little self-consciously. "My apartment isn't anything to write home about."

"I'm sure it's fine."

He huffed out a breath. "It's adequate. That's about it."

"Vincent, I don't care where you live. I don't care how much you paid for your furniture. I don't even care if your bedroom is full of stuffed animal heads on the walls and guns and knives displayed on every available surface. All I care about is that *you're* there."

He chuckled and squeezed her fingers. "No dead animals on the walls, and my weapons are in lockboxes."

She smiled at him.

"I just want you to be comfortable. To feel safe."

"When I'm with you, I do," Remi said, hoping she wasn't being too mushy.

The smile on his face assured her that she wasn't.

"You are, you know. When you're with me, you're completely safe. I'll never hurt you, sweetheart. With words or fists. And I'll do everything in my power to keep others from doing the same. But the truth of the matter is, I won't always be around. I know I keep mentioning that, but you need to be aware."

His worry was easy to hear. And it made her fall for him more, not less.

"I've lived on my own for a long time, Vincent. I'm used to it. My parents aren't too far away, and trust me, they know a lot of people. If I truly need something, all it'll take is a call to them and I'll have a handyman or plumber or someone out to my place immediately. And believe it or not, my life is actually pretty boring. Being left in the ocean and tonight notwithstanding. I can handle your job. Promise."

"I hate not being there for you," he admitted. "I never thought twice about it with other girlfriends, but with you? It makes me feel itchy inside. I love being a SEAL, but this past week has made me see how much others sacrifice for me. I should've met your family by now. Hung out with you and Marley. Taken you to dinner. Sat on your couch and watched a movie. And we haven't even come close to those make-out sessions I promised."

"It's not a sacrifice, it's a part of life. There will be times when I'm on a deadline and I can't talk to you. Won't *want* to talk to you. When I'll lock myself in my room in order to concentrate on what I'm doing. I'm a perfectionist, and I get irritated with myself and everyone else if I get distracted. Honestly? If you were an accountant or a car salesman, I'd be annoyed by now if we hadn't gone on a date or if I thought you were dodging meeting the people most important to me. But you aren't. You're a freaking SEAL. You're planning a very important mission to somewhere dangerous to keep others safe. I'll never, ever be pissed about that, Vincent. I'm proud of you and your teammates."

He gave her a look full of an emotion she couldn't read. But he didn't speak, simply squeezed her hand and turned his attention back to the road in front of them.

They pulled into a small parking area behind his building and he cut the engine before opening his door. Remi followed suit, and he already had her suitcase in his hand before she could even try to grab it. Then he came around to her side and took her hand in his before walking fairly quickly toward the building.

Remi's lips twitched. He was being bossy without saying a word. It was actually kind of impressive. But since she didn't mind, she didn't call him on it. It felt good to let him take control, even if it was over something as simple as carrying her bag and escorting her toward his apartment.

He led her up a set of stairs and down the outside walkway. His apartment was the last one at the end of a long row, and he only dropped her hand long enough to unlock his door before pocketing his keys and grabbing her once again, towing her inside.

Remi looked around with curiosity. Vincent didn't flick any switches inside the door, but since he'd left a kitchen light on when he'd last been here, she could see just fine. She caught a glimpse of a huge bookshelf stuffed with books, a giant TV against the wall, and a beat-up old couch, one that looked extremely comfortable, before Vincent walked her down a small hallway.

"Vincent?" she asked, confused about why he hadn't spoken. He still had her suitcase in his hand, so she figured maybe he was bringing her to a second bedroom.

But when he pushed open the door at the end of the hall, she realized they weren't in a guest room. This was *his* room. She knew it without him saying a word, because it smelled like him. The dark, woodsy scent that she attributed to him was strong in the decent-sized space.

"Vincent?" she said again, when he stopped and put her suitcase on the floor. But he didn't say a word, simply turned to her and took her face in his hands. Then he kissed her. It wasn't a short, gentle kiss. It was hard and rough...and claiming.

By the time he pulled back, she couldn't think straight. He'd scrambled her brain with a simple kiss. No, not simple. There had been nothing simple about that kiss.

"You have a choice," he said in a low voice. "You can sleep in here, in my bed, by yourself. I'll sleep out on the couch and in the morning, I'll make us breakfast, then bring you back to your condo before I head back to the base for my meetings."

When he didn't continue, Remi found the courage to ask, "Or?"

"Or we can both stay in here. And I'll make long, slow love to you all night. I'll taste every inch of your skin and get so deep inside you that you'll wonder how you ever survived without me. Then in the morning, we'll shower together, I'll make breakfast, set up my second bedroom as your work space, and you can stay here while I go to the base for my meetings. And when I'm done, I'll come home to you and we'll pick up where we left off."

Remi could feel her body tingling. Preparing itself for everything he'd just offered.

"I need you, Remi," Vincent admitted. "But everything I said last week still applies. If we do this, if you let me in, I'm not letting you go. I'm not like your idiot of an ex. I know a good thing when I see it, and I'm also aware that you could do so much better than me. But I'll spend the rest of my life making sure you don't regret choosing me. I'll make the time we *do* get to be together worth your while, so hopefully the times we're apart won't seem quite so bad."

Remi couldn't help it, she laughed. Snort-laughed at that.

Vincent frowned.

"I'm not laughing at you," she reassured him as she wrapped her arms around his neck. "I'm laughing at the fact you'd think for one second I'd choose box number one.

I want you, Vincent. All of you. The good, bad, and ugly. My parents are going to love you, and Marley has already told me if I don't jump your bones soon, she's going to arrange to have us locked in a room together in some mountain cabin with the snowstorm of the century approaching." She wrinkled her nose. "She reads too many forced-proximity romances, but it's part of her charm, and I can't say that the scenario she proposed is all that awful."

When she realized she was babbling, and that the worried look on Vincent's face hadn't dissipated, she said quickly, "I choose *you*, Vincent. Your bed. Both of us. You inside me, hard, deep, and slow. Or fast. Whatever."

If she wasn't halfway in love with this man, the intense look on his face might've scared her, but this was Vincent. The man who'd saved her life in Hawaii. Who didn't even flinch when she snort-laughed. Who didn't give a rat's ass about her bank account. Who came tonight as fast as he could when she called.

He started pushing her backward. "You need anything from your suitcase?"

"Um, no?"

"Good. Because I'm two seconds from ripping your clothes off and having my wicked way with you."

Remi smiled. "Okay by me."

Before she could blink, he'd done just that. Not literally ripping her clothes, but he somehow managed to strip her shirt and jeans off in seconds. She should've felt self-conscious, but she felt nothing but a need to have him as naked as she was. She wasn't as smooth as she struggled to get his shirt over his head, but thankfully, he helped. Then he was pushing her onto his bed.

Scooting backward, Remi couldn't take her eyes off the man crawling over her.

Vincent was gorgeous. And he was all hers. It was hard to believe, but the look of lust in his eyes was for *her*. It was a thrilling feeling.

Feeling confident for the first time ever, Remi arched her back and put her arms over her head as she preened for her man.

"*Fuck me*," Vincent breathed as his gaze roamed over her body. "I don't know what to look at or touch first. I knew when I saw you in that wetsuit that you were perfect for me, but I didn't know *how* perfect."

With every word out of his mouth, Remi fell harder.

Then he climbed over her and straddled her hips. His cock was hard against her belly, and he certainly wasn't self-conscious about *his* naked body, but why should he be? He was all lean, hard muscle.

He wasn't smiling, had an intense look of concentration on his face as he lifted a hand and lightly traced her nipple with his fingertip. As if it had a mind of its own, and like it had been waiting for his touch, it hardened.

A small smile formed on his lips as he watched.

"Beautiful," he whispered as he continued to play with her nipple. He continued to use one finger, and Remi craved more.

"Vincent, please," she begged.

"Please what?" he asked.

Her stomach tightened at the satisfied sound of his voice. "Touch me."

"Where?"

"Anywhere. Everywhere!"

"I might be rushing this, taking you to my bed, but I'll be damned if I rush our first time."

"There's rushing, then there's being slow as a grandpa," she grumbled, putting her hands on his thighs and caressing up and down. To her delight, his dick twitched and a small bead of precome appeared at the tip.

"There won't be slow *anything* if you keep touching me," he grumbled.

"If you think I'm gonna complain about that, you're wrong," she said. This was actually kind of fun. It was hard to believe anything about being naked with a man was fun. In the past, she'd always been too nervous, too self-conscious for any teasing. But there it was. Proof that Vincent really was made for her.

He flexed his thigh muscles under her palms and reached for her breasts. His large hands covered her completely, and the feel of his calloused skin against her nipples made Remi arch up again.

"More?" he asked.

"Yes. Please," she breathed.

He kneaded and caressed her breasts as if he'd never get enough. Other boyfriends had touched her the same way, but for mere seconds before crawling up her body and thrusting inside her. Vincent was content to take his time. Remi could feel the wet spot on her stomach where his cock rested, but he didn't seem in any hurry to "get to the good stuff," as one ex had called sex.

He scooted backward minutes later, and Remi held her breath, thinking this was it...but instead of ramming himself inside her, he lowered his head.

The next ten minutes were mind-blowing, and such a new experience for Remi. Vincent did his best to lick and suck every inch of her chest, pinching and nibbling, feasting on her as if she was a meal to be savored.

Every time he pinched her nipple, harder than she thought could ever be pleasurable, a corresponding pang shot down between her legs. It wasn't long before she was writhing under him. Her legs were spread wide and she was humping against him in desperation.

She would've been embarrassed, but every time she looked into his eyes, she saw nothing but lust and pleasure reflected back. He was doing everything in his power to turn her on...and it was working.

"Vincent, please! I need more. I need you inside me."

In response, he finally sat up and reached over to the little table next to the bed. He opened the drawer and pulled out a condom. He quickly rolled it down his cock and Remi couldn't take her eyes off him. If she'd thought he was big before, it was nothing compared to the monster between his legs now. He was bigger and thicker than anyone she'd ever taken, and she began to wonder if this would even work.

She jolted when a drop of something cold fell onto her chest.

"Sorry," he murmured. "This'll be cold at first."

She wasn't sure what he was talking about. Then she saw the bottle of lube in his hand.

When she lifted a questioning brow, he gave her a shrug. "Masturbating is better with lube," he told her.

Surprised that he would be so open about something so personal, Remi could only give him a small smile.

He squirted a dollop into his hand and explained, "In the future, I'll eat you out until you orgasm, make sure you're wet enough to take me. But I can't wait. I need to be inside you right now. I don't want to hurt you though, so I need to make sure you're ready."

Remi wanted to reassure him that she was ready, she was wetter than she could ever remember being, but he'd already scooted back so he was straddling her thighs, then his hand was between her legs. She jolted at the first touch, and he said, "Easy, sweetheart. I've got you."

And he did. His fingers spread the lube around her pussy lips, then he began to caress her clit. Remi gasped and tried to spread her thighs to give him more room, but he wouldn't move his legs.

"You're so beautiful. So sensitive. Does this feel good?" he asked as he slowly circled his thumb over her clit.

Remi could only moan. She reached down and grabbed one of his thighs as he caressed her.

She vaguely heard his chuckle, but all her senses were centered between her legs. Her nipples were rock hard on her chest and she felt as if she was going to shatter into a million pieces.

"You're close, aren't you?" he asked, and she heard the surprise in his voice.

She refused to be embarrassed. Hell, he'd been teasing her for the last fifteen minutes. Had gotten her all hot and bothered. Of *course* she was on the edge of a climax. She was in Vincent Hill's bed, and he wanted her.

"Yes," she said, looking up at him. "Harder," she ordered.

He smiled. "Yes, ma'am."

He squirted more lube onto his finger, then surprised her by slowly easing it inside her body as he caressed her clit with his other hand.

"Oh!" she exclaimed, squeezing his finger with her inner muscles.

It was his turn to groan. "So hot. So tight. You're gonna squeeze me so damn hard when I get my cock in there."

It was kind of a crude thing to say, and Remi had never been so turned on.

"Come for me, Remi. Cream all over my fingers so I can give you my dick."

She wanted that. Wanted *him*. She arched her back as her orgasm approached and didn't think twice about what might be jiggling or what her lover might think about it. All she could focus on was the hands between her legs and how good they were making her feel. Between the lube and her juices, she was wetter than she'd ever been in her life.

As she flew over the edge, she felt Vincent moving. Then he was there. Pushing between her legs even as she shook and trembled through the most intense orgasm she'd ever had.

* * *

It took everything within Kevlar not to come right then and there. He'd never been with a woman more sensual than Remi, with her arms thrown over her head and her body arched into his touch as she moaned through her orgasm.

He was a big man, and the last thing he wanted to do was hurt her. Which was why he'd gotten the lube. He wanted to make sure she was nice and slippery so he could get inside her without causing any pain. He hadn't expected her to orgasm, but the second he'd touched her clit, he could tell she was close.

He'd never seen anything so damn sexy in his life. As her thighs shook and she cried out, he moved without thought. Notching his cock between her legs and pushing inside.

She was tight. Almost too tight. And the fact that she was orgasming wasn't helping, her muscles clenched and working against him. But Kevlar couldn't stop. The way she squeezed his cock made his eyes roll back in his head. He was doubly thankful that he'd gotten her so wet and slick before attempting to penetrate her.

She felt tiny under him, around him, but he couldn't stop until he'd bottomed out inside her. It wasn't until he felt his pubic hair meshing with hers that he opened his eyes and dared to look down. He held still, loving the feel of the small contractions deep within her body, massaging his cock.

Remi had grabbed hold of his arms as he'd pushed inside her, and he could feel her fingernails digging into his skin. His heart was beating so hard, he was sure she could see the blood pulsing through the artery in his neck.

"Vincent," she whispered.

He'd never get tired of hearing his name on her lips. The way she said it turned him on every time.

"Remi," he returned, sounding just as breathless.

"Are you...all the way in?"

He smiled down at her and nodded.

"You aren't moving," she commented.

"You're tight, sweetheart. I'm giving you time to adjust."

She took a deep breath. "Yeah, okay. Thanks. I, um..."

Her inner muscles flexed around him, and it was Kevlar's turn to inhale. "Do that again," he ordered.

"What? This?" she asked with a grin.

This time, she rhythmically squeezed him several times in a row.

"Damn, woman! That feels...you have no idea how good you feel. You're like an oven, so hot around me." Kevlar flexed his ass and shifted inside her.

Now she gasped.

"You good? I'm not hurting you?"

She lifted a hand and speared it through his hair. "No.

You definitely aren't hurting me. You're big and I feel full. Almost too full, but it's so good."

Kevlar couldn't stop the satisfaction that rushed through him. "I want to move. Can I move?" he begged. This wasn't like him. He was a man who took what he wanted, what he needed. But he'd cut off his own dick before he hurt this woman.

"Yes. Please, Vincent. Move!"

Slowly, he pulled his cock out of her warm body until only the tip remained, then he sank back inside.

She moaned. "More! Harder," she insisted.

Kevlar began to thrust in and out—and he realized that his life was completely and utterly changed. She was his. He'd never be intimate with anyone other than Remi, ever again, and the thought made him groan in ecstasy. He didn't need anyone else. Just her. Just this pussy. She was made for him.

"Vincent, *harder*," she ordered, digging her nails into his ass.

The little pain sent pleasure shooting up his cock. His balls let loose a spurt of come inside the condom. He didn't want this to be over yet. He needed more. Wanted to stay inside her hot, wet body for as long as possible. But he also wanted to please Remi. Wanted to give her the most pleasurable experience she'd ever had.

He scooted up farther, spreading her legs even wider around his hips. Then he leaned back.

Remi groaned in protest. "Vincent, please! I want it hard. I want to feel you deep inside."

"You will," Kevlar promised. "But first I want you to come again. Around me this time."

"I can't," she protested. "I'm too sensitive."

Kevlar knew he was a dick for ignoring her protests. All he wanted was to feel her ripple around his cock. He lowered his hand and found she was still plenty slick from the lube he'd used earlier. He ran his thumb around her opening until it was slippery and set to work making her come again.

At the first touch of his thumb to her clit, she jerked under him, and he couldn't stop smiling.

"No, too much!"

But he still ignored her. He'd had no idea he had this in him. He'd seen porn depicting forced orgasms, but figured the women had simply been acting. It hadn't turned him on or off, it was just mildly interesting. But with Remi under him, twitching around his dick, trying to get away from his touch and failing, he found himself spurting more precome.

He wasn't going to last very long, not when he looked down and saw himself buried to the hilt inside her. Her flesh was stretched around the base of his dick, and it was hard to believe she'd been able to take him into that tight pussy. Was *still* taking him.

"It's not too much," he told her.

Her hips were bucking constantly now, and both her hands were on his thighs, digging her nails in as he continued to stroke her.

"Ahhhh!" she screamed as she writhed under him.

Kevlar closed his eyes as he felt her orgasm around him, under him. Then he lunged forward. Braced himself on his forearms and fucked her hard, fast and deep, just like she'd begged for.

And with every thrust, she moaned in his ear, her pussy milking him as she continued to come. Every time he bottomed out, he rubbed against her clit, prolonging her orgasm. *Nothing* felt like this. Not the adrenaline high he got from a mission. Not the pride he felt when he'd earned his Budweiser pin. Nothing.

Groaning, he shoved himself as deep as he could and let go. Spurt after spurt of come left his cock. The orgasm seemed to go on and on, and it was all he could do to hold himself up, to not fall onto Remi and crush her beneath him. His arms shook, he saw black spots in front of his eyes, and through it all, he felt Remi's hands on his back, on his ass, caressing him, pulling him closer.

When he could finally breathe again, Kevlar rolled to his back, taking Remi with him so she was sprawled atop his body, his dick still tucked deep inside her. She giggled against his chest as he settled but didn't pull away.

Relief swam through Kevlar's veins. The last thing he ever wanted was to hurt this woman, and for a moment he thought he'd gone too far. Forcing her to orgasm, taking her as hard as he had, but when he heard that sweet giggle, he sighed in relief.

"That was...wow," she whispered.

"Yeah," he agreed.

She lay boneless against him, and Kevlar had the satisfied thought that *this* was what would be waiting for him when he came home from his next mission. Not just the sex, but his woman lounging against him, skin-to-skin, caressing him with her soft hands, happy to be with him. Not for what he could do for her, not because he was a SEAL. But for him. Just him.

He'd fight and kill to keep this.

"I need to get up," he said after a long moment.

"Oh, um, okay," she said, sounding unsure.

It occurred to Kevlar that she didn't realize why he needed to move. "The condom. As much as I want to stay right where I am, with my dick snug inside your body, I need to take care of the condom."

"Oh! Right. Yeah," she said, lifting her leg to climb off him.

But Kevlar held her against him, not willing to pull out of her just yet. It was stupid, could have serious consequences, but he dreaded leaving her warmth.

"I thought you said you needed to move," she said with a small huff.

"I did. I do. But I need you to tell me you're okay first. That I didn't hurt you."

"I'm more than okay," she reassured him immediately. "That was...intense, but great. Really incredible."

"I made you do something you weren't sure you wanted to do," he pressed. Kevlar had no idea why he was pushing this, just that he wanted to be completely sure he hadn't done anything she'd resent later.

"It was a little uncomfortable. Kind of hurt, but in a

good way," she hurried to say, when she saw the frown on his face. "No one's ever done that to me. I've never felt that way before, ever. Never had such an intense orgasm. And having you inside me when it happened...yeah, it was amazing, Vincent. Promise."

She was bright red by the time she finished speaking, but he couldn't have been prouder—of her, of himself—than he was at that moment. "All right," he said. "I just wanted to be sure."

"I'm sure. I'm *really* sure," she told him.

Kevlar kissed her. Hard. "Lift your leg, sweetheart. I'll be right back."

She did as he asked, and they both groaned when he slipped out of her body.

As he stood, Kevlar noticed that his come was leaking out the end of the condom, and he grimaced. He walked into the bathroom, removed the condom, and threw it away. Then he wet a washcloth and quickly cleaned himself, before rinsing the cloth and walking back into the bedroom.

Remi had covered herself with his sheet, and he had a moment of dismay that she'd hidden herself from him, but he pushed it down. It would take time for her to become fully comfortable around him. At least she hadn't jumped out of bed to put her clothes back on.

He climbed under the covers with her and braced himself on an elbow as he rested the warm washcloth on her belly. "May I?" he asked softly.

Remi nodded shyly, and it was all Kevlar could do to

control himself as he wiped the excess lube and her juices from between her legs. He threw the washcloth to the floor and pulled her against him once more. To his delight, she hiked one leg over his thigh and wrapped her arm over his chest.

She felt so right against him.

"Vincent?"

"Yeah, sweetheart?"

She paused for a long time. Then..."Nothing."

He turned a little, so she was more on her back, and stared down at her. "What, Remi? You can tell me anything. Ask me anything."

"I...I'm scared."

"Of what? Me?" Kevlar asked, appalled.

"No! I mean, maybe? But it's me, not you. I just...this was so good. You're so amazing. I'm afraid it's *too* good."

Kevlar relaxed. He understood that feeling. All too well. He settled onto his back and encouraged her to snuggle against him once more. "I feel the same way," he admitted.

"About *me*?"

She sounded so surprised. So floored, he could only chuckle.

"Yeah, you. You scare the shit out of me, sweetheart. I'm afraid you'll come to your senses and realize that being with me is more of a pain in the ass than you're willing to put up with."

"I'm not her," Remi said fiercely. "Or any of the other stupid bitches you dated who didn't know a good thing when they had it. I can handle you and your job, Vincent."

Her words sank into his psyche, and they were said with such conviction, he couldn't help but believe her. "Okay. So we agree that there's nothing to be scared about. Right?"

"Right," she said with a sigh.

"Sleep, sweetheart," he whispered.

"You too?" she asked.

"Me too," he agreed.

Kevlar fell asleep with a smile on his face, and a bone-deep knowledge that his world had just tilted on its axis... and he'd never been happier to be turned upside down as he was right then.

* * *

Howler paced his small apartment in agitation. He'd had Safe drop him off at The Golden Oyster, but he hadn't stayed. As soon as his teammate left, he'd ordered an Uber and gone home.

He was worried. Tex was obviously looking into Remi's ex, but he wouldn't find anything, because there was nothing there *to* find. And when he came up empty, he'd widen his net. Even with how careful Howler had been, the possibility that Tex would come up with something to tie him back to Hawaii made him increasingly paranoid.

Yes, he'd taken care of the boat captain, and he trusted his contact in Hawaii, but there was still a tiny chance that one remaining connection could come back to bite him in the ass. And time was running out. The day when they'd be leaving on the mission to Chad was quickly approaching. If he wanted to be team leader, wanted Kevlar to be too emotionally unstable to continue the role that was meant to be Howler's, he had to act now.

He had his plan, was ready to implement it, had finished the prep work. But he hadn't managed the last step—getting to Remi.

That was turning out to be the hardest part, and it was all because of fucking Kevlar. The asshole kept them in meetings about their upcoming mission from morning until night, day after day. As if they hadn't already planned everything from what they'd eat to where they'd take a shit. Taking out an HVT wasn't this difficult. If *he* was team leader, they'd already have killed the son-of-a-bitch and been on their way home.

It was just one more reason why Kevlar had to go. Immediately.

He needed to be a little more creative if he wanted to get to Remi before they left for their mission.

As he paced, his thoughts went back to Aces again...and suddenly, he knew just how to do it.

Blink.

The SEAL was still a mess. Everyone knew when he wasn't at Aces, he sat at home, wallowing in self-pity. Probably going over and over in his head how he'd fucked up on the mission that killed half his team. Howler had heard through the grapevine that the man obsessively watched everyone who came and went from his apartment complex, as if someone might plant an IED in the parking lot or some bullshit. And conveniently for Howler, Blink lived in the same complex close to base as several other military members—including Kevlar.

Anything out of the ordinary that happened outside Blink's apartment would likely catch the man's eye. And he seemed to have a soft spot for Remi Stephenson. It made Howler want to barf, but whatever. He could work with it. Surely if anything went down with the woman on his watch, he'd feel the need to insert himself into the situation.

At least, Howler was counting on it.

His plan was tricky...might not even work. But if Blink did what Howler expected, he'd have someone mentally unhinged to point to; someone to blame for what was about to happen to Kevlar's bitch. A handy scapegoat. Someone he wouldn't even have to *pay*.

Collateral damage. As a SEAL, Howler knew it was inevitable. To get the job done, there was always collateral damage. That's what Blink would become. If he was a stronger man, a better SEAL, he wouldn't involve himself. But he was weak. Perfect for Howler's plan.

And Remi Stephenson was just another Frog Hog. She might not admit it, but she was the same as every other bitch who wanted to fuck a SEAL. She'd get what she deserved—just as Kevlar would.

CHAPTER FOURTEEN

Remi woke to the sound of a phone ringing. She reached out to slap her cell, which she always kept by her bed, but jolted awake quickly when she encountered not her table, but warm flesh instead.

"Morning," Vincent murmured sleepily.

My God, the man was hot. Even half asleep, he was beautiful. And even though she'd woken up with him in the same room once before, this time was so different. She was in his bed, they were both naked, and she could still feel him between her legs. She was sore, which wasn't surprising considering how big he was. But it was a good sore. An ache that reminded her of the mind-blowing way he'd made love to her.

He'd woken her up in the middle of the night, and they'd had round two. It had been less intense, almost sweet. He'd still made sure she was lubed up enough to take him without pain, and insisted on her coming before he did.

"Morning," she mumbled into his chest. Then she lifted her head and said, "Your phone is ringing."

"I know."

"Aren't you going to get it? It could be an emergency. Isn't there a chance it's your boss calling you to come in? That you have to leave on your mission early?"

"Would that bother you?"

Remi frowned. "Well, yeah, but only because I'd worry about you getting in trouble for ignoring the phone that's rung four million times and *still* the person isn't giving up."

He chuckled, and the sound rumbled through her. "It's not work."

"How do you know?"

"Because I've programmed a different ringtone for my team and the commander."

"Oh."

A moment passed. The phone rang again. Remi couldn't help but press the issue. "But aren't you curious? Something could be wrong."

"What's wrong is that my one morning to sleep in is being disturbed by someone who isn't taking the hint that I don't want to talk to them," he grumbled.

Remi grinned.

Vincent sighed and rolled over to grab his phone, but he didn't let go of Remi when he did, so she went with him.

She was still laughing when he answered tersely, "What?"

"I can't fucking believe you!"

Remi blinked at the vitriol coming from the feminine voice through the phone. Even though Vincent hadn't put the call on speaker, she could clearly hear what the woman was saying.

"You have some nerve sending the cops to my house to accuse me of trying to kill you! Are you insane?!"

"Hello, Bertie," Vincent said with a sigh.

Remi's eyes widened.

"I'm serious! Why would I do that? I mean, you're an asshole for not letting me go to Hawaii with my friend, and it probably serves you right, but *seriously*? You think I'd pay someone to leave you in the ocean? You could swim back to shore with one hand tied behind your back—at least that's what you always said. Were you lying? Maybe you *did* almost die and you're pissed because your precious reputation is in danger if someone on base finds out you're not as macho as you claim to be."

"It's routine, Bertie. Nothing personal."

"Not personal?" she screeched. "They said that since I'm your ex, and I'm pissed at you, that I have motive. If I was going to kill you, I'd come to your house and blow you away the second you opened the door!"

Remi stiffened against Vincent, but he didn't seem concerned in the least.

"Careful, that could be construed as a threat," he drawled.

"It *was* a threat!" she practically screamed. "You're a dick! If word gets out that I'm being questioned, I'll be ruined! You need to fix this. Tell the cops that I had nothing to do with your fucking problems!"

"But I don't know that you didn't."

"Maybe you shouldn't antagonize her," Remi whispered.

"Who was that? Oh my God, do you have a chick with you? It's seven in the damn morning... Wait—she spent the night? You never let *me* spend the night! You sure moved on fast enough. You were probably cheating on me the whole time. You fucking Navy SEALs...such assholes! Maybe *she* set you up. Hey, bitch," she called out loudly, obviously speaking to Remi, "he's not worth it. He might have a big dick, but he doesn't know how to use it!"

Remi knew her eyes were huge in her face. Was this woman kidding?

"She didn't set me up. She was stranded in the ocean *with* me," Vincent said calmly, his gaze on Remi's as he spoke.

Bertie laughed, a bitter, ugly sound. "Right, so your hero complex kicked in, and she sees you as her savior. Take it from me, mystery woman, he's no hero. Not even close. Run while you still can. Before he accuses you of something heinous too and sics the cops on you!"

"Not a hero? Are you kidding me?" Remi said. She couldn't help it. She was pissed on Vincent's behalf.

"She must have a golden pussy to earn the privilege of sleeping in your bed," Bertie snapped. "I don't give a shit. Leave me alone, Kevlar. I mean it. Call the cops off or you'll regret ever getting involved with me."

"I already do," Vincent assured her. "This conversation

is done. If you didn't do anything, you have nothing to worry about. Just answer the police's questions and they'll be done. The more pissed you get, the more they'll think it's you. Goodbye, Bertie. Don't ever call me again."

He clicked off the phone, cutting off Bertie's pissed-off sputter. Then he clicked a few more buttons before throwing the phone onto the table and turning, pushing Remi until she was on her back.

"I blocked her number so she can't call back. Are you okay?"

"Me? Are *you* okay? She said some mean things."

To her surprise, Vincent smiled.

"This isn't funny," she said with a frown.

"It's a little funny," he returned. "Your ex pitching a fit. Mine doing the same. Sounds like something a guilty person might do."

"Which one do you think did it?" she whispered, staring up at him.

"Honestly?"

"Of course."

"Neither."

Remi felt relief course through her at his answer, but on the heels of that was confusion. "If it wasn't either of them, then who set it up, and why?"

"I don't know. Tex is still digging into it. But I know it's no one in your life."

"How do you know that?" she asked.

"Because you're too nice. You make friends wherever you go. I think you were just in the wrong place at the wrong time. You got caught up in my shit, and I'll never forgive myself for that."

"You're nice too. Who would want to hurt you?"

Vincent barked out a laugh. "I'm not nice, Remi."

"Yes, you are," she protested.

"God, you're too good for me," he told her. "But I'm not letting you go. You go right ahead and keep on thinking that I'm a nice person. I need you to do me a favor though."

"Anything," she said without hesitation.

He smiled a little sadly. "See? Too good for me. If someone is pissed at me for some reason, I need you to be extra careful. Just being around me could put you in danger."

A shiver ran through Remi. Not at the thought of someone wanting to hurt her to get to Vincent, but because someone might be out there with a vendetta against him. "Okay."

"I mean it," he warned.

"And I heard you. Vincent, I don't go anywhere. If you want me to hang out here in your apartment, I will. It's not a hardship. I can draw Pecky anywhere. I can get Marley to go with me if I need to go to the store or something, and worse comes to worst, I can hang out at my parents' estate. They have enough security to keep even a cockroach from farting."

Vincent stared down at her without saying a word.

"Vincent?" she asked, getting worried.

In response, he said, "I know you're sore, but exactly

how sore are you?"

"Oh, um...not sore enough to say no," she told him.

"I need you. Need to show you how much you mean to me."

"Okay," she said, completely onboard with that.

"I'm on this," he told her. "Tex will eventually find something. I just need you to be cautious in the meantime. I think whoever set up that shit in Hawaii is a coward. Doesn't want to directly confront me. Which means you're probably good, but just in case, be careful."

"I will."

Then he sat up and threw the sheet back, exposing her body to the morning light.

"You have a problem with oral?" he asked as he crouched over her.

Remi smiled. "No. As long as I get to partake too."

"You want to suck my cock, Remi?" he growled.

Vincent had a way of making her feel utterly shy, yet turned on at the same time. "Yes, although there's no way I can take all of you. You're too big."

"The thought of just your tongue on me makes me hard as a pike. You can do whatever you want, take as much or as little as you want...after I'm done with you."

He grabbed her hips and pulled her down, making a small shriek escape Remi's mouth. Then she snort-laughed as he made motorboat noises against her belly. But she wasn't laughing when he spread her legs and lowered his head.

* * *

Hours later, after Remi had given him the best blowjob he'd ever received, after they'd showered together, after he'd made them a late breakfast and gotten her set up at his desk in the second bedroom of his apartment and made her promise to be there when he got home that night, Kevlar drove toward the base feeling both happier than he'd ever been in his life...and more worried.

Something Bertie said wouldn't stop running through his head. Not the shit about him or the way she'd tried to warn Remi, but something she'd said about her setting up the Hawaii thing—that she knew what he was capable of. He hadn't been bragging when he'd told her that he could swim for at least twenty miles if he had to. She'd have known that leaving him in the ocean off Oahu wouldn't do a damn thing other than piss him off. He was certain she hadn't been responsible for what happened.

So if it wasn't her, and it wasn't Douchecanoe—he honestly didn't believe that twit had the brains to plan something like that—who had it been? Kevlar couldn't think of anyone who might try to get rid of him by stranding him in the ocean. No one who knew his skills in the water, anyway. Another former girlfriend? A different jealous boyfriend? Neither made sense, as he hadn't been with anyone for months before hooking up with Bertie, and Remi said her boyfriends were few and far between.

He'd been honest with Remi, he was sure it was someone who'd been trying to piss him off, not someone who was targeting her. She was good down to her core. He'd previously had no thought that she could be in danger just being around him, but now the idea wouldn't leave him. He wondered briefly if he should break up with her, for her own good...but screw that. He wasn't going to risk losing the best thing that ever happened to him over an unconfirmed threat.

No, he'd just have to figure out what that Hawaii thing was about and nip it in the bud.

He needed to call Tex, but he didn't have time right now. He was already cutting it close to being late to the base. He'd lingered too long making sure Remi was set up and good to go in his apartment. Until he could contact his friend, he'd just have to be extra vigilant and check in with Remi more than he had been. At the slightest hint something was wrong, he'd act. And he knew if Tex learned anything important, he'd reach out to Kevlar first.

He hoped the man found some intel, because Kevlar had a feeling he and his team would be heading to Africa sooner rather than later. And he'd prefer to have answers before he left. If something happened to Remi because of him, he'd never forgive himself. Ever.

CHAPTER FIFTEEN

Three days later, Remi couldn't stop smiling. She'd never been as happy as she was now. Even Marley had commented that she didn't remember ever seeing Remi so content. She and Vincent had finally had a chance to have dinner at Marley's house with her family. Vincent had spent a lot of the time in the backyard with her husband and son, throwing a football. Then after dinner, he'd played gin rummy with her daughter and gotten his ass handed to him.

Needless to say, he'd fit in perfectly and had gotten a huge thumbs up from not only Marley, but her entire family. When she'd used the restroom before she and Vincent left, Marley had intercepted her upstairs to tell her how happy she was for her. That things with her and Vincent would work out, she just knew it.

Remi hoped her friend was right. They were still in the

honeymoon phase of their relationship, and Remi had no illusions that things would stay shiny and rosy, but she hoped they could weather any storms that might come their way.

She'd talked with her parents last night, and Vincent had a chance to meet them...sort of...over the phone. He'd been polite and respectful, and Remi had high hopes that when they did finally get a chance to meet in person, things would go just as well.

The plan for today was for her to get a drawing done that morning, then Caroline was going to pick her up and take her to Aces, where they'd meet Vincent for lunch. She'd argued that he could just come back to his apartment, but he'd said that he didn't want to keep her a prisoner in his place and mentioned that Wolf had said Caroline would love to hang out with her again.

She couldn't say no to that.

Being in Vincent's space wasn't a hardship. Yes, his apartment was smaller than her condo, but it was very Vincent—no frills. She'd spent a few hours poring over the books on his shelves and checking out the shows he'd saved on the streaming apps he watched on TV. They were amazingly similar in their likes and dislikes, and as she'd told him, she could draw anywhere. And she liked being surrounded by his things. Liked being there when he got home at night. It was obvious he was stressed about the mission he and his team were planning, but she hoped being there for him, talking about her day to take his mind off things, cooking dinner for him, was helping at least a little bit.

And the nights...she'd never slept so well, or been loved so hard. She had no doubt that Vincent liked having her in his bed, though he never made her feel as if she was there simply for sex. In fact, he'd admitted that she was the first woman who'd ever spent a night in his bed.

Remi had almost blurted that she loved him more than once, but she didn't want to be cliché. Didn't want to freak him out. Although she'd caught him watching her with a longing in his eyes that she was sure echoed her own gaze, something held her back from saying the words. Maybe once they'd made it through his first deployment, she'd feel more confident in sharing her feelings.

Until then, she'd show him nonverbally that she was fully committed to being with him.

Two nights ago, she'd shyly shown him the cartoon she'd drawn Kevlar into, and he'd been silent for two whole minutes as he'd taken it in. Just when she was worried that he hated it, that he thought it was silly and stupid, he'd put down the paper—careful not to wrinkle it even one little bit—then dragged her into their bedroom and shown her *exactly* how much it meant to him to be drawn into her world.

Remi checked her appearance in the mirror one more time. Vincent never complained about her penchant for wearing T-shirts and sweats when she was in the house. He actually loved that she didn't wear a bra, because he said it gave him instant access to her tits. It was such a guy thing to say, but since Remi benefited from the pleasure he gave her when he got his hands on her, she didn't complain.

But today she wanted to look nice. Put in the effort to show him that she cared about how she looked when she was out with him. She was wearing her usual jeans, but she'd chosen a new pair of skinny jeans that clung to her curves more than she was normally comfortable with. Though with Vincent as a lover, she was beginning to adore her body. He certainly showed her in no uncertain terms how much he appreciated her curves.

She'd paired her jeans with a V-neck shirt that dipped low enough to show off some cleavage, but not low enough to be sleazy. It was yellow with pale blue flowers on it and it made her feel pretty and feminine.

Glancing at her watch, Remi saw she was ready too early. Caroline wouldn't be there for another thirty or forty minutes. The anticipation of seeing Vincent in the middle of the day was too much for her to resist, and she'd gotten ready way before she had to.

She'd just sat on the couch to find something to watch for the next half hour when her phone rang. She smiled. Vincent had been checking in with her as often as he could, usually during breaks from his meetings.

But it wasn't Vincent's name on the screen—it was Howler's. Frowning, wondering why he was calling, Remi unconsciously braced herself as she answered. "Hello?"

"Hey, Remi, it's Howler. Kevlar's been hurt. I'm on my way to get you to bring you to him. I'll be there in two minutes. Meet me in the parking lot."

"What?! What happened?"

"No time to talk now. I'll tell you everything when I get there. Be ready, Remi. It's serious."

"I will. Drive safe—don't *you* get in an accident or anything."

She couldn't read the tone of his voice when he said he'd be fine, then abruptly hung up. But Remi couldn't dwell on that. She was freaking out that Vincent had been hurt. It had to be serious if Howler was coming to get her, if Vincent hadn't called himself to break the news.

Remi stood, then spun in place, not even sure what to do for a second. Then she took a deep breath. She had to get herself together. Vincent would need her to be calm. He'd be okay. He had to be.

She grabbed a long-sleeve cardigan from the back of the couch, thinking that hospitals tended to run cold and she'd probably need it, before heading for the door. She didn't bother with her purse. Her only thought was to get downstairs to meet Howler. To get to Vincent. Nothing else mattered.

Nate "Blink" Davis watched as Kevlar's girlfriend paced the parking lot in front of his apartment. He and Kevlar lived in the same complex, although their paths didn't cross much, probably because Blink spent most of his time inside his apartment or at Aces.

But today, he'd been staring out at his vehicle...contemplating whether or not to go to the base to work out, something he hadn't done in weeks. He was sick of himself. Sick of spending so much time in his own head.

Intellectually, he knew he hadn't done anything wrong on that last mission. The one that had taken out so many of his teammates. Sometimes things just went to shit. Bad luck, being in the wrong place at the wrong time. And that's what happened in Iran.

It had been a long time coming, but Blink was finally pulling his head out of his ass.

Thanks to Remi Stephenson.

She'd approached him in Aces, braved his bad mood and glacial stares and babbled about nothing and anything. She'd been nervous, that much was obvious. But she'd stuck to her guns. Even sounded sincere when she'd called him a hero.

Blink didn't feel like a hero. Far from it. Didn't want to hear that kind of thing, from her or anyone else. But that wasn't what made the fog in his brain finally clear.

It was her cluelessness about the Long Island iced tea. And her laugh. And the way she looked at Kevlar when she didn't think anyone was watching. The woman didn't have an artificial bone in her body. She was exactly what she seemed—sweet, kind, and willing to do whatever it took to heal a stranger's fractured heart.

But it was her touch that really broke through.

No one had touched him in weeks. It was as if they were afraid to. Yes, he'd put up one hell of a shield, effectively keeping everyone away, including his own twin brother. But it was as if Remi hadn't even noticed his remoteness. Or she just didn't care. Her gentle hand on his arm broke through his shields as if they were made of paper. And then she'd kissed him. *Him*. The fucked-up SEAL who others were afraid to approach.

But not Remi. She'd done it without a second thought. It wasn't sexual. It was a small gesture of friendship, of caring...that made Blink feel human for the first time since shit hit the fan on that mission.

Now he was staring at her pacing in agitation in front of his apartment—and he knew something was wrong. Something big.

As soon as Blink saw Howler's beat-up old pickup truck pull into the lot, his oh-shit radar kicked into gear.

No way in hell would Kevlar send *Howler* to get his girl. He'd heard the rumors. Had seen first-hand the disrespect Howler had for his teammate and friend.

No. The man was up to no good.

Making a split-second decision, relying on the skills he'd spent his entire adult life honing yet ignoring in recent weeks, Blink strode for the door. Whatever was happening, he wanted in. He might not have a team anymore, but he'd be damned if he stood by and watched bad things happen to good people ever again.

* * *

Remi bit her thumbnail as she paced and waited impatiently for Howler to arrive. With every second that passed, her imagination threatened to overwhelm her. She couldn't guess what might have happened. Had Vincent gotten into a car accident? Was there a shooting on the base that he'd been involved in? She hadn't heard any kind of alert on her phone, but that didn't mean something big hadn't gone down.

When she finally saw Howler's older-model pickup pulling into the parking lot, she was both relieved and even more scared. She walked toward the front passenger seat, ignoring the sound of an apartment door slamming behind her. She tried the handle and was annoyed when the door didn't immediately open.

She waited for Howler to unlock the door, and when he finally did, she quickly opened it and got in without a moment's hesitation. "What happened? Where's Vincent?"

Howler didn't get a chance to respond because suddenly the door behind her opened and someone slid into the backseat.

Whipping around, Remi saw it was Blink. The SEAL from Aces. The one who some claimed was days away from being committed because he couldn't snap out of whatever had happened on his last mission.

"Get out," Howler told him.

"I want in," Blink said.

"No."

"I want in," Blink repeated firmly. "Whatever it is, I'm *in*."

Remi looked from Blink to Howler, then back to Blink.

She didn't understand the undercurrent between the two men.

"You get spit in the face enough, you want to show the spitter that you're more than the dirt under his shoe. I don't know what's going on, but I'm in. I've watched you, Howler. You're better than the hand you've been dealt. You're a born leader. If I was still able to be on a team, I'd want to be on yours."

Remi's brows drew down in bewilderment. She had no idea what Blink was talking about. Who spit on him? And he wanted to be on a team? *What* team? Was Howler in charge of a team now? She was so confused.

"If you think I'm afraid to get my hands dirty, you're wrong. They're already dirty. Filthy. I'll follow a good leader anywhere he wants to lead me," Blink said calmly.

A strange smile formed on Howler's lips. A smile of... satisfaction? "I planned to do this alone, but I'm thinking I *could* use some help. All right, you can stay. But you do what I say, when I say it. Understand?"

"Yes," Blink agreed, and shut the door behind him.

"What's happening?" Remi asked.

"I'll tell you, but I need to make a stop first," Howler said.

"A stop?" Remi practically yelled. "No! We need to get to Vincent."

"And we will, after I make a stop," Howler said somewhat brusquely.

"But—"

That was all she got out before Blink said, "Hush," in a low, scary voice.

Turning to look at him, seeing the coldness in his blue eyes, Remi did the only thing that seemed smart at that moment—she hushed.

She held her tongue as Howler drove them down a few streets to another apartment building not far from Vincent's. He parked and handed his phone to Blink. "Take this and your cell to my apartment. Number one-oh-two. First floor. Go to the sliding door in back, it's unlocked. Keep them on, but put both phones on the table in the kitchen."

Without hesitation, Blink nodded and held his hand out for Howler's phone.

"This is a test," he said, his voice hard, before releasing the cell to the man.

"And I'm going to pass," Blink assured him, before opening the door and heading toward the side of the building.

"Howler, seriously, what's happening? Why are you leaving your phone behind? What if someone tries to call you about Vincent?"

"Nothing you need to worry about," he told her.

But Remi was plenty worried. Howler was acting weird, Blink didn't seem like the same man she'd met in the bar the other night, and she was freaking out about what could have happened to Vincent.

Moments later, she saw Blink headed back in their direction. She was relieved that he'd returned so quickly, that they'd finally be on their way to see Vincent and she could find out for herself if he was all right.

Blink got back in the truck and said, "Done."

Howler smiled. Then he put the truck in reverse and backed out of the parking space.

"*Now* will you tell me where Vincent is and what happened to him? If he's okay?" Remi asked.

Howler didn't respond. It was as if she wasn't even there.

For the first time, Remi felt seriously uneasy. But... Howler was a member of Vincent's team. Was one of his oldest SEAL buddies. They'd been through the iconic Hell Week together. She hadn't hesitated to get into his truck, because why would she?

"Howler?" she asked.

"What?" he answered in a harsh tone.

Remi winced. "What happened to Vincent? You're taking me to him, right?"

"Of course. Patience, Remi. All will be revealed soon."

His words didn't make her feel better. Not at all.

Realizing she was still holding her phone in her hand, she made a split-second decision to try to call Vincent—which she should've done already. He might answer, or one of his other friends would, and she could tell them to let Vincent know she was on her way.

She unlocked the phone and had clicked on the icon that would bring up the keyboard when something hit her in the face.

It was sudden and unexpected, and Remi cried out in pain.

"Give me that!" Howler ordered.

Blinking in confusion, she looked over at Howler. He was scowling at her. As she stared, his fist flew toward her —and she realized in the second before he connected, *that's* what had struck her face the first time. Howler had punched her.

She tried to jerk away from his fist but it was no use. His knuckles struck her cheek again, in the same place as before.

Remi groaned, dazed and unable to fight when Howler pried the phone out of her hand.

Then she cried out in shock when arms from behind grabbed her and manhandled her into the backseat of the truck. She hadn't put on her seat belt earlier, completely forgetting in her panic.

She was slow to react to being dragged over the seat, but now she fought. She had no idea what was happening, but it wasn't good.

"I've got her," Blink said as she struggled against him, to no avail. He was bigger and stronger than she was, and she quickly found herself on his lap, her back against his chest, his arms around her like steel bands. She wiggled and squirmed, but with her arms pinned to her sides, she couldn't get any leverage to try to fight the muscular SEAL.

"Let me go! Stop it!" she yelled.

Then one of Blink's hands covered her mouth, effectively cutting off any further protests she might make.

"*Fuck*. What a cunt," Howler muttered from the driver's seat. He met Remi's gaze in the rearview for a moment before returning his attention to the road. She stilled at the pure hatred she saw in his eyes. Was this the same man she'd met at Aces? The guy Vincent said was one of his best friends?

"This is *your* fault," Howler said. "If you'd behaved, I wouldn't have had to hit you."

Anger swam in Remi's veins. Figures he'd blame *her* for his violence. She tried to get Blink's arms to loosen again, but it was a wasted effort. He had a firm grip on her and she wasn't going anywhere.

The feeling of betrayal hit her out of the blue. She'd thought Blink was a good guy. Had done her best to befriend him, to be kind to him. And this was how he repaid her? What a dick!

Her anger made her renew her struggles. She called him and Howler every bad name she could think of, but the hand over her mouth made her efforts fall a little flat, since the men couldn't understand her.

"Settle, Remi," Blink growled in her ear.

For some reason, she froze.

"You got her?" Howler asked from the front seat. "The last thing I need is the bitch getting free."

"She's good," Blink told him.

As she struggled to get her panicked breathing under control...Remi realized that while Blink was holding her immobile, he wasn't hurting her. The hand over her mouth wasn't covering her nose, so she could breathe easily. His arm around her was tight, but not painfully so. He'd also wrapped one of his legs around hers, so she couldn't kick him or use her feet to try to escape.

She was more confused than ever.

She thought about Vincent. Was he okay? Had his so-called *friend* hurt him too?

"Vincent?" she mumbled behind Blink's hand. Somehow, Howler understood her.

"Kevlar's fine. For now," he muttered darkly. "I just needed a way to get you to come with me on short notice. We don't have much time to get this done. I have to be back on base for the afternoon meetings. So you need to cooperate. Understand me?"

Cooperate, her ass. If he was supposed to be somewhere, and she could prevent that from happening so someone might ask questions, she was all for it. And now that she knew Vincent was all right, she was all the more determined to get away from these psychopaths.

She realized they were driving west, and Howler was definitely speeding. She prayed that he'd get pulled over, that would be her best chance at getting away. But of course, the farther they drove from the city, the lower her hopes got.

"What's the plan?" Blink asked after ten minutes or so.

"I've got a place already prepped. We'll leave her there, then get back to the city. Our phones are our alibis. We'll leave hers with her so she'll be found. I'll join in the search parties for her. Of course, when her body's found, I'll be just as devastated as everyone else." An evil smile spread over Howler's face. "But the show must go on, right? We're supposed to leave for that mission in Chad in three days. Kevlar will be too devastated to go, I'm sure. So I'll take over as team leader. We're gonna need a seventh man. You in? You over whatever bullshit had you all tied up in knots?"

There was a lot to dissect in his little speech, none of which Remi liked. Her heart was beating as fast as a jackrabbit's and she couldn't believe Howler was...what was he doing? It sounded like he was taking her somewhere to *kill her*!

No. That couldn't be right. And why? Just so he could take over Vincent's SEAL team? That was...completely insane!

"As I said before, I'm in," Blink said in a calm, even tone.

"Everyone said you were done for, man. That you'd be chaptered out. But I had a feeling they were wrong. I saw something in you, something I recognized in myself. I need strong people at my back, because Lord knows the fucking team I'm on now are a bunch of pussies. They'd rather sit around like old men at Aces than partake in the buffet of pussy elsewhere. Don't know why you were wallowing in that place. Everything seems better when your cock is deep in a chick's hole." He grinned at Blink in the rearview. "Maybe I'll take Kevlar's bitch for a spin, see how she got him wrapped around her finger so fast."

Remi stiffened. Her anger was fading and panic was quickly returning. There was no way she could overpower

Howler. Especially not with Blink holding her as easily as if she were a child.

"I'm thinking we don't have time for that," Blink told the other SEAL.

"Damn. That's probably true. I'm on a timetable here, just over an hour to get this shit done and return to base," Howler muttered.

"So you were responsible for the Hawaii job, then," Blink said almost nonchalantly.

"I don't know what you're talking about," he retorted.

"Right. Well, it was brilliant, if you ask me."

"Fucking captain," Howler muttered. "If he hadn't fucked up and stopped too early, it would've worked."

"Kevlar's one of the best swimmers on the team," Blink argued.

"He is. But twenty miles would be tough at the best of times. He had his wetsuit and scuba gear, but those wouldn't have helped him against a shark. And if the boat captain had done his job, it would've been dark by the time Kevlar got even close to land. At worst, he would've been exhausted, maybe even injured and unable to assume his duties. At best...Well, you know."

Remi felt sick. The things Howler was saying—they were horrible. Especially about someone who was supposed to be his friend. His teammate.

"Fucking asshole captain," Howler mumbled as he drove. "If he'd just listened to the instructions he'd been given, we wouldn't be here now." He looked in the rearview at Remi. "With you along, Kevlar would've played the gallant hero he thinks he is, which meant you *both* would've died out there. You weren't part of the plan, but honestly, I should've thought about including a civilian from the start. A helpless chick, someone he wouldn't be able to leave behind to save his own ass. Kevlar's always been the noble one, which makes him a shit team leader."

Remi's fists clenched. She was back to being pissed. Her emotions were all over the place.

Then she felt something against her arm, and her breath caught. She wanted to look down, to make sure she was feeling what she thought she was, but Blink's hand was still covering her mouth. She couldn't move her head, which rested on his shoulder. All she could do was stare straight ahead.

Then she felt it again.

Blink's thumb...gently stroking her arm. As if he was trying to soothe her.

But that couldn't be right, could it? Remi was utterly baffled.

Howler was driving even faster now. Her face was throbbing where he'd hit her—*hit* her, twice—and he was taking her who-knew-where to do who-knew-what before going back to the base and pretending he was as worried as everyone else when it was discovered that she was missing.

Well, screw that. If she got any chance, she was taking it. She wouldn't go down without a fight. At the very least, she'd get Howler's DNA under her fingernails so the crime lab would know she'd fought someone. If she could, she'd run, but with Blink helping him, she wasn't sure that would happen.

Screw him. Screw them both.

"Thanks for taking control of...*that*," Howler said, his gaze flicking to Blink.

"Would've been hard to drive and subdue her," he replied emotionlessly.

"True. I'm thinking it was a good thing you snapped out of your shit and decided to come along."

"Me too," Blink said.

Remi wanted to plead with Howler to let her go. Promise that she'd leave the Riverton area. That she wouldn't see Vincent anymore. Anything that might prolong her life. But she couldn't say anything with Blink's hand over her mouth, and she didn't think there was anything she could say that would change Howler's plans.

But mostly, she knew that she could never give up Vincent.

She swallowed hard and tears sprang to her eyes, but she blinked them back. She had to stay alert, ready for anything. For the smallest chance to escape. Remi had no idea what Blink would do if she ran, but she had no doubt Howler would do whatever he could to prevent her from getting away.

The next sixty minutes would be the most important of her life. She could give up and accept whatever Howler had planned, or she could fight. And while she might be an introverted nerd, she wasn't ready to die.

* * *

"What do you mean, she's not there?" Kevlar asked Caroline in confusion. She was supposed to pick up Remi at his apartment and drive her to Aces, where he would have met them for lunch.

That was the plan, anyway. But the meetings had run late that morning and he'd had to cancel. Which pissed him off, but it couldn't be helped. It looked like they would be going wheels up in thirty-six hours or less, and he wasn't satisfied with the latest intel they'd received. He wasn't sending his team into a situation without as many concrete facts as possible, if he could help it.

The HVT they were being sent to neutralize had several safe houses in the city, and while they had good intel on the one where he'd most likely be hiding, they needed to know the layouts of *every* house. Just in case. There were dozens of things that could go wrong, and it was his job as team leader to mitigate as many of the roadblocks as possible.

He'd texted both Caroline and Remi about the change in plans twenty minutes ago...and now that he thought about it, Kevlar hadn't heard back from Remi after he'd sent that text. Which wasn't common. He'd been so intent on figuring out egress routes for the team, it hadn't hit him until right this moment that she hadn't texted him back.

"She's not here," Caroline told him again. "I'm at your place, and she isn't answering. Her car is here though. Maybe she got a ride from someone else?"

But Kevlar was already shaking his head. No, she wouldn't do that without letting him know. When he brought up their text string, his message to her was the last one.

Kevlar's mind immediately went into planning mode. His team was on a much-deserved break. They'd left about half an hour ago and weren't required to be back for another hour. "If you could head to Aces and see if she's there, I'd appreciate it," Kevlar told Caroline calmly. If his team was here right now, they'd know immediately something was wrong, because whenever shit hit the fan, while others might get hyped up and excited, Kevlar did the opposite. He got hyper *focused*, almost unemotional.

"Of course. I'm sure she's fine," Caroline said.

"Yeah," Kevlar agreed, but deep down he knew something wasn't right. He didn't know what, but Remi wouldn't change plans without letting him know. He may have only met her a short time ago, but he knew that without a doubt.

"Kevlar?" his commander asked when he'd hung up with Caroline. "What's wrong?" Just like his team, Kevlar's commander could also read his moods.

"I don't know," he admitted. "Remi's not home."

"And that's unusual?"

"Yes."

"What do you need from me?"

That was the thing—Kevlar had no idea what he needed to do, or what anyone else should do, for that matter. All he knew was that every fiber of his being was screaming that something was wrong. That Remi was in trouble. "Can you call the team? See if they can come back from lunch early?"

"Of course."

Kevlar took a deep breath. Everything within him was telling him to leave, to find Remi. To confirm with his own eyes that she was all right. But that would be a mistake. Without any intel, without knowing where to start looking for her, all he'd be doing was spinning his wheels.

He closed his eyes and took a deep breath in through his nose and let it out through his mouth. He couldn't panic. Not now. He prayed there was a good reason Remi was in the wind. That she'd tease him later for his overreaction to her not being at the apartment when Caroline got there. He hoped against all hope that she'd simply gotten the plans mixed up, and had maybe called an Uber to take her to Aces instead of waiting for Caroline. That she'd roll her eyes at the fuss when she was discovered at the bar, safe and sound.

But deep down, he knew she wasn't there. Something had happened...and his gut told him it had to do with Hawaii.

He'd been an idiot for not taking her safety more seriously. If someone was after him, it only made sense that they'd try to get to him through Remi. It wasn't as if he'd hidden how much she was coming to mean to him.

How much he loved her.

He wasn't even surprised at the thought. He loved Remi. Hell, he'd basically moved her into his apartment without a second thought and had every intention of convincing her to stay. He couldn't wait to see her at the end of each day and lived for the cute texts she sent him randomly while he was working.

The thought of something happening to her because of him was unacceptable. She didn't have an enemy in the world. She was in trouble because he hadn't worked hard enough to figure out who wanted to hurt him.

The phone rang in the silence of the conference room, bringing Kevlar back to the present. He ground his teeth together. No one hurt his woman and got away with it. He'd find Remi and fucking destroy whoever it was who dared try to take her away from him.

CHAPTER SIXTEEN

The truck slowed, and Remi braced for whatever was to come. Howler had obviously scoped out where he was going before today, because he didn't hesitate to turn down a series of roads that got smaller and smaller. First asphalt, then gravel, then dirt, and now they were driving on two-tracks in the grass that couldn't even be described as a road. He stopped the truck at the edge of a huge forest.

He turned around and said, "Now the fun starts."

"Asshole," she mumbled from behind Blink's hand. The other SEAL hadn't taken his hand from her mouth during the entire voyage. It was annoying, and she'd tried to bite him several times, but Blink had merely pressed down on her mouth until she stilled, then loosened his hold once more. He hadn't hurt her. It was still confusing as hell. What was the point of being gentle with her if Howler was just going to kill her anyway?

Blink finally took his hand off her mouth after Howler exited the truck. He opened the door, slid across the seat and stood, all the while holding Remi as if she was nothing more than a toddler. Which was actually pretty impressive, considering her height and weight. But Blink maneuvered her seemingly without any effort...which kind of pissed Remi off again. Her emotions were on a roller coaster, and the adrenaline in her veins was making her feel kind of sick, but she had to stay alert. Ready for anything.

"Come on," Howler said. "We don't have a lot of time."

Remi noticed he had her phone, and she desperately wanted to get her hands on it. To call 9-1-1, Vincent, Wolf, *anyone*. Of course, she had no idea if there was any cell service out here, but she'd walk however far it took for her to be able to get through to someone, if only she could escape.

"Walk," Blink ordered, gripping her upper arm in his left hand and wrapping his right arm around her waist, holding her against his side.

Remi wiggled, trying to see if she could possibly get away, but of course Blink had a firm hold, and she didn't see how she could get him to let go of her. He was stronger and taller.

She tried to scream, but Blink quickly covered her mouth with his hand, even has he forced her to walk. Not that it mattered; there wasn't anyone around. It was just her, Howler, and Blink. The only sound was the leaves blowing in the breeze. Wherever Howler had taken her, it was certainly deserted.

It was crazy, but she was actually glad for Blink's physical support as they walked into the trees, as it didn't seem as if her legs wanted to hold her up. She almost cried at the thought. Remi needed her muscles to work if she was going to get away from these assholes.

"Please let me go, Howler. I promise I'll leave. Move away from Riverton. Whatever you want me to do."

But the SEAL leading the way to whatever destination he had in mind just shrugged. "Sorry, but that won't work. I need Kevlar broken. Need him unable to function so I can take his place. Prove that I can do a better job at leading our team than he does. And the only way to do that is to hit him right where it hurts most."

"He and I, we...it's not serious." The lie felt wrong on her lips, but Remi would literally disown her entire family right now if she thought it would get her out of this situation.

"That's not what he says," Howler informed her.

Remi's heart nearly stopped, it ached so badly. She didn't need to ask what Vincent might've said about her, because Howler seemed happy enough to keep talking.

"All he talks about is you. Remi did this, Remi said that...*barf*. You should hear him go on and on about that ridiculous cartoon you draw. He acts as if it's the funniest thing ever when it's just fuckin' stupid. Shit, he actually claimed you were the best thing that ever happened to him. That being stranded in the water in Hawaii with you was actually kind of fun. Fun!" Howler yelled, suddenly spinning to face her and Blink.

"He was supposed to fucking die! And he thought it was *fun*!" He stomped forward so he was right in front of her, and Remi could feel Blink tensing against her side. She didn't dare move. Didn't dare say anything. It was obvious Howler was losing it, and her cheek still hurt where he'd hit her before. She didn't want to antagonize him further.

"With you gone, he won't be having any more *fun*. He'll be crying over your coffin, doing everything he can to figure out who killed you and why, and I'll be with *my* team in Chad, kicking ass and taking names. His plans are ridiculous, too conservative. The only way to deal with terrorists is to go in hard and fast. All the planning and contingencies and twelve-hour days are just fucking stupid. We need to get over there and do what we've been trained to do—kick some ass. I'll show the commander and everyone else how a *real* SEAL leads a team. Your death will break Kevlar. I'll finally get my shot. We'll see what kind of *fun* he's having then!"

Remi was appalled. But she did her best to keep the horror from showing on her face. That's what Howler wanted, for her to be scared. To beg. But it wouldn't do any good; it would just make him more satisfied.

"You'll get caught," she said after a moment, with only a small tremor in her voice.

"No, I won't. My phone is on and transmitting my location back at my apartment. I went home to eat lunch, and by the time Kevlar raises the alarm that you're missing, I'll be rushing back to base to help along with everyone else. Blink will be my alibi. My truck is old enough that it doesn't have a GPS. There are no tolls on the roads to get here, and I've got another set of clothes in my truck, just in case things get...messy."

Remi had to admit that it sounded as if he'd thought this through—to a point. But her fingerprints would be in his truck. Possibly even her DNA. And he'd called her. There would be a record of that as well.

Howler thought he'd planned everything perfectly...but he'd still messed up.

Then she had a thought. "My phone," she whispered.

"Yep. Your phone," Howler said, glancing at the device he was still holding. "It's probably transmitting even now. Although the cops will still have a large area to search because the pings aren't precise. By the time they even think to trace it, even if fucking Tex steps in to help, Blink and I will be long gone. And I *want* the authorities to find you, Remi. I need you to be found so Kevlar can fall apart. Oh, I'll smash it before we leave. All the police will find is plastic bits. No tire tracks, no footprints. Just your poor dead body.

"You'll end up in the cold case files and no one will ever know who killed you or why. They'll be forced to assume it was a random abduction. Maybe you opened your door to someone who kidnapped you. But...time's a tickin'. No more time to stand here and chatter with you. I have a mission to Africa to plan. Bring her," Howler said, nodding at Blink.

This time when he urged her forward, Remi's legs refused to work.

No, she wasn't going any farther into this forest of death. She wasn't going to let Howler get away with his plans. He was acting like a jealous kid, stomping his feet and crying because he wanted to be in charge of a SEAL team. It was insane. *He* was insane.

But her refusal to walk didn't faze Blink. He simply lifted her off her feet and strode into the trees after Howler.

"Please, Blink—don't do this! You don't have to do this!" she babbled. "You're a good man, a good SEAL. What happened wasn't your fault. You can still stop this. Please don't let him hurt me!"

Blink didn't respond. His lips were pressed tightly together and she could see a muscle tic in his jaw as he carried her. She kicked and writhed, tried frantically to get out of his hold, but he only tightened his grip and said, "Stop it, Remi."

"No! Let me go! Blink, this is crazy! You can't kill me! Help! Someone help!" She resorted to screaming because she was out of ideas.

Howler spun and before she could react, he punched her again. Blood dripped from her lip down her chin, but she barely noticed. His fist reared back and he tried to punch her again, but this time he only got her shoulder because Blink had turned with her in his grip.

Remi grunted at the pain that shot down her arm.

"I got her," Blink huffed, before putting his hand back over her mouth.

No! She had to be able to speak! To talk her way out of

this. To *beg*! But Blink's hand was immovable. She tried to twist her head but his arm was wrapped around it, holding her cheek against his shoulder.

"Fucking bitch. Keep her quiet and come on. I'm behind schedule," Howler complained. "It's not far now."

Remi was kind of straddling Blink's hip as he carried her and kept her quiet at the same time. She dug her fingers into his arm, trying to dislodge him, with no luck. She prayed she was getting some of his DNA under her nails. Anything that would help the cops figure out who kidnapped her.

Then Howler stopped walking—and if she was scared before, it was nothing compared to how she felt looking down at the hole in the ground that Howler had obviously pre-dug.

There was what looked like a footlocker sitting in the hole, with a padlock hanging open in the latch.

"No!" she screamed behind Blink's hand.

"Put her in," Howler ordered.

Remi struggled as hard as she could against Blink. If he got her in that box, she was as good as dead. She supposed she could be grateful that he hadn't simply pulled out a gun and shot her in the head, or stabbed her twenty times before locking her in...but then again, was being buried alive any better?

It was almost pathetic how easy it was for Blink to subdue her and shove her into the metal box. She tried to get up on her knees, not wanting to make it easy for these men to kill her, but Howler came over and added his weight to Blink's as they pushed on her shoulders, forcing her to fold into the box. She was screaming at the top of her lungs and flailing as she did her best to escape. It was no use.

The sound of the box slamming shut seemed loud in the tiny space. But it was the sound of the lock engaging that had every muscle in her body freezing in terror.

This was it. She was going to die. Right here and now.

She heard Howler say, "Fill it in," before a loud thud made her locked muscles jerk. There was another thud on top of the box—and that's when the tears started.

She was being buried alive. By a man Vincent trusted with his life.

Awkwardly, Remi struggled onto her side and curled into a small ball as she sobbed uncontrollably.

She wanted to live. She hadn't gotten a chance to tell Vincent she loved him. That he was the best thing that had ever happened to her. And it was likely he'd never know one of the men he'd been to hell and back with had been the one who'd killed her.

"Vincent," she cried. "I'm sorry. I'm so sorry. I tried to fight...I did." No more words would come out through her sobs as she lay in the metal box that would become her coffin.

* * *

"I've asked everyone, and no one has seen her," Caroline said in Kevlar's ear.

His shoulders sagged. He'd hoped against hope that Remi would be at Aces, even though he knew it was unlikely. "Thanks for looking."

"What do you need from me? From Wolf?" Caroline asked. "He can call the guys and I can get in touch with the girls. We can start looking. Just tell us what you need."

This was why Kevlar never regretted becoming a SEAL. The unwavering support. Even from men and women who were no longer active duty. It meant the world to him. He just wished he had something for them to do. At the moment, he had nowhere to start a search for Remi. It was as if she'd disappeared into thin air.

"If you could just call Wolf and let him know that Remi's missing, I'd appreciate it," Kevlar told Caroline. "But that's it for now. I'll be in touch if I get any intel."

"All right. We'll find her, Kevlar."

Would they? Those were words everyone said when someone went missing, but they sounded so hollow at the moment. "Thanks," he managed to say before hanging up.

He stared at the table, feeling frustrated and lost. He was a SEAL. He should be *doing* something. Should have some ideas about where to start looking for Remi. He still held out a small glimmer of hope that she was simply out shopping or something. That's what any normal person would assume when they couldn't get a hold of their girlfriend when she was an hour late, but after what happened in Hawaii, and with how new their relationship was, he didn't think she'd up and leave without telling him where she was going. Hell, she'd barely left his apartment since she'd arrived. She always said she was more than comfortable hanging out in his space, drawing. Occasionally text with him and...

Marley!

Kevlar reached for his phone. Stupid! He needed to call Remi's best friend. If she'd gone anywhere, surely she would've told Marley.

Three minutes later, he'd only managed to freak someone else out, and hadn't learned anything else about where Remi could be. Marley hadn't heard from her, and the last she'd known, Remi had been looking forward to seeing Caroline again and having lunch with him.

The door behind him burst open, and Flash and MacGyver were suddenly there.

"What's happening?"

"Got here as soon as the commander told me Remi was missing."

Just having his teammates there to have his back made Kevlar feel much better.

Then Preacher, Smiley, and Safe arrived too.

Kevlar stood and faced the best friends he'd ever had... but he had nothing to say. Had no idea what to tell them. His mind was blank. He was supposed to be the team leader, but at the moment, he was lost. Frustrated and pissed off. And had no idea what to do next.

"Where's Howler?" Smiley asked.

"He didn't answer when I called him. Left a message," their commander said.

"I'm sure he'll be here as soon as he can," Flash offered.

"Probably went and picked up some Frog Hog to fuck during lunch," MacGyver muttered.

Kevlar couldn't argue that point. The closer they got to leaving on a mission, the more Howler felt the need to pick up women. He'd tried to talk to his friend about how fucked up that was, but Howler wouldn't listen. He was a little disappointed that the man wasn't there to help find Remi, but since he had no idea where to even start looking for her, he supposed it didn't really matter.

Safe walked over to Kevlar and put his hand on his shoulder, then turned him and forced him to sit. "Start at the beginning. What's happening, when did you last hear from Remi?"

Taking a deep breath, and thankful for his friend taking charge, because he wasn't able to do more than panic at the moment, Kevlar brought his team up to speed. He prayed they'd be able to think clearer than he could. That they'd come up with a logical reason why Remi wasn't answering her phone and was nowhere to be found.

Blink was hyper-focused. He needed a window so he could act. Just a small one. He was at a disadvantage here. Howler was an asshole, and obviously unhinged, but in hand-to-hand combat, the guy would come out on top. Blink had let his physical shape slide in the last few weeks. Sitting on his ass brooding hadn't done his body any favors.

And Howler would have been working out daily, preparing for the mission to Chad.

If they got into a fight out there in the woods, Blink would lose. And there was too much riding on him overpowering Howler for that outcome.

He'd *hated* seeing the terror in Remi's eyes as he'd closed that fucking lid on the footlocker. And while he'd done his best to protect her from Howler's fists, he'd still gotten in a few licks.

That outraged Blink. Pissed him off so badly that Howler was using his strength against someone physically weaker. Blink had manhandled Remi into the backseat of the truck to keep her out of range of the guy's fists. She didn't understand that he was helping her, of course. How could she? He'd had to go along with Howler's insane plan, not let his horror show over how callously and casually he'd planned another person's death.

He'd done what was necessary, including complimenting the man's leadership skills and promising to serve under him. No way in hell was that happening. Blink's SEAL team had been his family. He would've died for them, just as they'd died and been hurt to save *his* life. No fucking way would he sully their names and character to serve under someone like Howler.

The man was unhinged. Jealous as fuck. Blink had occasionally watched the team in Aces. He'd seen the looks Howler frequently shot Kevlar's way. No one thought he paid attention to anything when he spent hours at the bar... but he did.

Blink saw *everything*. Heard everything. He knew how people talked about him. Gossiped. Knew they thought he'd lost the will to live. But he'd simply been...recalibrating. Coming to terms with what happened. Mentally saying goodbye to his friends.

He'd also seen the way Kevlar couldn't take his gaze from Remi that one afternoon in the bar, and how she looked at *him* with longing when she thought no one was watching.

He saw how nervous Remi was, how uncomfortable she'd been at Aces, but she still charmed everyone and fit right in with Kevlar's SEAL family. And when she'd approached him, Blink had braced himself for the intrusive questions. For more insensitivity disguised as well-meaning concern.

But instead, he'd gotten kindness. She didn't know him, and yet she'd still wanted to make sure he was all right. Thank him. She'd made him almost smile for the first time in weeks.

She'd somehow gotten through to him, when nothing and no one else had.

And how had he repaid her? By scaring the shit out of her and making her think he was as bad as Howler.

She'd never forgive him. Would never be able to see him without remembering the terror she'd felt when she'd been abducted. And he couldn't do anything about that.

But Blink wasn't going to let Howler get away with his evil, outrageous plan.

He had no doubt the commander wouldn't make

Howler team leader, regardless of what this stunt did to Kevlar. Even if there was no other SEAL team available to go to Chad, the commander wouldn't send Kevlar's team without him. Howler was delusional. He wasn't going to be leader. Ever. He didn't have the right mindset or the skills. He only had his own conceit that made him think he could successfully do the job.

"*Shit*. Faster, Blink! I need to get back to base!" Howler ordered. "We need to get this box covered so she'll suffocate before anyone finds her."

His words horrified Blink even further. Glancing over his shoulder, he saw that Howler was standing behind him, close enough that he could see his progress. More than content to watch as Blink did the physical work of filling in the hole with dirt. Another sign this man could never be a leader. A true leader didn't just watch others do the work; he'd be right there helping.

Remi was pounding on the locker now. Blink winced, imagining the damage she was doing to her fists as she unsuccessfully tried to get out of the locked box.

It was now or never.

Tightening his hands on the shovel, Blink took a deep breath—and moved.

He swung the shovel like a baseball bat, putting all his strength behind the hit.

It took Howler by surprise, scoring a direct hit to his face. Blink felt the bones in the other man's face crack as the metal shovel found its mark.

Howler cried out in pain and fell onto his back with a

hard thump. "You asshole!" he shouted, rage filling his features as his hand went to his nose. "You were the perfect fucking pawn—"

Without hesitation, Blink was on Howler in a flash. He straddled his waist and attacked.

Over and over, he punched the other SEAL in the face, letting all the grief and rage he'd felt for weeks pour out through his fists. He struck so fast and furious, the man didn't have a chance to fight back. Pummeling him until his knuckles were covered in blood...and Howler was no longer moving.

Panting, Blink rose on his knees, hyper alert, ready to do whatever it took to make sure Howler couldn't get up. Wouldn't get away with his crazy fucking plan to kill Remi. He'd thought it was sheer luck, him standing at his window, seeing Howler pull up at the apartment complex. And after what Howler said about being a pawn, he knew he was right...but it wasn't lucky for *Blink*. It was lucky for *Howler*.

He'd been set up. Howler had obviously heard about his so-called paranoia. The ridiculous rumor that he spent all his time at his apartment windows, watching his neighbors. And he'd obviously hoped to use that to his advantage, letting Blink take the fall for Remi's death. He'd fallen right into the asshole's hands.

Even knowing that, Blink was so grateful that he hadn't hesitated to get in that truck. To put himself in the middle of Howler's plan.

Remi would hate him, and Kevlar would forever be pissed that he hadn't done more to prevent things from getting this far. But Blink had done what he could in the situation.

Taking a deep breath, he looked down at Howler—and froze.

Shit.

The man wasn't moving—at all. Wasn't moaning, wasn't trying to get up. He just lay in the grass, limp and bloody.

Moving slowly, Blink reached out a shaky hand and put his fingers on Howler's neck.

Nothing. No pulse.

Falling to his ass and backing away from the body, Blink swallowed hard. He didn't regret killing the man, but he knew it would cause problems. *He'd* be accused of everything. Kidnapping, attempted murder. Remi would recount everything he'd said and done, and he'd be found to be as guilty as the asshole lying dead on the ground.

He didn't care. He'd accept the ramifications of what happened here today. Because Remi would be alive. That was all that mattered.

As thoughts of Remi entered his brain, Blink realized that he couldn't hear her pounding on the footlocker anymore. Was she okay? He hadn't put more than a few shovelfuls of dirt on top of the box. But he had no idea if Howler had done something to make the locker water or airproof. Was she suffocating already?

Blink crawled back over to Howler and frantically dug in the front pocket of his jeans. He had to have the key on him. He *had* to. But he came up empty.

The asshole had the key to the padlock somewhere, but

Blink didn't have time to find it. He couldn't go back to the truck or, God forbid, all the way to the man's apartment to search for it.

He had to get that lock off. Now.

Looking around, Blink spotted the shovel he'd used to bash in Howler's face. He stood and reached for it, hurrying back to the hole. He used all his strength to bring the shovel down on the lock. It made a clanging noise as it hit the side of the footlocker, but didn't come off.

"Come on, you asshole. Break!" Blink murmured as he hit it again. And again. He was blind with desperation and fury. He had to get that lock off and get Remi out of that box. He wouldn't stop until she was free.

His hands were slippery on the handle because of the blood from Howler's face, but Blink refused to give up. Splinters from the cheap wooden handle dug into his palms, but he didn't even feel them. All his focus was on breaking that lock. He couldn't save his teammates, had watched as they'd been shot by the enemy, but he'd be damned if anyone else died on his watch.

CHAPTER SEVENTEEN

Remi had finally stopped pounding on the lid of the box. It wouldn't do any good, and the angle was awkward anyway. Even lying on her side with her knees drawn up to her chest, she still barely fit and could get no strength behind her efforts. If she was petite like Marley, she might've felt less claustrophobic. But at five-eight and plenty curvy, it was a very tight squeeze.

She had the momentary thought that if she was bigger, she might not have fit inside the damn footlocker at all, and then what would Howler have done? If he couldn't get the box shut and locked.

A snort-laugh escaped, which turned into another sob. But she forced herself to stop. She'd already had her crying fit. She didn't want her last moments on earth to be spent bawling.

She held her breath, trying to hear what was happening

outside her prison, but she couldn't pick up anything. After just a few thumps of what she assumed was dirt being thrown on top of the box, they'd stopped. Had they left? Only half buried her so she'd be easier to find?

How long could the human body go without water? Remi thought it was three days. She could do that. But the more pressing problem would be oxygen. As soon as the box was covered in dirt, her air would quickly run out. It was unlikely Vincent and his friends would find her before she suffocated. Even if they got his computer genius friend to track her phone. Howler had expected the police to do just that, so they'd find her before the team was supposed to leave on their mission.

Stupid Howler! What a dick. Asshole. Fucking lunatic!

She wanted to get out of this box to warn Vincent about his unstable teammate. So she could press charges. Face him in a courtroom and tell everyone how he'd tried to kill her.

A sudden loud noise right by her head scared Remi so bad, she jerked and smacked her bruised cheek on the top of the locker. "Shit!" she cried out, before the sound came again. And again.

It sounded like someone was hitting the footlocker as hard as they could. She had no idea why. Maybe Howler wasn't satisfied with leaving her alive in the box? Maybe he wanted to open it and kill her outright, just in case, before burying her again.

Whatever was happening, it couldn't be good. As much as she wanted out of this tiny coffin, she didn't want to come face-to-face with Howler again. Or Blink. Nothing good could come out of the lid opening so soon after she'd been forced into the box.

The loud banging continued—and then suddenly, it stopped. She heard scraping sounds, metal on metal, then the lid was flung open.

Springing to her knees, Remi blinked in the sudden bright light of day after being in the pitch dark for what seemed like hours, but was only minutes. She tried to focus, wanted to run, but she needed to know what she was facing before she tried to fight her way out of the box.

At first, her brain refused to comprehend what she was seeing.

Howler was lying a dozen feet away, on his back, unmoving. His face was covered in blood. There was so much, at any other time the sight would've made her sick. But she must've been in shock, because the blood barely registered, other than her brain making note that he likely wouldn't be getting up to hurt her anytime soon.

Then she focused on Blink. He was backing away from her slowly with a faraway look in his eyes. There was a shovel on the ground near the hole, and the broken lock lay in the dirt next to the box.

She looked from the lock, to the shovel, to Blink, then back to the lock.

He'd broken it. Opened the lid. Had clearly beaten the crap out of Howler. And even as she sat there, putting the pieces together, Blink tripped over a log or something and fell to his ass. But he didn't move to get up.

They were both frozen, staring at each other with wide eyes.

Then Blink rasped, "Run, Remi. He left the keys in the truck. Drive back to town. Get the cops."

She should do exactly as he ordered. But for some reason, she couldn't. Instead, she climbed out of the footlocker onto her hands and knees began to crawl toward Blink.

Everything that happened swirled through her brain like a bad B movie. Howler arriving at the apartment by himself. Blink showing up, and how pissed Howler looked when he'd first gotten into the truck. Blink holding her tightly, but not enough to hurt her. Turning when Howler tried to punch her in the face again.

She was probably losing it, having some sort of mental break that happened when people began to trust their kidnappers—but with sudden clarity, she knew that Blink had saved her. Had been *trying* to save her all along.

He'd hurt—*killed?*—Howler, and had broken the lock to free her.

He looked scared...of *her*. Broken.

Remi was shaking so hard, it was difficult to keep moving, but she couldn't stop crawling toward Blink.

He was shaking his head. "Go, Remi. Get out of here!"

But she ignored him.

When she got close enough, Remi threw herself at him. Needing human contact. She'd almost *died*. Been buried alive! She needed to anchor herself to another human being. To know for a fact that she wasn't dreaming. That

Blink had saved her. Yes, he'd said and done some scary things, but he'd been as helpless as she was.

He was her guardian angel.

Letting out a soft grunt, Blink caught her in his arms and somehow stayed upright as she clung to him like a baby monkey holding onto its mother.

She buried her face in the space between his head and shoulder and began to shake violently. "Thank you, Blink! Thank you," she whispered.

His arms tightened around her, but he didn't speak.

They sat together on the ground for a long, silent moment before Blink finally said, "You should be pissed at me."

"I'm not."

"I let that go too far. I'm sorry. I'm so sorry."

"You did what you had to do, and you stopped him when you got the chance."

"It wasn't enough."

Remi took a deep breath and pulled back. She should be embarrassed at the fact she was straddling this man's lap. He was practically a stranger, after all. But they'd just been through hell together, and she needed him right now. Needed his warmth. Needed his strength. His safety. "I'm breathing, and not in that box in the ground covered with dirt. It was *more* than enough."

Her words seemed to affect him greatly, because he closed his eyes and shuddered in her grip. For the first time, Remi realized that he probably needed human contact as much as, or even more than, she did.

"I thought you'd run away from me screaming," he told her.

"Thought about it," Remi admitted. "But when I stopped for two seconds to think, I realized you'd actually been protecting me this entire time."

He stared at her for a beat before saying, "We need to call Kevlar."

"My phone!" Remi exclaimed. "Where is it? I can't believe I forgot Howler had it."

"Stay here," Blink ordered in that low, rough tone of his.

But this time, it didn't scare Remi.

As if he could see that she had no intention of sitting there like a good little girl, he added, "Please? I don't want you near him."

"Is he...is he dead?" she asked with a stutter.

"Yeah."

Remi swallowed hard. She should be more upset that there was a dead body less than ten feet from her. But honestly, what she mostly felt was relief. She nodded solemnly at Blink.

He stared at her for another moment, as if making sure she'd stay put, then gently eased her off his lap to stand and walk over to Howler's body. He turned him and reached into his back pocket, and when he straightened, her phone was in his hand.

Blink returned to where she was still sitting on the ground and held it out to her.

Remi's hands shook as she took it from him and

unlocked it. Then she looked up at Blink in frustration. "No signal."

"Let's get back to the truck. Maybe we'll have better luck there."

Nodding, Remi held out a hand so he could help her stand. She wasn't sure she could do so on her own. The adrenaline dump she'd had the moment that box lid opened was fading, and she still felt shaky as hell.

Blink stared at her hand for a long moment, then clasped it in his own. Once she was on her feet, Remi leaned against him, and his arm went around her shoulders, holding her steady. Other than his hand not being over her mouth, the walk back to the truck felt very similar to the one they'd taken into the trees not so long ago.

But everything had changed. Remi felt like a different person. She'd had a close call, and thanks to the man at her side, she was alive to get the second chance she'd prayed so hard for.

When they got to the truck, Blink opened the back door and helped her sit on the seat with her legs dangling out the side.

"Any luck?" he asked.

Looking down at the phone, Remi smiled. "Yeah. One bar."

"It'll have to do."

"Should we drive back to the city?" she asked.

Blink sighed. "Probably not a good idea. Not with...you know," he said, looking behind him into the trees. "But you need to get in touch with Kevlar before we do anything else."

"He might not even know anything happened," Remi told him.

"Oh, he knows," Blink told her. "He probably felt a shift in the space time continuum the first time Howler hit you."

Remi stared at the man in front of her. She couldn't decide if he was kidding or not.

"Call him, Remi," he ordered.

Nodding, she clicked on Vincent's name and brought the phone up to her ear.

Kevlar paced the lobby of the police station. When his phone rang an hour earlier, and he'd seen Remi's name on his screen, he'd nearly had a heart attack.

But that was *nothing* compared to how he felt when she'd told him the basics of what had happened, and where she was.

All he'd wanted to do was jump in his car and race into the hills to get her. To see for himself that she was all right. But his commander and team had convinced him it would be faster if he went straight to the police station. Because that's where the cops would be taking her in order to get her statement.

So now, here he was. Waiting to put his hands on her. To see with his own eyes that she was okay.

Knowing it was Howler, his own teammate, his friend, who'd taken her...tried to *kill* her...had Kevlar nearly at his breaking point, along with the rest of his team. How could Howler have done this? What the fuck was he *thinking*?

He needed answers, and he had nothing but questions.

But honestly, all he needed right now was Remi. He could work on getting answers after making sure she was all right.

"Easy, man, she'll be here soon," Safe said.

Kevlar nodded, but he barely heard his friend.

His entire team was at his side, and as appreciative as he was, he felt as if he was going to jump out of his skin if he didn't see Remi in the next few seconds.

"Vincent Hill?" an officer asked. She'd come through a door that led to the bowels of the police station.

"Yes, that's me," he said.

"If you'll follow me."

"Go," Smiley said. "We'll be here."

"Should we call her parents?" Preacher asked.

"Oh, shit, Marley, what about her?" Flash added.

"I'm sure she's called them, or will soon," MacGyver said calmly. "Go, Kevlar. Get to Remi."

He didn't need to be told twice. Kevlar followed the officer down a long hallway. She led him to a door and opened it. Looking inside, Kevlar shook his head. "No. Where's Remi? I need to see her."

"She's fine."

"Not what I asked," Kevlar growled, refusing to step

foot inside the small room. "Please," he begged. "I need to see her. See for myself that she's okay."

The woman smiled slightly, then she got serious again. "You sound as stubborn as she is."

"What do you mean?"

"She refused to leave the scene in a different car than Nate Davis."

"Who?" Kevlar asked.

Now it was the officer's turn to look confused. "Nate Davis? The man she was with?"

It dawned on Kevlar then—Blink. He wasn't sure he'd ever heard his full given name. Remi had briefly told him that Blink saved her life. He didn't know the details, knew nothing other than his Remi had been abducted by Howler, and Blink had somehow been there and saved her. But he didn't care. He owed the man *everything*.

"Right, Nate. Please, where's Remi?"

"She's coming," the officer told him. "She and the others will be here momentarily. You can wait in this room and we'll bring her to you."

But Kevlar didn't want to go into the room. He wanted to wait in the parking lot. See her as soon as possible.

A noise at the other end of the hall drew their attention, and when Kevlar looked up, he saw the most beautiful sight he'd ever lain eyes on.

Remi. She was standing on her own two feet—thank God—with one of those silver emergency blankets around her shoulders and Blink's arm around her waist.

Kevlar was moving before he even registered the

thought. He was halfway down the hall before Remi noticed him. When she did, she shrugged off the blanket and broke into a run. Okay, it was more like a wobbly jog, and she only got four steps in before he was there.

He gently wrapped his arms around her and pulled her against his body. Kevlar realized he was shaking like a leaf. Even without knowing the details, he knew he'd almost lost her.

"Vincent," she whispered against his neck as she clung to him.

"I've got you, you're okay," he murmured.

He quickly pulled back, his gaze scanning her from head to toe. He saw bruises on her face and her arms, a busted lip, dirt on her knees and legs and hands. Everything about her appearance made him want to find Howler and kill him all over again. But it also made him so damn grateful that she was here. In his arms. Alive.

"I love you!" he blurted. Not caring that the hallway of a police station probably wasn't the best place to let her know how he felt. But then again, it was also perfect. "So much," he told her. "I'm so sorry I wasn't there! That I didn't keep you safe."

"I love you too," she said with a watery smile. "And it's okay...Blink was there." She turned her head to look at the man now standing behind her.

Straightening, Kevlar stared at the SEAL, seeing him in an entirely new light. Blink wasn't smiling. Looked pretty damn grim, in fact. And regret and pain filled his eyes...but then Remi held out her hand.

He took it without hesitation, and Remi pulled him forward. "I know we have a lot to talk about, but you need to know. Blink saved me. Without him, I..." Her voice cracked, and she cleared her throat before she continued. "I wouldn't be standing here right now."

Kevlar felt his throat close up. He couldn't speak. The magnitude of what he owed this man was overwhelming. He'd never be able to pay him back. Ever. Reaching out, he grabbed Blink's shoulder and squeezed. Hard.

Blink didn't speak, but Kevlar saw a riot of emotions on his face. Disbelief, concern, relief, fear.

"Anything you need," Kevlar told him, "you've got it. It's probably too early, but if you want back on the teams, I'll welcome you on mine with open arms. Anyone who goes to the lengths you did to protect an innocent life is someone I want at my back. I'll talk to whoever it takes to make that happen. I just...thank you, Blink. Thank you."

"I didn't do anything anyone else—"

"Yes, you did," Remi interrupted.

Both men looked at her to see tears streaming down her cheeks.

"Remi?" Kevlar asked.

"I'm okay," she told him with a small smile. "I'm just so happy to be alive."

Dropping his hand from Blink's shoulder, Kevlar pulled Remi into his embrace once more. He wasn't sure he was going to be able to let go for a very long time.

"Excuse me," interrupted one of the officers who'd

escorted Remi and Blink into the station. "We need to get official statements."

"I'm not leaving her," Kevlar warned.

"You don't have to. Ms. Stephenson, if you would head into that room on your right. Mr. Davis, we'll talk to you in this other—"

"Wait! Why are we being separated? You aren't going to arrest him, are you? Because he did nothing wrong! He saved me! Yes, he killed Howler, but it was justified! He'd locked me in a box and was trying to bury me alive!"

Kevlar's entire body stiffened. *What the fuck?*

The officer didn't seem surprised in the least by what Remi said. "We just need to get your statements, ma'am."

But Remi was too panicked to listen. She turned to Kevlar, gripping his shirt. "Do we need lawyers? Should we call Navy NCIS or something?"

"We've already gotten in touch with them," another officer said. "They're on their way. And this isn't an interrogation, Ms. Stephenson, we just need to get both your sides on what happened today."

Remi didn't look any less concerned. But she finally nodded and turned to Blink. "Don't worry. I'm gonna take care of this. By the time they're done hearing my story, they're going to be giving you a freaking medal."

Blink's lips twitched, but he controlled his reaction almost immediately. "Don't leave anything out, Remi. Tell them *everything*," he ordered.

"Of course I will," she huffed. "Why wouldn't I?" Then she pulled away from Kevlar and hugged Blink. Hard. She looked up at him and put a hand on his cheek. "Thank you for being observant. For watching me out your window like a creeper." She smiled at him, letting him know she was joking. "I'm sorry about everything you've been through, but I'm a big believer in things happening for a reason. Me breaking up with Douchecanoe, going to Hawaii, meeting Vincent, you sitting in that bar day after day, watching and listening, and you being there when Howler arrived to pick me up. Thank you."

Blink visibly struggled to control his emotions, but finally nodded at her.

Remi backed up, and Kevlar wrapped his arm around her waist, pulling her against him.

"I'm ready," she declared, nodding to one of the officers.

Two hours later, Kevlar wasn't sure if he wanted to snatch Remi up and take her to his apartment and never leave again, or hunt down Howler's body and desecrate it.

It had taken every ounce of control he'd cultivated over the years to sit in that small interrogation room and listen to Remi explain everything that had happened.

He was outraged that Howler had pretended Kevlar was hurt, playing on Remi's emotions to get her to go with him willingly. But that was nothing compared to how he felt when Remi calmly talked about Howler punching her in the face, shoving her into a footlocker, locking her in.

He trembled when she described what the dirt sounded like, landing on top of the box, and how even though she knew it was futile, she couldn't stop herself from pounding on the lid to try to get out.

Throughout the retelling, he held onto her hand. Squeezing it in support when she faltered and wrapping an arm around her when she shivered. He'd never been as proud of anyone as he was of his Remi.

But more than that, he realized just how big of a debt he owed Blink. He itched to hear his side of the story, to find out how he knew Howler was up to no good and what happened after Remi had been locked in that box. But there was no denying that regardless of how Blink came to be involved, Remi owed her life to the man.

The officers had asked her to repeat various parts of the story several times, most likely to see if her details changed at all. He had no doubt they were comparing what she said to what Blink was saying in the next room.

"So he said he wanted to be the leader of a SEAL team?" the detective asked for the second time.

"Yes. He was jealous of Vincent. Said if I was dead," she shuddered in Kevlar's grip, and he wanted to kill Howler all over again for being a fucking idiot and a psychopath, "that Vincent wouldn't be able to cope, and he'd be able to take over the team when they went on their next mission in a couple of days. That Vincent would be too broken from his grief over what happened to me. He wanted the police and the team to find me, which was why he left my phone on."

"And he had Mr. Davis bring both their phones into his apartment, so he'd have an alibi?"

"Yes," Remi said a little impatiently. "I already told you that. If you go to Howler's apartment I'm sure you'll see them in there, just like I told you. Oh! And you can also check my phone. You'll see that he called me this morning. And my fingerprints are in the truck too."

"Talk to me more about Mr. Davis holding you hostage in the vehicle and carrying you to the hole Mr. Starrett had dug in the woods."

Kevlar hadn't been thrilled hearing that part of Remi's story. He was almost overwhelmed with anger at Blink when she'd described how he'd kept his hand over her mouth and basically helped Howler kidnap her. But Remi's defense of him had been so absolute, so firm, he was able to think a little clearer about everything when she described the details a second time.

"This again?" Remi asked with a sigh. "Right, *fine*. Yes, Blink pulled me out of the front seat and into the back with him. Yes, he held me against him so I couldn't move, couldn't try to open the door and jump out, and yes, he had his hand over my mouth. But he was doing it to keep me safe from *Howler*. He got me out of range of Howler's fists after the jerk punched me in the face twice, and he kept me quiet so I wouldn't say anything else to antagonize him. Trust me, if it had just been me and Howler, I have no doubt he would've beaten me unconscious to keep me compliant.

"Blink didn't hurt me," she insisted. "Even though he

held me, he didn't hurt me while he was doing so. I didn't know it at the time, but now I realize he was figuratively and literally standing between me and Howler. Keeping him from hurting me as best he could. When he carried me into the woods, he even twisted his body when Howler tried to punch me again, so he'd miss my face."

The detective made another note on the pad in front of him.

Remi sighed again. "Is that enough? I've told you several times what happened. I want to go home."

The last five words were almost a whine, and Kevlar realized how exhausted she was at that moment. He was about to insist the detective let her leave, even if he had to make Remi exercise her Fifth Amendment rights, when the man closed his notebook and nodded.

"Yeah, I think we've got enough here."

"And Blink? He's done too?" she insisted.

Kevlar was as proud of her as he could be. Even after all she'd been through, she was still worried about the other man.

"Because I'm not leaving until he does," Remi added firmly.

"I'll check in with the detective talking to him," the officer told her.

"You do that. I'll be waiting right here," she said, crossing her arms in front of her.

The detective grinned. "Can I get you anything? Another water? A snack? We have a vending machine down the hall."

"No. Thank you, though."

Kevlar wanted to laugh. His Remi, so polite and kind, even when she was exhausted, probably hurting, and worried about others.

The officer nodded at them and left the room. As soon as he was gone, Kevlar tugged on Remi's hand. "Come here," he said.

"What? Where?" she asked, but stood at his urging. Kevlar took her hips and pulled her down onto his lap. She sat across his legs and leaned into him, putting her head on his shoulder.

"I love you," he said, repeating his earlier words. "When I couldn't find you, didn't know where you were..." He shuddered.

"I know. I knew you'd be worried."

"Worried doesn't even begin to cover how I felt," he said, exhaling a huff of breath.

Remi picked up her head and stared at him. "I didn't even think twice about going with him," she said, her voice quiet. "He was your teammate. I trusted him. I thought you were hurt and all I could think about was getting to you."

"We need a fucking code word," Kevlar growled. "To make sure this doesn't happen again."

"Yeah, I think we do. Vincent?"

"Yeah, sweetheart?"

"I'm sorry about Howler."

"What do you mean?" Kevlar asked in confusion.

"He was your friend. You guys have been through so much together. You have to feel a little sad that he's gone."

But Kevlar shook his head. "I don't. Not one ounce. He clearly wasn't the man I thought I knew. He wanted to be team leader? All he had to do was talk to the commander about it. He could've been transferred to another team, gone to a Navy school, taken the initiative to get what he wanted. Instead, he stewed about it, let his resentment build up, then came up with a completely insane, unforgivable plan. He was a *coward*. A jealous asshole. I'm not sorry he's gone. Not at all. What I'm sorry about is that I wasn't there when you needed me most."

But Remi shook her head. "You kind of were. If you weren't the man you are, if Blink didn't respect you so much, didn't think you were a great leader, a great *person*, he wouldn't have done what he did. So, in a small way, you were there. Because of his respect for you, Blink went out of his way to protect me when he didn't have to get involved.

"Besides...you're always with me, Vincent. Here." She tapped her chest over her heart. "I tried to be strong, for you."

"I don't deserve you," Kevlar told her, lowering his forehead to hers.

"And I don't deserve you. So two negatives make a positive...or something like that. I wasn't that good at math growing up. I was always doodling in my textbook, making pictures that corresponded with the word problems we were supposed to be solving."

"I really do love you, you know," Kevlar told Remi. "I was waiting to say it because I didn't want to freak you out."

"I was waiting for the same reason," she admitted.

Kevlar kissed her. Soft and gentle. The feel of the scab forming on her lip from where Howler had punched her making his fury rise all over again. But he kept his emotions to himself. She needed his care right now. Not his anger.

"I need to call Marley. And my parents. They've got to be freaking out after those texts I sent them."

She wasn't wrong. She'd had time to send the most important people in her life a short note, letting them know she was all right and that she'd talk to them later. But she was exhausted. Dead on her feet. And probably hungry to boot. Kevlar needed to get her home and taken care of. While she was sleeping, he'd call her family and Marley and tell them what happened.

"And, Vincent?"

"Yeah?"

"Can we...is it okay if, maybe...we went back to my place? Just for tonight? I know I've been staying at your apartment, but I keep reliving what happened and—"

"Of course," Kevlar said, interrupting her. Of course the place where she was kidnapped would make her uneasy. He had no problem staying at her condo for as long as she wanted. Forever if needed. Her place was nicer than his anyway.

The door to the room opened once more and the detective stuck his head in. "Mr. Davis is ready to go."

Remi practically leapt off Kevlar's lap, promptly swaying when she was on her feet. Steadying her, Kevlar had the fleeting thought that some men would definitely be threatened by their woman's sudden interest in another man, but he couldn't find it in him. As far as he was concerned, Blink was his new blood brother.

They walked out of the room, and Blink was waiting in the hallway. He looked as wiped out as Remi.

"You're coming home with us," she declared when she saw him, obviously realizing the man was at the end of his rope, just as she was.

"I'm not—"

"You're coming back to my condo," she said sternly, interrupting his refusal. "If you think I'm letting you go home to your empty apartment, just so you can torture yourself all night by thinking about what happened, you don't know me that well."

"I *don't* know you that well," Blink countered with a small smile.

"Well, hold on, bub, because that's about to change," Remi told him.

"You're really bossy," he said.

"Actually, I'm not. I'm meek and mild. Ask anybody. I'm a cartoonist who sits at home with her head stuck in her sketchbook. But right now, I'm not about to let you be by yourself...and with you and Vincent with me, I feel safe."

The last bit was said in a soft tone, and Kevlar tightened his arm around her. His Remi was strong, but she'd also been through a horrific, scary experience. If she needed him *and* Blink with her to feel safe, that's exactly what she'd get. Even if he had to hog-tie Blink and force him into her condo.

But to his relief, Blink gave a brief nod. "If that's what you need."

"It is," Remi insisted.

"Come on, sweetheart. Let's get you home."

The trio was escorted by an officer to the door that led into the lobby, and when they entered it, Kevlar was surprised by what he saw.

The lobby was completely full. Not only was his team still there, but Wolf and his team had arrived, along with their wives.

"Remi!" a woman cried out, and before he knew it, Remi was pulled out of his arms and into Marley's.

The two women cried against each other as they hugged.

"I can't believe that asshole took you!" Marley exclaimed when she'd gotten a semblance of control over herself.

"I know, right? Who would've thunk it?"

"Left in the ocean *and* kidnapped. No more! You hear me?" Marley barked, shaking her finger in Remi's face.

She smiled at her best friend and nodded. "I hear you," she said softly.

Then the two women hugged once more.

"My turn," an older man said gruffly, and when Kevlar

turned, he knew with one glance that he was Fernando Stephenson, Remi's father. The mogul who'd started Crown Condoms, turning it into the powerhouse brand it was today. He didn't look anything like the reserved businessman he portrayed to the world. He looked like a father who was devastated to learn his little girl had been hurt and almost killed.

Remi's tears started up again as she turned to her dad. Mr. Stephenson was a big man. Remi looked tiny against him, but the way he held her, as if she was the most cherished thing in his world, nearly brought Kevlar to tears himself.

He then passed her over to a woman, who Kevlar could see was her mother; they had the same nose and eyes.

Kevlar was overwhelmed by everyone showing up to show their support. He kept his gaze on Remi as she was basically passed from one person to the next. Everyone wanted to hug her, tell her how relieved they were that she was all right.

And he didn't miss how his team closed ranks around Blink. Even with only knowing the bare-bone details of what happened, his team was treating the SEAL like the hero he was.

"So, you're Vincent," Mr. Stephenson said.

Kevlar turned to look at the man and nodded. This wasn't how he'd planned to meet Remi's parents, but now was as good a time as any. The older man held out his hand, and Kevlar shook it firmly.

Remi's dad didn't let go for a long moment, studying

him intently as he stood there. Then he nodded. "I expect this to be the last time you and I are standing in a police station together because of Remi," he said firmly.

"Absolutely. And for the record, I love your daughter. She's too good for me, but I'll spend the rest of my life making sure she doesn't regret choosing me anyway."

"See that she doesn't."

"Fernando! You're being rude," Remi's mom scolded.

And suddenly, Kevlar had a flash of what things would be like years from now with him and Remi. She'd call him out when he was being less than congenial with others. But she'd also look up at him the way Mrs. Stephenson was looking at her husband. With love and affection. It was clear where Remi got her kindness; she'd learned it from her mom.

"Ma'am," Kevlar said, nodding to her. "It's good to meet you, but I wish it wasn't under these circumstances."

"Remi's talked about you a lot," she said graciously. "While I'm not happy this happened to her, I'm so relieved she's all right. It looks like she's found a group of friends who appreciate her exactly how she is. And who will keep her safe."

"She has," Kevlar said as he looked across the room and saw Wolf hugging Remi tightly. Her eyes were closed, and she was listening to something Wolf was murmuring into her ear as they embraced. Again, Kevlar wasn't jealous, not in the least. He was happy she had people to look after her when he couldn't. And it sucked that there would definitely be times when he couldn't be at her side, like earlier today.

But she'd be looked after by his Navy family, and he couldn't ask for anything more.

"If you'll excuse me, I need to get Remi home. She's had a hard day and I need to feed her and get her to bed."

Mr. Stephenson nodded in agreement. "Two days."

"Excuse me?" Kevlar asked, itching to head across the room to claim Remi and get her out of there.

"Two days. Then her mom and I will be by to check on her."

Kevlar smiled. "She'll be happy to spend some time with you," he said with a nod.

Then he turned toward Remi. Today had been one of the scariest in his life, and he never, ever wanted to go through anything like it again. He needed to get Remi home, hold her tight, and try to forget what happened.

EPILOGUE

Remi sat in Aces surrounded by all her new friends. Two SEAL teams and all the SEAL wives. Marley. Even her parents and grandmother had wanted to come. The get-together was an impromptu celebration—a celebration of life for Remi, and for the fact that Vincent and his team had arrived home safely from another mission.

It hadn't been fun when he'd had to leave just a few days after her kidnapping, but Remi had sucked it up. This was her new life. Being a Navy SEAL girlfriend wasn't easy. But she'd quickly realized that just because Vincent was gone, it didn't mean she was alone.

Blink was a constant in her life now. She'd stayed in Vincent's apartment while he was deployed—he felt better leaving her, knowing Blink was right downstairs. And she'd do anything to ease his mind, so he could concentrate on work. Blink had come up to visit them both before the mission, and while the team was gone, he came up every night. They'd watched TV. Talked. She'd sketched some Pecky the Traveling Taco cartoons while he read books. Being around him was very calming, and despite what Marley had feared, spending time with Blink didn't bring back any bad memories for Remi.

He'd been cleared of any wrongdoing after an investigation, which was a huge relief for both of them. She'd been ready to hire one of the best lawyers in the state if there had been even a hint of Blink being charged with anything.

Tex had called one night and apologized for not being able to discover Howler was behind what happened in Hawaii. He seriously doubted the police's assumption that the boat captain had died from an accidental overdose. He also managed to learn Howler had bought a dozen burner phones, with cash, and he'd obviously sent one to Hawaii, because the police confiscated it in the boat captain's apartment when they found his body. It had been bagged as evidence, just in case.

How he learned *any* of those things—let alone accessed a phone that was still in some evidence locker—Remi had no idea, but Vincent told her not to even bother asking. Tex was almost scary with the information he could find.

Marley had hovered since her kidnapping, insisting Remi call or text her every hour, until she'd put her foot down and refused. They'd had a pretty big fight about it, actually, but like the best friends they were, they'd made up within minutes of hanging up on each other.

And while Vincent and the rest of his team had been

gone, she'd had lunch with one or more of the SEAL ladies almost every day. Caroline and Fiona one day, Summer and Cheyenne the next. Alabama another day, and Jessyka had invited her to Aces to try her hand behind the bar...which had been a hilarious disaster.

All-in-all, Remi reflected, as she looked around her and saw all the people who'd become very important to her in such a short time, she was blessed. Yes, bad things had happened to her, but she'd gotten through them with the help of her friends, and come out stronger on the other side.

Her gaze went over to the pool tables, where her dad had teamed up with Dude and Preacher, and they were currently beating the pants off Benny, Cookie, and Flash. She never thought she'd see the day her rich, refined father hung out in a military bar with a bunch of rough and tumble SEALs, but she loved that for him.

Loud laughter had her attention turning back to the table, and she found her grandmother and Cheyenne both cracking up. Probably because of something inappropriate her grandmother had said. The older woman wasn't afraid to say whatever came to her mind, and she'd been welcomed into Remi's new group of friends without hesitation.

Her gaze roamed over to the bar, and she saw Blink standing there with Vincent. For a moment, she worried that Blink had reverted to his old habits, sitting alone, shutting himself off from others, but then she smiled when Vincent reached out and gave Blink one of those weird man-hug things that guys did. Both of them were smiling, which made her relax.

Vincent had told her before they'd left for the bar that he'd gotten word from his commander—Blink passed his psych eval and he'd been added to Vincent's team. It warmed her heart that none of the other guys held what had happened against Blink. Yes, he'd scared her, had held her against her will, but they understood as well as she did that if he hadn't, if he hadn't gotten into that truck, the outcome of that day would've been much different.

So the man-hug must've been because Vincent told Blink that it was official. He was part of a team again. Relieved that Blink looked as satisfied as her man, Remi slid off her chair and headed toward the bar.

She hooked her arm in Vincent's as she snuggled against him. "You told him?" she asked.

"He told me," Blink said with a small smile and nod.

"And you're happy?" she pressed.

"Yeah."

"Good. Me too."

"I have no doubt if the paperwork didn't go through, you would've stomped into the commander's office and demanded he bend to your will," Vincent said with a chuckle.

"Me? I'm an angel. I never would've done that!" Remi protested. "I would've sent my grandmother. Or maybe Dad's goons."

Both Blink and Vincent burst out laughing.

"Fernando doesn't have *goons*," Vincent said with a shake of his head.

"I think he does," Remi said with a shrug. "But I'm glad we didn't have to use them. Now I can shred that cartoon I drew where Pecky and his friends snuck onto base one night and burned the SEAL headquarters to the ground in protest."

She smiled as, once again, Blink and Vincent laughed. She squeezed Vincent's waist with happiness. Her life felt... complete. Full.

"I'm gonna go see if MacGyver and Mozart need a third on their team," Blink said. He nodded at Vincent, then leaned in and kissed Remi's temple before sauntering toward the pool tables with his beer.

She loved how affectionate Blink was with her after their shared ordeal. He was still grumpy. Still prone to disappear into his head. But they'd forged a bond that could never be broken. Even better, her boyfriend didn't seem the least bit jealous over her relationship with his fellow SEAL.

"I'm going to marry you, you know," Vincent said nonchalantly.

Remi's gaze flew up to his. "What?" she asked.

"I'm going to put my ring on your finger, my baby in your belly, and glower at anyone who dares to even look twice at my beautiful wife."

Butterflies swam in Remi's stomach at his words.

"But before I ask, I want to make absolutely certain you know what you're getting into if you tie yourself to me.

It's not easy being with a military guy. You've been through hell, *twice*, all because of me. And you've only been through one deployment. I want to make sure this is what you want. *I'm* who you want, before I make things official."

"You're what I want," she told him firmly. "I don't need to go through any more missions. And what happened to me *wasn't* your fault. It was his." Remi didn't say Howler's name out loud. No matter how much Vincent swore he wasn't upset over his friend and teammate's death, she had a feeling it was painful for him to think about the man. "And you know what? If it wasn't for him, we wouldn't be together."

But Vincent was shaking his head even before she was finished speaking. "I don't believe that for a second. We practically live in the same town. Our paths would've crossed at some point...at the library, sitting in our cars next to each other at a stoplight, something. I would've known you were it for me even if we hadn't spent that time in the ocean."

"Vincent, that's sweet," Remi said, feeling overwhelmed.

"That's me, Mr. Sweet," Vincent said sarcastically, with a small chuckle.

He was right. Vincent was a little rough around the edges, got irritated with people fairly easily, but he was hers. And she wasn't giving him back. "For the record," she told him. "When you ask, I'm going to say yes. To it all. The ring, the baby, and even though no one looks at me any kind of way except to wonder what the gorgeous military guy is doing with a frizzy-haired nerd like me, I'll let you glower at anyone you want."

The look on his face made her lady parts sit up and take notice. Their love life was good. More than good. Vincent was the most attentive and unselfish man she'd ever been with. He always made sure she came before he did. And the night he returned from his mission?

She still blushed just thinking about it.

Looking around, Vincent muttered, "I wonder if there's a closet around here we could use."

Remi giggled. "I'm not having sex in a closet in a bar," she told him firmly. "What was it Meg Ryan said in *Top Gun*? Hey, Kevlar, you big stud, take me to bed or lose me forever," she said with a huge smile.

"Show me the way home, honey," he returned with a look so full of lust, it was all Remi could do not to spontaneously combust right then and there.

She grabbed his hand and pulled him toward the door.

"Where are you going?" Marley called out.

"Home!" Remi returned without stopping.

She heard laughter all around them, but she ignored it. She didn't care what anyone else thought. She needed her man. Now.

"Remember, we've got PT at oh-six-hundred!" Safe yelled.

Remi had no idea what kind of response Vincent gave his friend to that, but assumed he'd flipped him the bird. Still smiling, she got them out of the bar and into the parking lot before Vincent took over. He tugged on her hand, stopping her in her tracks, then he spun her toward him and bent over, throwing her over his shoulder and continuing toward his car.

Remi snort-laughed and propped herself up with her hands on his back. She stared at his perfect ass as he walked and smiled to herself. She, Remi Stephenson, had landed a SEAL. Growing up in the area, it was something all the girls in her high school class talked about when they were younger. About how sexy they were, how awesome it would be to sleep with one.

And she was not only sleeping with one, she was with the best of the bunch. And he wanted to marry her. It was a dream come true. And while she'd marry Vincent tomorrow, she understood his need for her to be sure. His ex had done a number on him, and after what happened with Howler, he was still feeling raw over everything they'd been through.

But that was all right. Because Remi wasn't going anywhere.

The second he got them to the condo—after he'd returned from his mission, they'd ultimately decided to live there, since it was bigger—he picked her up again and headed straight to the stairs and up to their bedroom.

He carried her as if she weighed nothing, then threw her onto their bed. Remi kissed him with all the love she had in her heart. She hadn't said a word to Vincent, but the truth was, his missions scared her. She had to trust he and his teammates knew what they were doing. She felt better just knowing that Blink would also have her man's back.

But she'd never tell Vincent how scared she was for him when he left. She'd be the strong woman he needed. She was as proud of him as she could be. He was her hero.

After undoing the zipper and button on her jeans, he grabbed the material at her ankles and yanked. Remi snort-laughed again. Once she was naked, Vincent crawled over her and stared down into her eyes with a look of such love, it made Remi's heart lurch in her chest.

"I love you," he told her.

"And I love you too."

He lifted a hand and brushed a piece of hair off her face. But he didn't otherwise move.

"Vincent?"

"Just memorizing this moment. You. Here, under me. Seeing the love in your eyes."

Remi smiled. "Get used to it. The love, that is. Because it's all yours. *I'm* all yours."

His nostrils flared, and he eased down her body. "Hold on, sweetheart, because I'm thinking I want to take my time tonight."

Remi moaned as the man she loved made himself comfortable between her thighs. "Do your best, honey," she goaded.

"No, I'll do my worst," he said with a grin before lowering his head.

* * *

Wren sighed. She'd hoped the bar wouldn't be busy tonight. She'd chosen to meet her date at Aces because it was usually a pretty mellow and quiet place. She could talk to the man, get to know him, without feeling as if she was in the middle of some damn frat party. But tonight, there were a ton of people laughing, smiling, playing pool, making it almost impossible to have a normal conversation with the guy sitting next to her.

From what she could figure out after overhearing the toasts and speeches people had made, one of the women had actually almost died, and one of the other guys at the bar had saved her. But it was confusing, because the guy who saved her clearly wasn't the man she was dating. She was snuggled up to some other hot SEAL.

She knew they were SEALs by eavesdropping on other conversations around her. But the thing that made her heart twinge was seeing how close everyone seemed to be. They weren't all the same age, but it didn't matter. They were having a great time. Hell, there was even an elderly woman who seemed to be having the time or her life. Apparently the grandmother of the woman being celebrated.

It made her smile. Ache to be a part of something like that. But Wren led a solitary life.

She'd had to scrape and claw for everything she'd ever had. Why would love, acceptance, and family be any different?

"Are you listening to me?"

Wren internally winced at her date's question, because

she *hadn't* been. She'd been too engrossed in the conversations going on around her. The festive vibe. The men at the pool tables seemed to be having a blast. No hard feelings when one team won a game over another.

"I'm sorry, it's really loud in here," Wren told her date.

In response, he scooted his chair closer to hers, so he was practically sitting in her lap. It made her uncomfortable, but she didn't want to upset him by telling the guy to back off. That's how she'd spent her entire life...being compliant. Not rocking the boat. It was a hard habit to break.

"We could get out of here. Go back to my place," he suggested, putting his hand on her thigh.

Wren stared at him in disbelief. Where had the polite, almost nerdy accountant gone? When she'd first spotted him, she'd sighed in relief because he'd looked exactly like the picture on his online profile. She'd been half afraid he was catfishing her or something. But he seemed to be exactly what he'd portrayed on the dating app. A mild-mannered math geek who wanted to get to know her, rather than someone simply looking for a quick hookup.

But now, with his hand on her thigh, she was beginning to think there weren't any good men left out there. Anyone who wasn't just looking for sex.

"I'm not comfortable with that," she told him, moving her leg as far away from him as she could.

"Right, sorry," he said with a small smile as he leaned away from her.

Wren mentally sighed in relief that he'd taken the hint.

"You want something else from the bar? I'm going to get a refill," he told her.

"Um, sure. Maybe a lemonade?"

"A lemonade? You don't want another glass of wine?"

Wren shook her head. "I'm driving, so I can't."

"All right, one lemonade, coming up."

Her date smiled again, then headed toward the bar. It was busy. He'd have a bit of a wait, so Wren closed her eyes for a moment.

This night was a bust. She should've realized that online dating wasn't for her. But it wasn't as if she was meeting potential partners in any other aspect of her life. She'd just moved to Southern California for her new job, and even though she worked mostly with men, she'd always had a no-dating-coworkers rule. Besides, none of the men she saw on a daily basis appealed to her. Which was why she'd turned to the Internet.

Way before she was ready, Wren saw her date coming back toward her with a bottle of beer in one hand and a glass in the other.

"Here you go," he said, sliding the glass over. "What were we talking about before I so rudely left your side?" he asked with kind of a slimy smile.

Wren wasn't sure, because she'd been paying more attention to whatever celebration was going on around them than anything he was saying.

She took a large swallow of her lemonade as he launched into some boring story about the people he worked with.

She wasn't sure how much time had gone by, but it wasn't long before Wren began to feel strange. The room had gotten extremely hot all of a sudden, and she felt dizzy.

Fucking hell...The asshole had *drugged* her!

She knew without a doubt—because it had happened before.

Wren shoved at her date's hand, which had found her leg again. But now his fingers were on her inner thigh, coming way too damn close to touching her completely inappropriately for someone she'd just met.

"If you'll excuse me, I need to use the bathroom," she told her date, as she pushed at the hand that was already latched onto her leg once more.

"You feel okay? You don't look that good. Let me take you home."

Sure, asshole, she thought. *You'll get me in your car and won't fucking take me home. You'll rape me, slit my throat, then leave me in some damn alley to be found like the piece of trash you think I am.*

Wren shook her head, hating how that made the room spin even more. She just had to get to the bathroom. Lock herself in a stall, then beg for help from the first woman who came in. Another reason she'd come to Aces was because she'd read a story about the owner, a woman who said she was determined to make her bar a place where ladies could be safe when they wanted a night out.

She must've surprised the man, because when she shoved at him again, he scooted his chair back.

"Okay. I'll watch your purse," he said.

Wren didn't want to leave her things with him, but by doing so, it seemed to make the guy relax. Like anyone else, he thought she wouldn't leave without her belongings. He probably thought she'd splash some water on her face, then come back to the table to get her purse before he "helped" her leave.

Well, she wasn't that much of an idiot.

She stumbled across the room, knowing she was weaving like a drunk chick who couldn't hold her alcohol.

Changing her mind, Wren decided to go down the hallway where the bathrooms were located, then keep going—right out the back door, if she could find one. Her phone was in her pocket and she could call for a ride once she was outside and safe.

But as soon as she walked into the hallway, Wren knew she was already in trouble. She could barely keep her eyes open, and it was only a matter of time before she was out cold. Whatever the asshole had put in her drink was strong. And fast-acting. He'd been cocky. So sure she'd agree to let him help her. Well, fuck him.

As her vision doubled, Wren saw someone walking toward her. He was tall and good-looking. Had a closely cropped beard and mustache. She recognized him. He was one of the SEALs in the bar. He'd been playing pool with the others. But the thing that made him stand out in her eyes was his freckles. They were all over his face. So close together, if you didn't look closely, you'd think it was just a blotchy tan or something.

Something about those freckles made him seem safe.

She didn't know why; it was probably the drugs messing with her mind.

"Help me!" The words were out before she could think twice.

"Excuse me?" the man asked.

"My date put something in my drink. Wants to take me home. I'm about to...pass out... Please help..."

Wren felt herself falling—but she didn't hit the floor. The man caught her.

The last thought she had before her world went dark was that she hoped like hell she hadn't jumped from the frying pan into the fire.

* * *

"What the hell?" Bo "Safe" Cyders exclaimed as the slender —no, downright *skinny* woman in the hallway passed out in his arms.

His gut instinct was to carry her into the bar, to get help. But he instantly remembered what she'd said. About her date drugging her.

The very thought made his blood boil.

His sister had been drugged and raped when she was in college, and when Safe learned about it, he'd felt completely helpless. He'd always protected Susie, but he hadn't been able to protect her when she'd needed him most. It had eaten at him for years.

Turning, Safe acted without thought. He needed to get this woman out of here. Glancing at her, he recognized her as the woman sitting in the farthest corner from the pool tables, with a buttoned-up, shifty-looking asshole at her side. He'd pegged them as being on a first date with one glance. He hadn't liked the way the man was ogling the woman when she wasn't looking.

She had on a pair of slacks and a short-sleeve, scoop-neck blouse. She was dressed fairly conservatively, in his opinion, but that hadn't kept her date's eyes from locking onto her cleavage. The guy was practically drooling.

While Safe agreed that the woman was pretty, she definitely wasn't his type. She looked as if she'd blow away in a small breeze. He preferred his women tall and curvy. Not petite and skinny.

But as he easily held the woman while pushing the back door open, Safe couldn't deny the lady intrigued him. Not every person was astute enough to realize when they'd been drugged...or strong enough to get away from their attacker.

Shaking his head, he focused on the task at hand. She was extremely lucky. She hadn't come to him for help; they'd simply been in the hallway at the same time. He could've been anyone. Hell, he could be stealing her out of the bar to have his perverted way with her, just like her so-called date had probably planned.

But luckily for the woman, it *had* been him in that hallway. And he wasn't going to hurt her. No way in hell. He hadn't gotten his nickname because he was a danger to women.

Making a mental note to call Jessyka and tell her what was happening—she'd be pissed off, since she prided herself on running an establishment where women didn't have to worry about date-rape or any of that shit—Safe carried the woman to his Jeep.

He managed to open the passenger door without dropping her...not that it was all that hard. The woman didn't even weigh as much as the pack he carried on missions. He got her buckled into the seat, and her head lolled to the side awkwardly as Safe ran around the vehicle.

He questioned what the hell he was doing even as he started the engine.

As he drove out of Aces' parking lot, he pressed his lips together. He should turn around. Bring her back to the bar. Caroline, Jessyka, and the others would take care of her while he and the guys called the cops and forced her date to fess up to what he'd done.

But instead, Safe headed for his house. It was tiny, in a kind of rundown neighborhood. But it was his. Paid for by money he'd earned with his blood, sweat, and tears.

The mystery woman would be fine. He'd watch over her, make sure she didn't have any adverse effects from whatever drug she'd ingested. When she woke up...

Well, he'd deal with the repercussions of his choices then.

For now, every instinct was screaming at him to get the woman somewhere safe. And the safest place he knew of was his own humble home.

* * *

Not the best way to "meet" someone, but of course Safe is going to do whatever he can to help Wren. Get the next book in the SEAL of Protection: Alliance series, *Protecting Wren*, now!

Want to talk to other Susan Stoker fans? Join my reader group, Susan Stoker's Stalkers, on Facebook!

Sign up for my newsletter so you never miss a freebie, sale, or other Stoker news:
https://www.stokeraces.com/contact-1.html

Scan the QR code below for signed books, swag, T-shirts and more!

Also by Susan Stoker

SEAL of Protection: Alliance Series

Protecting Remi (July 2024)
Protecting Wren (Nov 2024)
Protecting Josie (Mar 2025)
Protecting Maggie (TBA)
Protecting Addison (TBA)
Protecting Kelli (TBA)
Protecting Bree (TBA)

SEAL Team Hawaii Series

Finding Elodie
Finding Lexie
Finding Kenna
Finding Monica
Finding Carly
Finding Ashlyn
Finding Jodelle

The Refuge Series

Deserving Alaska
Deserving Henley
Deserving Reese
Deserving Cora
Deserving Lara
Deserving Maisy (Oct 2024)
Deserving Ryleigh (Jan 2025)

Eagle Point Search & Rescue

Searching for Lilly
Searching for Elsie
Searching for Bristol
Searching for Caryn
Searching for Finley
Searching for Heather
Searching for Khloe

Game of Chance Series

The Protector
The Royal
The Hero
The Lumberjack (July 2024)

SEAL of Protection: Legacy Series

Securing Caite
Securing Brenae (novella)
Securing Sidney
Securing Piper
Securing Zoey
Securing Avery
Securing Kalee
Securing Jane

Delta Force Heroes Series

Rescuing Rayne
Rescuing Aimee (novella)
Rescuing Emily

Rescuing Harley
Marrying Emily (novella)
Rescuing Kassie
Rescuing Bryn
Rescuing Casey
Rescuing Sadie (novella)
Rescuing Wendy
Rescuing Mary
Rescuing Macie (novella)
Rescuing Annie

SEAL of Protection Series

Protecting Caroline
Protecting Alabama
Protecting Fiona
Marrying Caroline (novella)
Protecting Summer
Protecting Cheyenne
Protecting Jessyka
Protecting Julie (novella)
Protecting Melody
Protecting the Future
Protecting Kiera (novella)
Protecting Alabama's Kids (novella)
Protecting Dakota

Delta Team Two Series

Shielding Gillian
Shielding Kinley

Shielding Aspen
Shielding Jayme (novella)
Shielding Riley
Shielding Devyn
Shielding Ember
Shielding Sierra

Badge of Honor: Texas Heroes Series

Justice for Mackenzie
Justice for Mickie
Justice for Corrie
Justice for Laine (novella)
Shelter for Elizabeth
Justice for Boone
Shelter for Adeline
Shelter for Sophie
Justice for Erin
Justice for Milena
Shelter for Blythe
Justice for Hope
Shelter for Quinn
Shelter for Koren
Shelter for Penelope

Ace Security Series

Claiming Grace
Claiming Alexis
Claiming Bailey
Claiming Felicity

ALSO BY SUSAN STOKER

Claiming Sarah

Mountain Mercenaries Series

Defending Allye

Defending Chloe

Defending Morgan

Defending Harlow

Defending Everly

Defending Zara

Defending Raven

Silverstone Series

Trusting Skylar

Trusting Taylor

Trusting Molly

Trusting Cassidy

Stand Alone

Falling for the Delta

The Guardian Mist

Nature's Rift

A Princess for Cale

A Moment in Time- A Collection of Short Stories

Another Moment in Time- A Collection of Short Stories

A Third Moment in Time- A Collection of Short Stories

Lambert's Lady

Special Operations Fan Fiction

http://www.AcesPress.com

ALSO BY SUSAN STOKER

Beyond Reality Series

Outback Hearts

Flaming Hearts

Frozen Hearts

Writing as Annie George:

Stepbrother Virgin (erotic novella)

ABOUT THE AUTHOR

New York Times, *USA Today* and *Wall Street Journal* Bestselling Author Susan Stoker has a heart as big as the state of Tennessee where she lives, but this all American girl has also spent the last fourteen years living in Missouri, California, Colorado, Indiana, and Texas. She's married to a retired Army man who now gets to follow *her* around the country.

She debuted her first series in 2014 and quickly followed that up with the SEAL of Protection Series, which solidified her love of writing and creating stories readers can get lost in.

If you enjoyed this book, or any book, please consider leaving a review. It's appreciated by authors more than you'll know.

www.stokeraces.com
www.AcesPress.com
susan@stokeraces.com

facebook.com/authorsusanstoker
x.com/Susan_Stoker
instagram.com/authorsusanstoker
goodreads.com/SusanStoker
bookbub.com/authors/susan-stoker
amazon.com/author/susanstoker
tiktok.com/@susanstokerauthor

Made in the USA
Coppell, TX
30 June 2024